W9-AYD-931

A remote Scottish village.
A killer who hides behind the mists.
A murder that will push Seth Mornay
to the breaking point. . . .

Savor the atmospheric chills
of M.G. Kincaid's compelling debut
*The Last Victim in Glen Ross*

"All the charm of Scotland and all the edge of a great crime story—an irresistible combination."
—*Lee Childs*

"A polished, extremely well-written British police procedural filled with fully developed characters. There's more to [the protagonist] than meets the eye, and hopefully readers will find out what it is, in future books in the series."
—*Midwest Book Review*

"Kincaid's debut novel is an intricate mystery plotted in the spider-web style reminiscent of the golden age of crime fiction, brought right up-to-date with modern protagonists and a setting to die for—literally."
—*Deadly Pleasures*

"Intriguing. The end of the story solves the mystery in a most interesting fashion, however, it does not solve [Seth's] personal mystery. But then, I would not be looking forward to the next installment into the brooding Seth Mornay's life if it did."
—*Old Book Barn Gazette*

Also by M.G. Kincaid

*The Last Victim in Glen Ross*

Now available from Pocket Books

# LAST SEEN IN
# ABERDEEN

# M.G. KINCAID

**POCKET BOOKS**
New York London Toronto Sydney

The sale of this book without its cover is unauthorized. If you purchased this book without a cover, you should be aware that it was reported to the publisher as "unsold and destroyed." Neither the author nor the publisher has received payment for the sale of this "stripped book."

This book is a work of fiction. Names, characters, places and incidents are products of the author's imagination or are used fictitiously. Any resemblance to actual events or locales or persons, living or dead, is entirely coincidental.

An Original Publication of POCKET BOOKS

 POCKET BOOKS, a division of Simon & Schuster, Inc.
1230 Avenue of the Americas, New York, NY 10020

Copyright © 2004 by Moira Maus

All rights reserved, including the right to reproduce this book or portions thereof in any form whatsoever. For information address Pocket Books, 1230 Avenue of the Americas, New York, NY 10020

ISBN: 0-7434-6757-4

First Pocket Books printing November 2004

10 9 8 7 6 5 4 3 2 1

POCKET and colophon are registered trademarks of Simon & Schuster, Inc.

Cover design by John Vairo
Cover art by Lloyd Sutton/Masterfile and Lisa Pines/Photonica

For information regarding special discounts for bulk purchases, please contact Simon & Schuster Special Sales at 1-800-456-6798 or business@simonandschuster.com

Manufactured in the United States of America

For Lucas, Heather, and Alec—
I'd pick you again and again and again . . .

# Chapter One

Criminal Investigation Division Sergeant Seth Mornay jogged across the narrow road, leaning forward to keep icy November rain from blinding him.

His partner, Constable Claire Gillespie, had already arrived at the scene of the head-on collision just outside of Cordiff, a small village near enough the coast to lure in tourists, but not so close that it was overrun in the summers.

A Nissan four-by-four was upside down in the stream that ran parallel to the road. The Nissan had been pulling a battered, windowless horse box, which was also upside down. The other half of the head-on collision was a silvery blue Fiat with a crushed front end. It'd been spun around from the force of the collision and was now on the other side of the road, facing the wrong direction.

On the far side of the accident, parked on the grassy embankment next to the road, was a dark green Mitsubishi with HARRIS VETERINARY CLINIC painted on the driver's door. The vet was towing a white horse box. In front of the Mitsubishi was a construction crane—the sort used to lift heavy loads to second-floor building sites. The crane was parked directly in front of two Grampian Police cars. An ambulance and a mud-splattered tractor, hauling a wagon burdened with rusting acetylene tanks, were also at the scene.

"Where's the Nissan's driver?" Mornay asked Claire.

Claire's gaze took in his appearance: the gapping anorak, the slice of wrinkled shirt, and the tie that didn't match jacket or shirt. She fixed on the nick he'd given himself as he'd rushed through his morning shave. He'd have changed into a clean suit, but he'd forgotten to pick them up from the cleaners.

"How late did Gordon have you working last night?" she asked.

Laina Gordon was their new detective inspector, brought into their office to temporarily fill the void their former supervisor, DI Byrne, left when he was transferred earlier that year. Gordon was on the fast track to a carpeted office in Aberdeen, the top office if she got her way. Her father's position as deputy justice minister of the Scottish Executive didn't hurt her career goals.

"My shift ended at two."

"But did you leave when Taylor came on duty?"

"Taylor brought tea and rolls." He didn't need to tell her he'd fallen asleep after the early-morning meal; she could see he was still wearing yesterday's suit. Taylor woke him at nine when his pager went off.

A gust of wind scoured Mornay's cheeks, numbing them. He crouched to see his reflection in the car's window, in case there was anything he could quickly mend. He'd been working grueling hours since ten-year-old Matthew Adair's disappearance two weeks earlier. The long hours were taking their toll; his face was gaunt and pale, despite his dark coloring. His deep-set eyes always gave him a brooding expression, even when he was well rested. Before his service in the Royal Marines, his features could have, at best, been described as stern. Now, after being rearranged by several necessary surgeries, his features had a ferocity that seemed almost primeval. He pushed his damp hair off his forehead, quickly combing it with his fingers, trying to tame the waves the damp had brought out.

He turned away from the window as the crane operator started barking directions at Constables Dunnholland and Sahotra. The shivering men were standing on the edge of the stream's embankment, holding a heavy, rusted chain between them. On the crane operator's command they scrambled down the slippery embankment, managing to remain upright and keep their grip on the chain.

Mornay pointed to a couple huddled under an umbrella next to one of the police cars. The unpredictable gusts of wind were threatening to turn their umbrella inside out. "They were in the Fiat?"

Claire nodded. "Called from their mobile. Up from the borders. Both were near hysterics, because they couldn't find the driver of the truck. They said it came flying around that curve." Claire pointed to the curve just up the road. "There was no room or time for them to move out of the way."

The woman had a bandage on her forehead, and the man was pale. Given the condition of their Fiat, they were lucky that was the extent of their injuries.

"Shouldn't someone seat them in the back of a car, out of the rain?"

"They didn't want to get back into a car just now. I don't blame them."

"Is the horse box empty?"

"We don't know. The doors were crushed when the Nissan flipped. We need to cut it open."

Which explained the farmer and the acetylene torch.

Just then, a plump man in worn tweeds stepped in front of Mornay. "My name's Harris, are you in charge here? Because if you're in charge here, I want to make a report to your supervisor." The man's mouth was nearly hidden by a bushy white mustache. He must have been close to sixty, but he had the burly build of a man twenty years his junior.

"You'll have to leave the area," Mornay said, barely sparing him a glance.

"Your lot called me here over an hour ago, and I've seen nothing but incompetence since I arrived."

"We've got procedure—"

"Bugger procedure! You've got animals in that box, and I haven't been allowed near them."

The rain was plastering Mornay's shirt to his chest; he hadn't thought to zip up the coat before getting out of his car. He snapped it closed. "You'll need to remain in your vehicle until we're ready for you." Mornay stepped around the man, who sputtered under his breath before plodding, fists clenched, back to his Mitsubishi. Like the Nissan, it was a working vehicle with scratched paint, dented running boards and nicked front grills.

Mornay watched Dunnholland fumbling to loop the S hook at his end of the chain around the grill of the Nissan. The cold appeared to have stiffened his hands, making him more clumsy than usual. After he got it through, Sahotra grabbed the hook and shoved it back into one of the chain's links. The reinforced grill was the only place, short of the exposed drive-shaft and axles, that a chain would go around and support the weight of the vehicle.

Mornay glanced at his watch. It was half ten. This was a miserable way to start the morning when you'd slept propped against a cold window. If he were lucky, DI Gordon wouldn't find out he'd arrived at the scene late.

"Have you checked PNC for the Nissan's registration?" Mornay asked.

Claire nodded. "I've submitted the request. No one's gotten back with me yet."

The ominous sound of metal screeching on metal brought out a collective wince from the gathering, then the crane started lifting the vehicle inch by inch.

Mornay's gaze drifted into the rolling fields surrounding them. The fields were still green, a startling tropical shade of green, and were surrounded by low, drystone walls that formed meandering gridwork patterns across the landscape. In the distance, curls of smoke were drifting from the chimney of a white-washed farmhouse. The view would've been picturesque on a drier day.

Mornay shoved his hands farther into his pockets and tried to shrink down into his collar. At least the weather was keeping the gawkers away. The press wouldn't be interested in another collision on these twisting back lanes, not with Matthew Adair's parents giving regular briefings from their front garden, pleading for their son's safe return.

The crane lifted the crushed cab of the Nissan high enough off the ground so that Sahotra could nimbly slide down the embankment and search for the driver.

His head soon popped back into view. "There's no one here, sir," he shouted.

Mornay awkwardly slithered down the embankment, using his hands to steady himself. By the time he made it to the cab, his trousers were soaked to the knees, and his feet were numb from wading through the freezing water.

Sahotra was right. The cab was empty.

A stone turned beneath Mornay's foot, and he grabbed the open driver's door to keep from falling. The movement shook more chunks of bluish green glass loose; they sprinkled down into the water. He knelt to take a closer look into the cab. The seats were a dark blue canvas material. They were filthy. The dash was thick with dust. Most of the shattered windshield seemed to be lying on the stained canvas roof liner. There were two crumpled cigarette packs, Royals—the black-and-white SMOKING KILLS label covering half of the pack—and a red box of Kings. Ashes and butts were mingled among the chunks of windshield. He found a smear of blood on the interior of the driver's door. "Looks like there could've been two people," Mornay said when he straightened. "Two brands of cigarettes." "And one of them got hurt when he climbed out. But not seriously, if he could escape and disappear."

Sahotra straightened and glanced around him, as if he hoped to spot the driver lurking in the fields. The wall edging the side of the road blocked their view of the field behind them. And the grass was too thick to see any footprints, so they had no idea which direction the driver might've run.

"Think he's got a head wound?" Sahotra asked. "Maybe he was delirious?"

"He wouldn't have gone too far, then." Mornay pointed to the farmer driving the tractor. "Is he the owner of that property?" Sahotra nodded an affirmative. "We'll need to send someone to have a look around his buildings."

Harris had returned. "You've got to be careful!" he bellowed to the crane operator, his face a dark crimson. Claire had to lead him forcefully out of harm's way.

Mornay told the crane operator to lay the wreckage on the road so they could determine if there were any injured animals in the trailer. If not, the conjoined vehicles would then be lifted to the flatbed truck that was due to arrive at any moment.

Mornay and Sahotra scrambled back up the embankment and let the crane operator pull the wreckage out of the stream.

The farmer was tall and the wiry sort of thin that bespoke years of walking the surrounding hills. He wore an old set of coveralls whose original color might have been pale blue, but use had ground permanent brown streaks into the legs, arms, and back. The farmer sat comfortably on the seat of his tractor, his expression bland. Lying on the engine cowling was a well-behaved border collie that was sending beseeching looks in Claire's direction, his tail thumping against the cowling. The dog was too well trained to bound over to Claire and beg for her to scratch his ears.

When everyone had backed away from the horse trailer, the farmer reached for his cutting torch.

Cutting through the hinges was slow work, made even slower by the precarious position of the trailer, which lay on its side, balancing on a fender well, heaving with each gust of wind. From the trailer's list, it was obvious *something* was inside. Mornay thought it was late in the year to be moving animals, at least by owners who valued them. The weather and the road conditions were too unpredictable.

Mornay and Claire edged closer when the farmer stood on the tractor seat to work on the second hinge. Blue-white sparks hit the pavement with loud hisses, and a sharp, metallic odor filled the air. Once the hinge was cut away, the damaged door could be pried open with crowbars.

"Look," Claire said quietly. She pointed to a spot close to the road, near the most crumpled part of the trailer. Blood was seeping around the hinge and slowly dribbling onto the slick surface of the road.

When the farmer nodded, Dunnholland and Sahotra moved in with crowbars. They wrenched and heaved, and within moments had pried the doors apart. The bottom door fell open with a loud clang, splattering those nearest the door with blood. Dunnholland and Sahotra jumped back with startled shouts as gravity slid the carcass of a ram down the door that was now acting like a ramp. There was another dead ram inside, along with several bales of straw.

The woman from the Fiat screamed.

Mornay gritted his teeth. "Claire, would you kindly get rid of that silly woman?"

Some straw had come loose in the accident, and

gusts of wind scattered it, sticking bits and pieces of golden straw to everyone's wet slickers.

"Well, Dunnholland," Mornay said, giving Sahotra a wink behind Dunnholland's back. "Get in there and see if we've got any survivors."

"Survivors?" Dunnholland repeated. "Do I have to touch them?"

Sahotra had to turn around to keep from laughing aloud when Mornay said, "Just think of them as extra rare lamb chops. You're not afraid of lamb chops, are you?"

Mornay watched Dunnholland pick his way around the dead ram, then he turned and scanned the road for the truck that would haul away the horse box and the Nissan. A constable was leaning down to a car stopped by the roadblock, telling the driver he'd have to find another way around.

"Sahotra," Mornay said. "Get on the radio and find out what's keeping that flatbed. We can't hold up traffic all day."

"Sir," Dunnholland's voice echoed from inside the trailer. He swallowed hard when Mornay turned to stare at him. Dunnholland's gaze darted down to the bales of straw, then back up again. His face was pasty, which Mornay put down to the exertion he'd been through that morning.

"Sir," Dunnholland repeated inanely.

"What?"

"I think you should see this." Dunnholland bent down, taking a closer look at something near his feet.

Mornay stepped into the trailer, hunching over to avoid knocking his head on the riveted sidewall. "Don't touch it, whatever it is," he ordered automatically. Any other constable would've had the good sense to keep his hands to himself, but in times of crisis, Dunnholland tended to act like a curious bystander rather than a police officer.

Mornay stopped short.

A black plastic garbage bag had spilled from between two straw bales. A child's foot was sticking through the bottom of the bag.

The trailer shook as someone else stepped inside; Sahotra had joined them. He was the first to break the prolonged silence. "Now we know why the driver ran." He turned and stumbled outside.

The sound of Sahotra's retching nearly sent Mornay reeling out of the trailer.

"What is it?" Claire asked from inside.

"It looks like a child's body." Mornay clamped a hand on Dunnholland's shoulder. "Out, before we do any more damage to the scene."

"Is it Matthew Adair?" Claire whispered.

What was the likelihood they had two missing children?

"Probably," he replied. Mornay stepped out of the trailer, thankful for the brisk breeze. He put his hand firmly on the small of Claire's back and propelled her away from the trailer, guiding her toward the couple from the Fiat. "Look after these two," he said quietly into her ear. "I'll look after the rest."

# Chapter Two

Mornay parked behind the police car and lifted a hand to wave when Constable Dougie Brown glanced in his rearview mirror. The accident site was ten minutes away from the small village of Cordiff. Matthew Adair's parents would be devastated when they discovered how close to home their son's body had been found.

Dougie Brown worked in the Traffic Division of Mornay's office. He was a shy man, with a new wife who liked to bake sweets, and those sweets had taken their toll on Brown's physique. He'd been slimming for nearly two months, but Mornay could see no difference to the man's pear-shaped body.

Brown rolled down his window. "Is it true?" he asked.

"It's him."

Brown's face went slack. His wife was going to have a baby in five months' time.

Mornay nodded toward the house. "Our man been home all day?"

"And all night," Brown answered, his voice gruff. "Boring wee bastard keeps an eye on me through the kitchen window."

"Why isn't he at work?" Claire asked.

"You'll have to get him to tell you. Do I stay or go back to the office?"

"Stay, for now. Someone will radio to tell you what to do."

Jonathan Cross was a new teacher at the Cordiff Primary School. He was twenty-eight and Matthew Adair's English teacher. Matthew had written extensively in his journal about Cross, his favorite teacher. Though no charges had been made, they were keeping Cross under close surveillance.

Cross's front door opened before Mornay could knock.

The younger man was shorter than Mornay and more compact. His fair hair—kept slightly longer than current fashion—was artfully disheveled. He seemed to have an extensive wardrobe of suede jackets, close-fitting black T-shirts, and faded, baggy jeans. "More harassment?" Cross's full lips were trembling in rage. "Do you have any idea what it feels like to have to face that every day?" Cross pointed to Dougie Brown's car. "You people are ruining my life."

Mornay, still wet from his work at the accident site, stepped into Cross's foyer without wiping his feet on the doormat. Cross's fussy ways and breathless manner of speaking thoroughly annoyed him.

"We've just found Matthew's body. We need to ask a few questions."

Mornay walked through a doorway into Cross's lounge, a long narrow room dominated by a stereo system that had three remote controls. Cross had expensive tastes, and, as far as they could deduce, the young man did not have the income to support them. But so far their surveillance had produced nothing significant.

"Is it true?" Cross asked Claire, whom he'd wrongfully assumed was the more sympathetic of the pair. Claire ignored the question.

Cross collapsed into one of his black leather settees. "Oh, dear God. How awful for his parents. What happened?"

Mornay picked up one of the stereo remotes. "Why aren't you at work today, Jonathan?"

"I've been put on administrative leave until a decision is made to keep me on staff."

Mornay spotted a holdall on the floor next to the other settee. "Planning a trip?"

"A visit to my father. With the police cars out front, people assume I've something to do with Matthew's disappearance. I'll probably lose my job, though I've done nothing except grade Matthew's papers."

Mornay tossed the remote onto the table.

Cross jutted his square jaw forward, and said defiantly, "And I didn't even like him. Not really. I was only nice to him because I felt sorry for him."

"Why would you feel sorry for Matthew?"

"His parents. He couldn't make a move without one of them knowing what he was doing and whom he was going to be with. They were suffocating him, and he hated it."

"Did he ever mention running away?"

"What boy doesn't at that age?"

"He specifically spoke to you about running away?"

"I can't recall an exact date. Shortly after term started, I suppose."

"Curious you didn't mention this before."

"I've only just remembered."

"Don't leave town, Jonathan. If you do, I will find you. Not everything you hear on the telly is shite: I *really* am good at hunting men."

As they walked to the car, Claire said, "I thought you hated that advert." She was referring to the Grampian Police Force's newest recruiting campaign. They were using a real-life film of Mornay blocking an obnoxious reporter's access to Claire. The reporter, Ted Whyte, was from a news program that inundated its viewers with bizarre camera angles instead of actual news content. When the reporter switched tactics and began questioning him, Mornay, much to his disgust, had given a glib answer that had been recorded by the reporter's cameraman. The bosses at the news program had sold the film for an exorbitant sum to the Grampian Police, who, in a fit of logic understood only by the higher echelons, decided to use the film to draw in recruits.

"I do hate that bloody piece of film. But if it'll keep that Cross in his place, the public humiliation I've got to put up with will be worth it."

"Public humiliation? You've got your own fan club because of Ted Whyte."

"If I had it to do over, I'd break Whyte's nose and take my suspension."

Ted Whyte had asked Mornay if the skills he'd learned as a Royal Marine had helped him solve his last case. That case had gotten a lot of publicity, but the discovery of Matthew Adair's body today was going to trigger a media frenzy that would likely sweep across the whole UK. He'd had too many reporters after him these past weeks to relish the thought of having microphones shoved in his face while going in or out of the police office. Or of being stalked by the elusive Teddy Whyte, who'd probably turn into a permanent shadow.

Mornay had been outside so long that, as soon as he walked inside the police office, his skin started to ache from the warmth. It was a quarter to two. His only meal had been the rolls DS Taylor shared early that morning. The desk he shared with Claire was a depressing cluster of open cases. They had two missing persons that were probably runaways, and a handful of unsolved burglaries. Next week he was due in Sheriff's Court on a battery case. The paperwork was piling up faster than he could sift through it, since Matthew's disappearance. He was spending more time in the inquiry room set up next door, working on the Adair case, than at his desk.

Four months earlier, the building adjacent to the police office had been purchased for expansion and was halfway through the remodeling process. The top floor would be used for records storage, and the second floor had been promised to CID. No more sharing a desk; instead, he and Claire would share an office with a window. The bottom floor was to be turned into a proper inquiry room and two new interview rooms. A wide doorway had been knocked out of the common wall, and a temporary door of plastic sheeting had been hung. Since Matthew's disappearance, the entire bottom floor of the new building had been turned into a temporary inquiry room. Macduff's CID staff had been expanded by officers rotating in from other CID offices and from members of the Traffic Division.

Constable Sahotra approached. "The Nissan and the horse box are the property of a Harold Cosgrove from Turnhill. He's a horse trainer."

"Why was an English horse trainer carting sheep and straw through northern Scotland at this time of year?" Mornay picked up the stack of message slips and headed toward the inquiry room.

Sahotra followed. Of everyone at the station, he'd been the most hopeful that Matthew Adair would be found alive and well. "Cosgrove died over a year ago. His yard's been closed since his death, according to the land agent I spoke with. I've called the Durham Constabulary, who will make inquiries and see if anyone's been on the property. They'll also contact the family solicitor to do an inventory, find out if any vehicles are missing." Sahotra lifted a sheet of paper. "Cosgrove had a slew of vehicles; horse trailers and several work trucks."

Mornay held the plastic sheeting aside for Sahotra. The temporary door was useless at containing the construction dust; chalky white dust had settled everywhere on the old side. On the new side, a move couldn't be made without sending puffs of the fine dust floating into the air.

A jumbled assortment of six tables in the center of the large room seved as temporary desks for the officers assigned to the Adair inquiry—over thirty, at the last count. The wall at the far end of the room held boards that displayed the information they'd acquired so far: photographs, lines of inquiries, names, personnel assigned to particular tasks. A mass of computer cables and electrical cords and telephone lines as thick as Mornay's wrist snaked across the ceiling, and lines and cables dangled down from the thick mass. The cables were temporarily fastened to the exposed ductwork, held in place with plastic ties and silvery industrial tape. The skeletal boards that formed the outlines of the interior walls were as far as the workers had gotten before being called off the job due to the inquiry. The gritty, damp smell of new concrete almost overpowered the heavily sweet smell of Byrne's cigars.

Mornay's old nemesis, DI Walter Byrne, had been brought back to work on the Adair case and put at the back of the inquiry room. Byrne didn't like it that DI Gordon was in his old office, nor was he happy with Gordon's proximity; battle lines were drawn at every briefing.

Claire stood in front of a map taped to the unpainted wall. Next to the map was a board that listed every person they'd interviewed for the Adair case, over 150 names. Beside each name was a corresponding file number. He and Claire had conducted over a third of those interviews.

Claire lifted a finger and touched a point on the map. "The crash site is barely a fifteen-minute drive from Matthew's home."

"I know."

She marked the crash site with a red pin.

"Sergeant Mornay, Constable Gillespie," DI Byrne's gravelly voice sounded behind them. "A word in my office."

Byrne's office was primarily decorated with ashes from the cigars he chain-smoked, despite the strict no-smoking policy in the building. On the wall behind the door hung a massive framed corkboard. This was where he had tacked all of the Strategic Intentions literature headquarters printed. The literature outlined, in exhaustive detail, how everyone in the Grampian Police was supposed to perform their jobs. Next to the corkboard was a detailed map of all the land the Grampian Police covered. Byrne had put various colored pins across the map; only he knew their significance. He'd put up the map after his return to Macduff.

"Why's he back?" Mornay had asked Detective Chief Inspector McNab when word trickled down that Byrne was returning. He'd been assigned to the Scottish Crime Squad, and was supposed to have remained with them until his retirement the following year. "DI Gordon's doing a fair job."

"She is," McNab agreed. "It's her father that has me concerned. Lord Gordon is systematically tearing the force down every time he has a camera pointed his way. He was silent for so long after Matthew Adair disappeared, I thought we were finally going to be free of him. But now he's back at it."

Lord Murdo Gordon was one of the regional ministers in parliament for northeast Scotland and the deputy justice minister for the Scottish Executive. The cessation of his caustic interviews—which the media delighted in airing—had been viewed with relief by many on the force. On day eight of Matthew's disappearance, Lord Gordon began conducting daily briefings from the front garden of Matthew Adair's house. The resulting media blitz was unlike anything the

Grampian Police had encountered. Lord Gordon's hard-hitting tactics had skyrocketed his popularity.

"Is Gordon off the Adair inquiry, then?" Mornay had asked.

"She's put in too much work to be pulled off at this stage."

Mornay didn't follow the logic that put Byrne back in an office that was already adequately staffed by senior officers. "And Byrne will be working the Adair inquiry as well?"

"He's been around the force a long time," was McNab's nonanswer. "And we need a result."

"It hasn't been six months since that fiasco in Glen Ross. *His* fiasco, mind you. We're supposed to arrest people like Byrne—not let them run loose, endangering everyone who gets near him."

"He's good at bending the ears of the right people. And he's got a long memory."

Mornay realized McNab's words were meant as a warning. They had months to wait until Byrne retired. It was just a drop in the bucket to McNab, who was contemplating another ten or fifteen years on the force, at progressively higher ranks.

"You'll just have to make it work."

Claire closed the door to Byrne's office, jarring Mornay back to the present. Byrne plowed into the conversation. "You're positive the body was Matthew Adair?"

"Yes."

Matthew had gone missing two weeks earlier from Aberdeen, his disappearance led to a massive missing persons search. Matthew's parents had turned their house into a search headquarters. They'd brought in fax machines and printers and phones. They'd organized and fed an army of volunteers. *God be with them today.*

"Will the Adair briefing go as usual tonight?" Mornay asked.

Byrne fixed him with an unfriendly look and shoved his hands in his pockets. Except for the weight he'd lost, this was vintage Byrne. "I understand you were late arriving at the scene this morning."

"I wasn't home when the call came."

"That's why you're issued a pager and a mobile." Byrne's eyes narrowed. "Gordon's been keeping you out late every night?"

Byrne's tone implied there was more to the late-evening shifts than Mornay's being Laina Gordon's glorified chauffeur, but there was damn all he could do about it. "We interviewed Lynda Palmer again last night. She had no new information to offer about her daughter's disappearance. Then we went around to a few of her daughter's favorite clubs. Then I had a four-hour shift at Jonathan Cross's house."

"And had a grand time, I'm sure. Since you weren't at your desk this morning, where you should have been, Gillespie covered for you."

Mornay hazarded a glance Claire's way. There were bright spots of color on her cheeks. He studied her for a moment. She'd started wearing makeup recently, but she applied it with a light touch. She'd also put a rinse in her red-gold hair. He wondered if the changes were because DI Gordon was so fastidious with her own appearance. DI Gordon never had an eyelash out of place or wore anything that could've been bought on a DI's salary.

Or maybe the answer was simpler. Maybe Claire had a boyfriend.

Claire kept her gaze straight ahead, intending to get through the meeting with minimal friction.

"Just because Laina Bloody Gordon is on the Adair inquiry doesn't mean we're going to sit on our thumbs. Gordon's father is no friend to the force, and it's time someone went on the bloody offensive around here."

Lord Murdo Gordon was a friend of Matthew's parents. Gordon's briefings from the Adair's front garden over the past six days were undoubtedly the reason the country had galvanized so thoroughly behind the Adairs and the reason the police were being viewed with such animosity. The public was taking the criticism to the next level; they were equating the failure to find Matthew with a lack of effort.

"Gillespie," Byrne continued, "I want you to assemble a list of horse trainers in Scotland."

"We already know who owned the trailer," Mornay said.

"Do you have a problem with Gillespie's assignment?"

"What's the point of wasting time chasing down horse trainers when we know exactly where the Nissan came from?"

"Off you go, Gillespie," Byrne said without taking his gaze away from Mornay. "The sergeant will be along soon." To Mornay he said, "Where are you on the *Sunward* inquiry?"

"It's been turned over to the Scottish Drug Enforcement Agency. I'm special liaison. The Paisley brothers have never been known for their intelligence; they probably blew themselves up."

The *Sunward* was a nineteen-foot fishing trawler that had mysteriously blown up in the North Sea.

Another trawler had been nearby when the explosion occurred; the crew of the second boat had secured some of the *Sunward*'s wreckage after the destroyed trawler sank. Though there'd been three crew members aboard the *Sunward*—Trevor and Donald Paisley and Scott Gray—their bodies weren't found. In his pocket, Mornay was carrying a bit of what might have been the fish hold area of the trawler. The strange piece of metal was the reason Mornay didn't put up much of a fuss when he was told he'd been assigned as special liaison.

"The briefing tonight?"

Byrne puffed out his chest and swept his depressing little office with an expansive, proprietary gaze. "I'll attend. You'll do what you're told, and you'll do it with a smile. I don't want to hear another word about Harold Cosgrove. He's dead. That, coupled with the fact he's an English citizen, brings up a jurisdictional predicament that will make our bandy-legged superintendent's knees knock. So we'll run along in the direction I've just set and see what we find."

If Mornay pushed, he'd be charged with personally contacting each horse trainer. "What about Matthew Adair?" he asked.

"You'll find out what we're doing soon enough."

Mornay managed to keep his expression neutral. "So that leaves me with the *Sunward* and the missing Palmer girl."

"Tess Palmer has probably set up shop on a corner in Edinburgh or London by now." Byrne leaned back in his chair and smiled. "Which leaves you with the *Sunward*. Mind you come back in one piece; Gillespie can't do everything by herself, can she?"

Mornay delayed his trip to the boatyard long enough to gulp down a cup of coffee. DCI McNab called him into his office as he was leaving.

Byrne was seated in the corner of McNab's office, scowling.

"I'm glad we caught you," McNab said, his gaze avoiding the corner where Byrne sat.

"Sir?"

"The *Sunward* inquiry can wait. There's a briefing I want you to attend in two hours' time. I want you to pick up the Adairs. Take Gillespie with you. The Adairs seem to prefer you two over everyone else." McNab let the statement hang in the air for Byrne's benefit, then focused on Mornay's wrinkled suit. "You've something better to wear than that for the briefing, I hope?"

# Chapter Three

In the northeast part of Scotland, November was the damp segue Mother Nature used between the brisk months of fall and the frigid months of winter. Inhabitants resigned themselves to a world reduced to a gray skullcap of clouds, biting winds, and the occasional watery ray of sunshine that managed to squirm through the tightly knit heavens.

David Lockwood stared down at Cordiff's thick-walled cottages, which huddled in the bowl-shaped valley. Gray, squat, and square, the cottages were built to withstand the fierce gales that blew in from the North Sea. Each cottage looked like the next; individuality was expressed through the spot one chose to park the car, or the color one painted the front door, or what one did with the minuscule front garden. Smoke chugged out of chimneys, and lamps, glowing behind double and triple glazing, were lit early to ward off the gloom.

Everyone in the valley wanted to be somewhere warmer, and David was no exception. He was an expert at ensuring he was always somewhere better than there, whatever the time of year. He'd rather be home or in his air-conditioned office overlooking Sydney Harbor, or playing one of his biweekly golf games beneath the blistering Australian sun. But this time there'd been no escaping.

It was only half past three, and it looked like dusk. David scrutinized the hills surrounding the valley and wondered where the hell his seventeen-year-old stepsister could have wandered to. Why would she *want* to wander anywhere outside in weather like this? He'd been walking for an hour. If he didn't find her soon, it would be dark when they returned to the castle.

David followed one of the drystone walls that marked the eastern border of the property. His stepsister, Lady Eilish Lockwood, mistress of Finovar Castle, claimed to be familiar with every square meter of her estate.

He came upon his quarry quite suddenly. She was sitting on a drystone wall, blending quite well because she wore an inordinate amount of muddy earth on her body between chin and ankles.

"Birding again, Lee?" David asked, managing to restrain his smile of amusement.

"Actually, I was walking along the walls, looking for damaged bits. We're repairing them next spring." Eilish solemnly watched David as she kicked the heels of her oversized Wellies against the wall. The

Wellies were his castoffs, according to Eilish. In reality, they'd been innocently passing the time in his cupboard until she pounced on them and pronounced them hers. Mud splattered off their cleated soles with little plops.

David inspected her, from the muddy damp spots at her knees to the snags in her sweater. The bits of dun-colored mud on Eilish's cheeks were at odds with her flawless ivory skin.

"It's Thursday. You were supposed to come home tomorrow," Eilish said.

David clutched his chest with a theatrical flourish. "Such a warm welcome. I should return early more often."

Eilish turned her head, presenting him with her profile. "You-know-who is cooking tonight, and you know how annoyed he gets when he's surprised."

"Lord Gordon might not make it tonight." Murdo Gordon was going to marry their stepmother in April. He'd become a fixture at Finovar over the past year, a development neither of them cared for, though Deborah wasn't related to them by anything more than a name. The semantics of their family was strange, but it worked for them.

"Why not?" Eilish asked.

"The police found that boy that went missing from Aberdeen this morning."

"He was dead?"

"Unfortunately."

"Then you-know-who will be in a state when he does finally arrive. He always is, after he gives one of his interviews criticizing the police." She hopped off the wall. They started walking across the field.

"What sort of state?"

"Frothing-at-the-mouth angry. He's been horrid to Deborah these past two weeks. I'd have chucked him by now." She picked at some of the mud on her pullover. "Matthew was a local boy, did you know?"

"They mentioned it."

"Where did they find his body?"

"Near John White's farm. There was an accident of some sort. That's all they would say."

"My God, so close to home."

"Just shows you that we're vulnerable every-where, even in the one place we should feel most secure." Before she could ask what David meant, he reached out and plucked at the neck of her pullover. "I was wondering where this had gone."

"If you wanted it back all you had to do was come and get it."

David grinned. "I've seen the state of your cup-boards. The QE2 could be buried at the bottom, and no one would be the wiser."

She noticed the white bandage around his hand. "What happened?"

"A nasty accident with a paring knife. The doc-tors are almost positive I'll survive."

The castle came into view. Finovar was built out of massive granite blocks, and the central part of the castle shot five stories up into the sky. Built as a fortress in the late 1200s, it had a crenellated roofline with a crenellated tower at each corner. The central tower had slotted archer's windows and nar-row circular staircases and low, narrow passages to prevent easy access to the interior if invaders breached the massive main entrance. Several later additions were more hospitable, the largest having been added in the late 1700s. The rooms in those

additions were airy and pleasant and neatly sandwiched the central tower, forming the letter H if one
were to view it from overhead. The family quarters
were located in the south wing. The areas used for
entertaining—billiards room, library, lounges—were
located in the north wing, which had the more spec-
tacular views of the North Sea.

"When are you returning to Australia?"

"Sunday."

Eilish halted her loose-limbed gallop. *"Sunday!*
That's only three days. Why do you never want to
stay longer?"

They were crossing the last bit of field to the west
of the castle. David steered Eilish toward a narrow
bridge that led to the carriage yard and stables, and
eventually to the present front entrance to the castle.
The bridge, installed half a century before the First
World War, spanned a deep, steeply sided chasm.
David always got vertigo if he looked over the side
of the bridge, though the drop below them wasn't
nearly as harrowing as the drops that surrounded
Finovar's peninsula. He resolutely kept his gaze on
the gravel square that served as the public car park.

An older Mitsubishi was parked behind his car.

Eilish cursed. "I've forgotten about Calvin." She
glanced down at her muddied clothes and cursed again.

"Calvin?" David's question echoed behind Eilish,
who was trotting over to the Mitsubishi, which had
HARRIS VETERINARY CLINIC stenciled in white letters
along its side. When had Eilish ever cared about the
state of her clothes?

Eilish was fairly skipping when she returned with
Calvin, which was quite the accomplishment in
Wellies four sizes too large.

David allowed his hand to be crushed and winced when he was clapped heartily on the shoulder while Eilish introduced Calvin Walsh; junior partner with Harris Veterinary Clinic. Broad was the best adjective to succinctly describe the young man: broad of face, shoulders, and hands, Calvin Walsh was conventionally handsome if you went for the outdoorsy type. And the animation in Eilish's face suggested she did. Naturally.

David followed the pair through the dark portal of the castle and wondered how the defenders of bygone years protected themselves against invaders of the heart.

Mornay loathed everything about the morgue: the lack of windows, the low ceilings, and the smells that seemed to permeate the very blocks that formed the walls. He lounged against a scarred black filing cabinet in the small office of Dr. Cedric Hall, the chief of the Forensic Science Laboratory for the Grampian Police, and took shallow breaths. The worst smell was the industrial-strength cleanser used throughout the basement morgue. Its chemicals weren't masked with lemon or pine scents to make it more tolerable. Every noxious breath seemed to scald the back of his throat.

If there was anything he could be grateful for, it was the fact he didn't need to spend very much time down there—this year there were only two homicides in his command area.

Three, counting Matthew Adair.

DI Laina Gordon led Charles and Rita Adair into the office. They were a handsome couple, despite the deep lines of anguish around their eyes and mouths.

"They've been mentally preparing themselves for this eventuality," Gordon had told him in the car park.

Mornay tried, but couldn't ignore Gordon's smugness. "That's as asinine as suggesting someone could practice drowning," he'd shot back. "How do parents *prepare* themselves for the worst kind of news? They don't; they fight its eventuality. Maybe not as thoroughly as the Adairs, but they fight it."

Gordon was not one of those officers who valued their subordinates' opinions, and she ignored him as she tried to make the Adairs comfortable. Her red suit and red nails were ghoulish under the bright fluorescent lights that dominated the Forensic Science Laboratory.

During his years on the force, he'd seen all sorts of families, most of them in the worst light possible: fathers who spent all their time in the pubs, mothers more interested in what Hollywood actresses were doing than what mischief their children were getting into. The Adairs had relocated to Cordiff from Portsmouth two months before their son was born. They'd chosen Cordiff because of its size, small enough to have the feeling of a country village, large enough to have a good school—the perfect environment to raise a family. And it was less than an hour from Aberdeen, where Charles Adair worked as an engineer at one of the North Sea oil companies.

Dr. Cedric Hall walked into the office. Though he was small and wiry, he would never be lost in a crowd. Born in Trinidad, he still carried a hint of a musical lilt beneath the Doric accent he'd picked up as a child in Aberdeen. If Dr. Hall was surprised to see the Adairs, he didn't let it show. Gordon shouldn't have brought them down there, but that was something else she hadn't wanted to hear from Mornay.

Hall sent a curt nod in Mornay's direction, then turned a compassionate gaze on Charles and Rita Adair.

"Is it definitely . . ." Charles Adair began, but let the words trail off as his wife squeezed his hand. Adair knew he and his wife wouldn't have been brought to Aberdeen if the police weren't sure. But he'd still been hoping. "What happened to Matthew?" he asked when he'd regained his composure.

"He sustained a massive blow to his right temple. Death would've been instantaneous."

The Adairs leaned closer together, supporting each other. Hall's words had severed all hope of the future they'd expected to have with their son. There would be no more skinned knees. No more muddy football matches to attend. The Adairs' grief radiated from their bodies like heat, scorching everyone in the room.

Mornay examined the tiled floor next to his feet. This was one of the times he wished he hadn't been forced to quit smoking; nicotine was exactly what he needed.

He wanted to remain exempt from the depth of their emotions, but it was impossible. Gordon appeared the only one impervious. His own child was in a hospital half an hour away, growing inside a woman whose hold on life was so tenuous, the doctors refused to speculate on the survival of either of them.

Charles Adair swallowed twice before asking, "Was he molested?"

"There are no signs that I can detect."

"That's not a particularly direct answer," Charles
Adair said.

"My examination hasn't been completed yet. If I
seem to be answering your questions obliquely, it's
because I don't want to give you false information."

"Can we see him?"

"Yes, you may. I'm afraid you won't be permitted
in the same room, however. We're still collecting evidence to discover, more clearly, what happened to
your son." Hall cast a withering glance in Gordon's
direction. "My assistant will take you now."

Charles Adair turned to his wife and seemed
silently to communicate a question to her with his
eyes. She nodded. They both turned to Mornay, and
Charles Adair spoke.

"We need you to find who did this to our son.
You said you hunt men; that it's what you're good
at. We need you to hunt down the person, the animal, who killed our boy."

Mornay could feel Laina Gordon's anger from
across the room. "Mr. Adair," she began, but
Charles Adair continued speaking, ignoring her as
completely as if she'd just been vaporized from the
face of the earth. It was a response Laina Gordon
rarely   encountered,   which   perversely   pleased
Mornay despite his apprehension regarding the
Adairs' expectations.

"We know you can find him," Charles Adair
insisted quietly.

In the face of such adamant need, Mornay could
only nod and say, "We'll do our best."

Dr. Hall motioned to someone through the window set in the door. Arthur, the lab technician
Mornay dubbed Lothario because of his eagerness to

assist Claire, entered the room. Beneath his open white lab coat, Lothario was dressed with his usual tasteless flair in a shirt made from a shiny black material that had lurid flames spurting down the front, black corduroy trousers, and black trainers. It was an outfit suited to a spotty fourteen-year-old, not a fortysomething computer nerd. On the plump side, Lothario made *whisk, whisk* sounds as he led the Adairs out of the room.

"They had a right to know, Dr. Hall," Gordon said, before the door had fully closed.

Hall's voice, low and angry, blasted across the room. "Yes, they did, Inspector, in the privacy of their own home. They should *never* have been brought here. There was no need for a formal identification. Now they'll have to fight their way through a sea of reporters to leave. But it'll make a good cover for the *Press and Journal,* won't it? The grieving parents being led to their car by a somber Detective Inspector Gordon, who just happened to be dressed for the occasion in smashing red."

Hall removed his lab coat and threw it on the desk. Below the coat he wore his usual work clothes: a heavily starched, long-sleeved white shirt, narrow silk tie, braces, and tailored wool trousers.

Gordon's face remained composed. "I resent the implications of—"

"I resent your lack of compassion, Inspector. I resent police officers exploiting the people they're charged with protecting, for personal gain." He held up a hand. "Don't insult my intelligence by suggesting it was in their best interest to be subjected to this cruelty. You can be assured I will be speaking to Superintendent Campbell about the matter. Now, do you want to hear what I've found, or would you prefer to attend your press briefing utterly ignorant of Matthew Adair's condition?"

"I'd be happy to hear what you've found, if you can manage it without sermonizing," Gordon said in the icy voice Mornay knew all too well.

He decided to speak before they went for each other's throats. "How severe was the blow?"

Hall's gaze turned to Mornay, and the small man took a deep breath. "You saw the damage at the scene, correct?"

Mornay nodded.

"Something punctured through the bone at Matthew's temple. The wound is roughly one and a half centimeters around and nearly as deep. There's odd bruising below the wound."

"Any idea about the weapon?"

"None, beyond the fact that it was a blunt instrument with an odd edging. What I find particularly troubling is the bruising on Matthew's arms and back. The boy put up one hell of a struggle with someone."

There was a sharp gasp. They turned. Charles and Rita Adair were standing in the doorway. Charles Adair's face had drained of all color; his wife was holding him by the arm to prevent him from toppling forward. Mornay rushed to his side and helped him into a chair.

"We didn't know where else to go," Charles Adair said.

His wife walked across the room and stood in front of Dr. Hall. "What else did you find?"

"I'm afraid it's too soon to say, at this point."

Claire chose that moment to enter Dr. Hall's

office, and Dr. Hall seized his opportunity to have the grieving parents moved.

"Christ," Dr. Hall cursed when the Adairs were gone. He stared hard at Laina Gordon, who merely returned the look.

Mornay repeated Rita Adair's questions: "What else did you find?"

"There's bruising on Matthew's elbows, shoulders, and forearms, as well as the odd bruising around the head wound. However, the more disturbing fact is that his body was thoroughly washed after he died. With bleach. Someone was intentionally trying to remove any trace evidence. Fortunately for us, they were less thorough with his clothing; it wasn't washed at all. Sorting the fibers we've found will take time."

Laina Gordon was impatiently pacing in front of Hall's desk, sending nauseating waves of a sweet perfume in Mornay's direction. "You told the Adairs he wasn't molested."

"I said he didn't appear to have been molested, which is what they wanted to hear, Inspector. All I was able to determine was that there appeared to be no penetration or any obvious trauma to his body."

"A child can be sexually molested without penetration."

"I'm aware of that, Inspector," Hall replied coldly. "Baldly stating that fact wouldn't have been very soothing to the parents, however."

"You've determined the extent of the boy's injuries from having had the body for only four hours?"

"I can assure you, Inspector, whenever *I* conduct an investigation, I am quite thorough. I wouldn't want to do anything that might hinder the efforts of the officers in the field. It's my job to assist them."

"How long was the boy held before he was killed?" she asked.

"Inspector," Mornay said, "his name was Matthew. You wouldn't want to make the mistake of calling him 'the boy' in front of the cameras. You'll come across as uncaring. And it'll do your career good to remember that Matthew liked to read. He liked to play games on his computer. He was too old to admit to liking dinosaurs, but he wasn't too old to give his mum a kiss before he went off to school every day."

Gordon held his gaze for several long moments. Somewhere else in the laboratory, a phone was ringing. She turned back to Dr. Hall. "About the suggestion that the body was cleaned," she prompted.

"I'm not simply suggesting. Someone did clean it. The odor of bleach on the body was unmistakable. Whoever cleaned him knew what they were doing. Particular attention had been paid to his nails."

"What else did you find?" Mornay asked.

"The angle of the wound was curious." Hall paused. "It angled up slightly." Hall put a pencil near his temple, the length of the pencil close to Hall's head. "Like this."

"He could've been struck while on the ground," Mornay said.

"Possibly, but given the fact he appeared to have fought back . . ." Dr. Hall shrugged. "I'll have to finish my examination before I can commit myself. It's possible he was injured in a fall. He had extensive bruising on his right shoulder."

"You're going to say he was killed by accident?" Gordon demanded. "Is that what you're going to put in your report? That he could've died from a fall?"

"I am going to state that it is possible for Matthew to have obtained his head wound in a fall."

"So the answer is yes," Gordon snapped. "I don't understand why you can't say yes when that's exactly what you mean. If you put that in your report, we might as well not go on with the bloody investigation. You've just given the defense agent a perfect out for his client, whenever we make an arrest. It was an accident."

Gordon glanced impatiently at her watch for the third time in as many minutes. "We're going to need that report as quickly as possible."

"You'll have the postmortem report by midnight. But it could take as long as two weeks to process his clothing."

Gordon pressed her perfectly outlined lips together, clearly choosing to fight her battle of wills later, after the press briefing. Obviously she wasn't aware of the danger of getting on Hall's bad side. Or, more likely, she thought she was impervious.

Mornay pushed himself away from the filing cabinet, eager to escape.

"Feeling squeamish, Sergeant?" Gordon asked.

"Aye," Mornay replied as he neared the door. "Some things, a man shouldn't have to stomach."

# Chapter Four

Deborah Lockwood moved the whiskey decanter out of David's reach. "You've had enough, don't you think?"

"Apparently not; I'm still conscious." David finished his fourth whiskey since dinner, and she watched him roll the cut-crystal tumbler between his hands. "Why didn't you tell me about Calvin the Magnificent?" David's words were slurring. He nodded in the direction of the kitchen, where Calvin Walsh, Eilish, and Deborah's fiancé, Lord Murdo Gordon, were putting away the dinner dishes.

"I suppose because I didn't think he would last this long. Eilish has always been so indifferent about boys and dating, as if she could take them or leave them."

Deborah glanced at her watch. It was just going on nine. If she was lucky, she'd have everyone settled in their rooms within the hour, before David said something they would all regret.

"She certainly seems decisive now," David said. "She was giggling at dinner. She looked utterly absurd."

"You sound jealous," Deborah remarked quietly.

She held his gaze until he broke it by standing and reaching across her for the whiskey decanter. David had been four when his mother married Gerald Lockwood. His mother was killed in an auto accident just before his fifth birthday, so he never found out who his biological father was. Gerald always claimed David's mother never got the chance to tell him. Gerald married again when David was six, but he lost his second wife in complications delivering Eilish.

Deborah had married Gerald before Eilish's first birthday. Their marriage had been for the purpose of providing David and Eilish a mother; Gerald had been clear on that point from the start. But that hadn't stopped her from falling in love with Gerald or the children. They were only married ten years when he died, but they'd become the best of friends in that time, a fact few wives could claim about their husbands.

Deborah studied David's tanned face as he stared at the whiskey in his tumbler, but she gleaned nothing from his expression. "Is that why you moved to Australia? Because of Eilish?"

"No." He had to force the word out. "I did not move because I was having indecent thoughts about my ten-year-old stepsister. I moved for an entirely different reason."

"Is Eilish the reason you're back?"

"I'm here because my therapist made me return." He finished his fifth whiskey.

"Therapist?" she echoed.

"Deborah," Murdo called out, "come see the surprise I've gotten for Eilish's birthday."

Deborah stood and followed Murdo out the kitchen door. She kept glancing furtively at David, but he refused to look her way.


"What do you think?" Murdo was clearly eager for praise. Eilish, David, and Deborah were huddled next to Calvin's Mitsubishi, using each other as a buffer to ward off the chilling breeze. The close proximity also served to keep David steady on his feet.

"Did you know about this?" Eilish whispered furtively to Deborah.

"I had no idea," she whispered back. "This is the car his father gave him when he graduated from Eton." Eilish's eyes grew rounder, and her lips moved silently. If Deborah had to guess at Eilish's comment, it would be *shit*.

Calvin and Murdo stood on the opposite side of the silver Jaguar; the polished chrome of the lustrous car glinted in the lights surrounding the graveled courtyard. Calvin ran his hand along the sleek bonnet, grinning, while he peppered Murdo with questions about the engine. David slowly walked toward the car.

"Lee," Deborah whispered. "Walk with him so he won't fall."

Eilish ran forward and linked arms with David as he began his own inspection of the Jaguar.

Deborah went to Murdo and slipped her arm around his waist. "This is far too generous a gift. You adore this car."

"My father gave it to me, and I can't think of anything I'd rather do than give it to Eilish. I know she and I have had our differences in the past, but I'm hoping to put that behind us."

She stood on her tiptoes and gave him a kiss. "Then you're a dear, dear man."

In front of the car, David was closely examining the Jaguar statuette leaping from the center of the hood, hands on either side of it to keep himself steady. When he straightened, Eilish had to grab him by the waist so he didn't pitch face forward onto the stones.

When he regained his balance, David said, "Pity Eilish doesn't drive." The remark was made with a mocking twist to his mouth. "You've a gouge here. A deep one, I can see bare metal."

Murdo's body stiffened. "I'm sure you're mistaken." He walked around the Jaguar to examine the spot David was pointing out.

"The light's bad, I'll grant you, but you can just make it out, there," David pointed to a spot just slightly in front of the leaping Jaguar.

"So it is," Murdo said after a quick glance. "Thank you for pointing it out. I'll have it put in the shop next week." He turned to Eilish. "So what do you think? A driving course won't be too difficult. You can have your license by the holidays if you work at it."

"I thought teaching Eilish to ride a horse wouldn't be too difficult either," David said. "What I didn't know was that she had an aversion to horses."

"I don't mind looking at them from across a field," Eilish said in her defense.

"You do want a car, don't you?" Murdo asked. He'd finally noticed Eilish's expression as she examined her gift. Deborah crossed her fingers, hoping Eilish would temper her customary bluntness.

"Of course, I do, eventually. And the Jaguar's lovely; it truly is."

"But," Murdo prompted.

"It's a bit posh for me, don't you think?"

David chuckled. "I think our Lee is more the dented Mitsubishi type, Lord Gordon."

The remark elicited a scowl from Murdo and a blush from Eilish.

Deborah clamped her arms close to her body. "I'm freezing, why don't we go inside and warm up. Eilish can decide later if she wants to keep the gift or not." With a look at David, warning him not to say another word, Deborah continued, "It's her gift; it should be her decision."

"Do you think he's disappointed I didn't want it?" Eilish asked David. They'd left Murdo and Deborah half an hour earlier. Calvin had gone home; he had calls to make early the next morning.

David walked slowly out of the bathroom. He'd showered and now wore tattered hiking shorts and an even more tattered black T-shirt. His hair was damp, and his eyes were bloodshot.

"He's probably surprised you didn't fall over yourself in gratitude," David answered. "Rejection is probably a foreign concept to a man like Murdo Gordon."

"I've never seen you drunk before."

"You weren't paying attention."

Eilish spotted dark bruising and scratches on his arm. She walked across the room and lifted his T-shirt before he could protest or pull away. There was extensive bruising across his rib cage; the dark marks extended below the waistband of his shorts.

"Just how long have you been back?"

David answered truthfully. "A week, tomorrow."

Eilish poked one of his larger bruises, making him flinch. Then she grabbed his hand to stare at his palm. The plasters had come off in the shower. The cut on his hand was raw and held together with four stitches. "A paring knife?"

"I had an accident training your horse."

She dropped his hand. "So you'd rather be trampled to death by those stupid horses instead of spending time here?"

"The castle has enough men roaming the halls; there's no need for me to crowd anyone."

She caught the undertone immediately. "You don't like Calvin now? You didn't even try to get to know him; you were buried behind a whiskey bottle all evening. You barely said a dozen words to him."

"Would you rather I'd done my Benny Hill impersonation?"

"How about an impersonation of a civil human being?" She held up her hands to stop his reply. "I refuse to be drawn into another argument. Are you going to tell me what really happened?"

"The horse spooked. I was thrown. Your horse wasn't injured, by the way."

"And what about you? What happens when you have one of these training falls and land on that bloody thick head of yours? How many bones did you fracture this time?"

"They're only bruises, Lee. And they always look worse than they actually are."

Tears spilled down her cheeks before she could wipe them away.

"Lee," he whispered, "you're getting upset over nothing. I'm fine." He cradled her head in his hands and turned her face to look at him. "You believe me, don't you?"

"I believe you're a great bloody id—"

David kissed her. He tasted of whiskey and toothpaste.

She pulled away and walked quickly to the window. "I don't like it when you're drunk."

"I'm sorry. You're right, I am an idiot."

She stared down into the courtyard. "David, someone's just come out the front."

"Gordon, probably."

"He's too small."

David joined her at the window.

The front entrance was wide open, and a man was jogging down the stairs. He wore jeans and a dark rain slicker with a hood. The hood obscured his face. He held a torch in his right hand that cast a powerful beam of light onto the stones of the courtyard.

"That isn't Murdo or Deborah," she said.

The stranger opened the driver's door of the Jaguar. By the time David reached the phone next to his bed, the powerful engine was being revved. Apparently, the stranger had little regard for anyone who might be within hearing distance.

The red pinpricks from the Jaguar's taillights had vanished in the distance by the time David finished his call to the police station.

Assistant Chief Constable Roger Donaldson was preparing to leave his office for the press briefing when Mornay knocked on his door. Donaldson was a jolly man with four grandchildren he doted on. He was the top man at CID.

"Sir, do you have time for a quick word?"

"Come in." Donaldson's greeting was friendly; the recruiting commercial using Mornay's impulsive remark to Teddy Whyte was Roger Donaldson's brainchild.

"Sir, the recruiting campaign—you said it would be over by late October."

"I know I did, but our recruiting numbers are up. It's hard to tamper with something that's working so effectively. In fact . . ." Donaldson deposited his briefing materials on his desk and went to his door, reaching behind it to pull out a large poster glued to a stiff backing. "These are hot off the presses."

It was a still photograph of Mornay, taken from Teddy Whyte's film footage. The words *Zero Tolerance* were written across the bottom in bold white letters. On the right side of the poster were smaller photographs superimposed over his image; they ran from top to bottom and featured action shots of other CID personnel.

"We need the public to see our tough stance against crime, but they can't relate to an entire organization. From the rise in new applicants, we know they can relate to one man. These new recruits, they want to be a tough-talking cop, just like you. We'll phase out the recruiting adverts in a couple of weeks. We're launching our *Zero Tolerance* campaign starting Monday."

"Someone's going to accuse you of false advertising."

Roger Donaldson laughed heartily. "I've already showed my cousin, Lord Gordon, the posters. He thinks they're a move in the right direction. Those are his words exactly."

Ultimately, this was the thing that Mornay liked least about the number one man in CID. Donaldson never failed to remind everyone around him he was the first cousin of an important man.

"Going to the briefing?" Donaldson asked.

"Yes, sir."

"Good, I'll see you there."

DI Gordon remained on the raised dais during the entire press briefing. In her heels she literally dwarfed DCI McNab, and she outshone every man in her vivid red outfit. Mornay was in his usual spot, behind Gordon and slightly to the right, in full view of the cameras. His last murder inquiry had given him unwanted notoriety after someone leaked details from his military career. Gordon had latched on to that notoriety, using it for her own self-promotion. She enjoyed flaunting the fact she had a decorated ex–Royal Marine working on the Adair case when she was in front of the cameras, but away from cameras he was her glorified errand boy: She took her coffee black, two sugars.

ACC Donaldson allowed Gordon to field half a dozen questions. She answered them competently and with a compassion that probably went over well with anyone who didn't know her personally. But then, she was a politician's daughter, an old hand at performing before the public.

Mornay longed for another cup of coffee as he stood, expression stoic, in his second-best suit. Claire hovered on the edge of the crowd at the back of the room. CID had its offices on the fourth floor, but she'd rejected the idea of going upstairs and talking shop. Whenever she was there, she was invariably asked out for drinks.

A young female constable entered the crowded room, a look of irritation on her features. She spotted Claire and handed her a note. Claire read it and gave Mornay a look, motioning for him to come over.

It was as good an excuse as any to escape the glare of lights in front of the dais.

The old Mornay would've chatted up the attractive constable. This one waited for her to speak.

The constable ignored him and asked Claire, "What shall I tell them?"

Claire handed him the note.

He quickly scanned it and answered. "Tell them Inspector Gordon will leave as soon as the press briefing is over."

The constable turned smartly on her heel and walked away.

Mornay ignored the view as he slouched against the wall, conscious of the curious glances from a knot of reporters to his right.

"We've got horse trainers to run to ground; we don't have time for a stolen Jaguar," he complained.

Claire grinned wickedly. "But you hunt men. It's what you're good at."

"You've an evil streak running through you, Claire Gillespie. Who is David Lockwood? How does he have the pull to get a detective inspector to drop everything and come running to his castle?"

"We'll find out soon enough, won't we?"

He followed her into the hall, dreading the prospect of another evening with Laina Gordon.

"Sergeant Mornay," a familiar voice called out behind him.

"Teddy," Mornay said as he turned. "Brave lad, you are. Who let you off your leash?"

"Ha-ha," Ted Whyte said. "It's still a free country, and I've got a pass." He held up the pass that let him attend the press briefing.

"If you're wanting a quote, you've followed the wrong cop."

"I want something better. I've a publisher interested in the Adairs' story. And they're particularly interested in the man who's going to find Matthew's killer."

"Piss off, Teddy. That, you can quote." He started to walk away.

"What do you think of the new, tougher face Roger Donaldson is trying to plaster on the force?" Teddy asked in a voice loud enough to draw bodies from the press briefing. "Zero tolerance is a load of shite."

Mornay turned around. Teddy was grinning.

"And you want me to do something for you?"

"I don't need you to do anything for me, Mornay. I don't need your cooperation, and I don't need your consent. So *you* can piss off."

Mornay was close enough to grab Teddy by the lapels. He slammed Teddy against the wall. "Could you repeat that? I didn't quite hear what you just said."

Teddy couldn't talk, since Mornay's forearm was pressed against his throat.

"Thought so." Mornay released Teddy, allowing the smaller man to fall to the floor. As Mornay walked away, some members of CID held off the gathering crowd while another helped Teddy to his feet.

"Feel better?" Claire asked.

"I feel fucking grand."

# Chapter Five

Finovar Castle was a privately owned castle that was maintained as a residence year-round, a rarity in Scotland. Mornay had heard once that there were over two hundred castles in Scotland. If pressed, he might've been able to name six. Many of those two hundred castles were in ruins or simply abandoned: Upkeep was too expensive, and the owners preferred having amenities like windows, electricity, and toilets that flushed in their homes. Many of the remaining castles were now museums.

According to the official Web site, Finovar, located 5 kilometers south of Cordiff, was a favorite with the schoolchildren because it was a working castle with sheep and Highland Kylies, the long-haired cattle most farmers preferred not to keep these days because they had deadly long horns and were exceptionally smart.

After the animals, it was the weavers that drew

the biggest crowds to the castle. In the summer there were weavers working in a lofty barn that reminded Mornay of a cathedral, with its high, airy ceilings. But the barn was brighter than any cathedral he'd ever visited: Its interior walls were painted white, and there were massive skylights in the ceiling.

Mornay turned onto the narrow road that led to the castle and drove for half a mile before crossing a bridge that linked the castle to the mainland. During his five-minute perusal of Finovar's Web site, he'd learned the single-lane bridge was built over a hundred years earlier. Before its construction, anyone wanting to reach the castle had to wind precariously across a narrow strip of land. Mornay glanced into the dark chasm as his tires clunked over the wooden-planked bridge.

The front of the castle faced the sea. Someone, years ago, had planted a stand of trees, but the harsh winds and rocky soil had stunted their growth, twisting their limbs.

Mornay followed the drive as drops of rain started smearing across his windshield. Bright lights were lit in the courtyard that dominated the front of Finovar Castle.

DI Gordon had been silent for the entire forty-minute trip. She'd chosen to sit in the backseat; Claire was up front with him. While they were waiting for Claire to fetch the car, Gordon said, "David Lockwood is a very good friend of mine."

"Friends or not, we've more important things to be doing with our time than chasing down stolen vehicles."

"I expect you to be professional while we're at the castle."

As soon as they got out of the car, Gordon expected

them to fall into step behind her. They did, ducking their heads against the rain, which was coming down more steadily now.

The door that was now used as the main entrance to Finovar was a later addition. Set into a grandly arched affair of stone, the massive wooden door was intricately carved. To reach the original entrance one had to walk up a ramp. That door was narrow and appeared to be built for dwarfs; the Web site said it was designed to hinder entrance into the castle should an attack occur.

The scent of damp stone surrounded Mornay. The walls were dark and deeply pitted. A dented and tarnished suit of armor with a ridiculously large codpiece greeted them as Gordon confidently walked straight on, leading the way into what must have been the great hall. A pair of fireplaces at either end dominated the room; both were large enough for Mornay to walk into without fear of smacking his forehead.

Gordon displayed her familiarity with the castle by veering to the right, into one of the newer additions. "Wait here," she commanded, then disappeared through an arched doorway.

Their entrance into the small lounge startled the room's occupant. The man, who was in his early thirties, quickly put back a statuette he'd been examining, knocking over a vase of dried flowers in the process.

Claire jumped across the short distance and rescued the vase before it crashed to the floor. She hefted the vase, testing its weight. "Waterford. It might be a wise idea for you to keep your hands in your pockets. Fewer bits to hoover that way."

"Walden," Mornay said. "I thought you transferred to Orkney."

The man jumped at the sound of Mornay's voice.

Constable Walden's black woolen sweater appeared to be stretched two sizes too big. But he was so thin, maybe that was the way the sweater fit normally. Mornay noted that Walden's clothes were dry; he'd arrived before the rain. Walden had watery blue eyes and a nervous habit of rubbing the half-moon crescent bald spot on the top of his head. He also had the well-deserved reputation for being a bumbling idiot.

When Walden spoke, his voice cracked. "No one wanted to take Kierson's place here, so they gave the duty to me."

"How is Kierson doing these days?" Mornay asked, though he knew the answer.

Kierson had been invalided out of the force after an accidental shooting. Kierson and Walden had been performing an inspection on shotguns for a new permit when Walden dropped one of the shotguns, which had been loaded. The blast nearly removed Kierson's right foot. Fortunately for Kierson, surgeons managed to reattach the foot, but he would need a cane for the rest of his life. There had been an investigation about the incident, and Walden was absolved of any negligence. But only in the eyes of anyone who didn't know Kierson, who'd been highly regarded on the force. Kierson's colleagues thought Walden had gotten off too lightly.

"Kierson won't speak to me," Walden explained.

"No surprise why."

"I've been here nearly ten minutes. The family asked that I wait, but I think they've forgotten about me. Is there something I could do?"

"I wouldn't mind a coffee. Think you could find

the kitchen and manage to boil up some water without maiming anyone?"

Walden's mouth opened and closed while a bright red flush spread from his neck to his pale, sunken cheeks. "Yes, sir." Walden turned and fled the room.

Gordon returned moments later and led them into a modern kitchen. Walden was nowhere to be seen; he'd probably slunk back home. From the comfortably shabby furniture in front of the normally proportioned fireplace, Mornay thought it was safe to assume this was one of the most used rooms in the house. It was certainly the warmest part of the castle he'd been through.

Two men and two women were seated in front of the fireplace. One man was immediately recognizable. Laina Gordon walked to her father and greeted him with a kiss on the cheek. The other man was tall, lean, dark-haired, and much younger. A clean white bandage was wrapped around his left hand; the color of the bandage stood out prominently against his tanned skin. He barely noticed when Laina Gordon next kissed him; his attention was on Mornay and Claire.

"Notice how friendly her kiss was?" Mornay whispered to Claire. "That must be David Lockwood. They're *very, very* good friends."

"So it appears," she whispered back, barely moving her lips.

"Gordon warned me to be on my best behavior."

"Think you can manage?"

The two women were now approaching, one of them very young.

Laina Gordon's voice was low and husky. "David, this is Detective Sergeant Mornay and Detective Constable Gillespie."

Though Murdo Gordon wasn't part of the introduction, his presence dominated the room. Mornay wondered how the man did it; there was nothing physically impressive about him. Same height as Mornay. His voice was deeper than that of many men, but that was probably an affectation so he could sound more authoritative.

Lord Gordon took over the conversation, introducing Deborah Lockwood as his fiancée and Eilish Lockwood as Deborah's stepdaughter. The distinction caused a negative reaction in both women, who seemed to recoil at the word *step*. Mornay found the reaction mildly interesting, and thought it curious that Murdo Gordon was apparently oblivious to it.

"The car was mine," the politician said. "It's quite valuable. I was going to give it as a birthday present to Eilish."

"Was it taken before you had the opportunity?" Claire asked. She'd been jotting notes throughout the introductions.

"No. Eilish declined the gift." He answered with the same stiff-lipped determination he used when wading through news briefing questions.

Lately, Gordon's open criticism of the Grampian Police was making him even more eagerly sought by the media, of course.

"David and I saw the man drive it off," Eilish offered.

Laina Gordon turned eagerly to Lockwood. "Did you get a good look at him?"

"The courtyard was dark," he replied. "We only use lights at Christmas or for special occasions, so we didn't see his face. He was moving briskly. He wore dark clothes. Maybe trainers."

"Where exactly were you when the Jaguar was being stolen?" Mornay asked Eilish.

"In David's room, on the second floor."

Mornay turned to Deborah and Murdo Gordon. "Where were you?"

"We were in Deborah's wing, which doesn't have a view of the courtyard," Murdo Gordon replied.

"We'll need to see your room," Mornay told David Lockwood.

They walked single file up a narrow spiral staircase to the second floor. The stone treads were dished in the centers from centuries of use, and the walls of the staircase had been worn smooth from being brushed against by countless bodies. The staircase was originally meant for the servants, Eilish Lockwood explained, her voice echoing off the cold stone. She maintained a running dialogue on the history of Finovar. One historical fact after another tumbled out in what appeared to be a nervous need to fill the silence.

"Have you always been keen on history?" Mornay asked, as they entered the second floor hall.

"She's mad about it," Deborah Lockwood interrupted smoothly, putting her arm companionably around Eilish's waist. "Consider yourself warned."

Mornay noticed the ornate lock on the outside of David Lockwood's bedroom door. "Who has keys to the exterior doors to the castle?" Mornay asked.

Lockwood held Mornay's gaze. "We have no locks on our exterior doors. They're rarely secured, actually. There are interior doors we secure, and we do have an alarm system in the rooms with the most valuable pieces of the family collection."

"Doesn't matter anyway, does it?" Eilish said.

"The man came *out* of the castle to steal the Jaguar. Not in, then out again."

"Are you sure he came from inside?" Mornay asked.

"He opened the door and walked outside."

Inspector Gordon stood at Mornay's shoulder, her body tense. What was she worried about? "Have you noticed if anything besides the Jaguar is missing?"

"We haven't looked," Murdo Gordon said.

Gordon was answering questions as if he owned Finovar, and David Lockwood's expression hardened. No one else seemed to notice the intensity of Lockwood's expression, or the fact that, of all the family members, he appeared to be the most on edge.

Lockwood's bedroom was smaller than Mornay expected. The handsome furnishings were obviously expensive, but there was a comfortable hominess about the cluster of photographs on the tall mahogany bureau and the inviting color scheme of smoky blues and ivory in the wallpaper, the curtains, and the upholstery.

There was one window on the wall opposite David Lockwood's bedroom door. Another door led into a bathroom.

Mornay crossed the room and looked out the window. The courtyard was just below, and he saw that the scene-of-crime officers were arriving just as the rain appeared to be strengthening. Mornay watched Constable Walden pointing the forensics officers in the direction of the front door.

"Our man came out that door?" Mornay clarified.

"Aye."

"Claire," he said, "tell forensics our man came out the front door, and they'll need to go over the front hall.

You'll need to hurry; Walden's just sent ten of them through the very door. And tell them we've all been that way. They won't be happy to hear it, but maybe we'll get lucky and find something no one's tramped on."

Claire rushed out of the room. Laina Gordon didn't seem to notice; she was sticking close to Lockwood and speaking with him in low tones.

Eilish Lockwood joined Mornay at the window.

"Where was the car parked?" he asked.

"Just in front of that left post."

The post she referred to was one of a pair; the posts were topped with stone urns. They flanked the flight of stairs that led to the main door. A ring of decorative iron lanterns surrounded the courtyard, and the light they cast was bright enough to make out the weathered coat of arms carved on the urns.

"All that you see below was added when the wings were built," Eilish explained. "Around the late 1700s. That's why they look different from the main tower."

"How many other entrances are there?"

"Five. This one. One to each of the kitchens; we have three. One through the conservatory and another through the chapel, though that one's blocked at the moment with packing materials." She leapt ahead to his next question. "Nothing that could be easily shifted. It took us two days to get all the boxes inside."

"Do you use all of the kitchens year-round?"

"We only use one throughout the year. It's the family kitchen. The original kitchen is open May through October; it's part of the tours. It's also open for the winter solstice and for Christmas."

"Are there any secret entrances?"

She shook her head, amused by the question.

"How can you be so sure? It's a castle; it isn't beyond the realm of possibility."

"This castle was built to be defended; no one would've been foolish enough to risk their defenses by building secret tunnels. And it would've been impossible to tunnel from below; Finovar is built on a solid granite peninsula. Their tools were very crude six hundred years ago. If any sort of passageway had been built beneath the main tower, it would've taken ages. There would be some record. I've spent the past two years poring over all the existing castle records, and there's no mention of any such construction."

"Finovar is on a peninsula. It would be possible to put a tunnel through it leading to a cave."

"Such an undertaking would surely have been mentioned somewhere, and as I've just said, I've found no references."

"Why are you going over the records?"

"Apart from a natural curiosity, I wanted to make some improvements in the central tower, like more electrical outlets. And I wanted the improvements to be as unobtrusive as possible."

Mornay turned back to the window. "Why didn't you want the Jaguar? Not keen on antiques or sports cars?"

"A Jaguar would've been impractical. It was a nice enough gesture, I suppose."

"Was your birthday today?"

"It's Saturday. I'll be eighteen, if you're wondering."

Mornay walked to a series of photographs arranged on the wall; there were an even dozen. The photographs featured David Lockwood astride various horses. Lockwood was wearing mud-spattered racing silks—he was a steeplechase jockey.

"Did anyone in the family know you were going to receive the gift?"

"I think it was as much a surprise to them as it was to me."

"I didn't know," David Lockwood added. The tone of his voice implied that he didn't approve of the gift or of the surprise.

Behind David, Mornay watched Claire quietly reenter the room. She gave him the okay signal.

"I didn't tell you, because I know how close you and Eilish are." Murdo Gordon's explanation sounded plausible enough, but clearly David Lockwood wasn't buying a word. "There were several in the village who knew I was going to give the car to Eilish. I needed their help to keep it a surprise. I told them last week so I could get their help with the arrangements."

Mornay had his notebook ready.

"Where did you keep the Jaguar?"

"Behind Fox's Pub in a garage."

"The owner's name?"

Murdo started ticking off his fingers. "John Fox."

"Any others?"

"Joan and Michael O'Conner. They work here at the castle."

"How many other employees are there?"

Murdo Gordon began to reply, but Mornay interrupted. "I was directing the question to Miss Lockwood."

"We have a staff of thirty from May to October; twenty are weavers, the rest work in the gift shop or giving tours here in the castle."

"How about frequent visitors?"

"There's Calvin Walsh, my boyfriend. He's a veterinarian assistant. Then there's Joan's sister, who visits every other day or so. Deborah's here when she's not with Murdo or traveling abroad."

"Did they know about Eilish's gift?"

"No," Murdo replied.

Mornay turned his attention back to the photographs of Lockwood astride the horses. "I knew someone who was in the racing business. He was a trainer down in England. Ever race in England?" Mornay asked.

Lockwood smiled wryly. "That's where I do most of my racing."

"The man I knew was Harold Cosgrove. Did you ever meet him?"

Lockwood's face split into a boyish grin. "You knew old Harry? Well, this is a small world."

"Small country, at any rate," Mornay said, ignoring the dagger-eyed look Laina Gordon was sending his way.

"It's criminal, what Harry's boys are doing," Lockwood was saying.

Mornay flipped a page over on his notebook to jot down the names of the horses in Lockwood's pictures. The owners' names were included.

"I didn't keep up with Harry these last couple of years, and after he died, well . . ." Mornay let the sentence trail away. It was easier for Lockwood to make his own assumptions than try to provide plausible lies. People lost contact all the time. Or at least they did in Mornay's world.

DI Gordon spoke from across the room, "Sergeant Mornay, let's stick with the subject at hand, if you please."

Mornay snapped his notebook closed. Either Gordon was ignoring the connection with Harold Cosgrove, or she'd forgotten about it completely.

"Just a few more questions, ma'am." Before she could deny him the opportunity, Mornay asked Lord Gordon, "Who owns the castle?"

He'd actually discovered a question that Murdo Gordon wasn't impatient to answer. The politician was silent as he looked to Deborah for guidance.

"Finovar belongs to Eilish," Deborah said after a moment's hesitation. "It has since her father's death."

"Lord Gordon said you were Eilish's stepmother. When did you marry her father?"

"When Eilish was a year old. David was seven at the time. David's mother was Gerald's first wife. I was his last." Deborah Lockwood was nervous; a flush spread across her skin. "I suppose those are irrelevant details. They won't help get the Jaguar back."

"But they might explain why it was taken. What did you do before you married Gerald Lockwood?"

"I ran a small antiques shop in town. I still do. That's how we met."

"I don't understand why you would need to know what Deborah did years ago," Murdo Gordon complained. "It's hardly relevant to having my property returned."

"Perhaps," Mornay replied. "Here's something you will find relevant. Eilish watched the Jaguar being taken through a well-lit window. It's possible the thief saw her."

"It doesn't matter; she couldn't see his face," Lockwood pointed out.

"But the thief doesn't know that. So if you do have locks, I'd use them."

# Chapter Six

"W hy did you mention Harold Cosgrove?" Laina Gordon asked. "Why do you continually have to be reminded what your duties are?"

They were in Finovar's main kitchen. Claire hovered close enough to catch the brunt of Gordon's tightly contained fury.

Mornay pitched his voice at a respectful level, though he wasn't feeling respectful. "The castle is half an hour's walk from the accident site. Fifteen minutes or less by car. I think it's too much of a coincidence that Matthew Adair was found in a trailer owned by a man that David Lockwood knew."

"Coincidence does not automatically mean complicity."

"You don't think it's an odd connection?"

"I certainly find it odd," Murdo Gordon said as he joined them. "It's a relief to see that some members of our illustrious police force actually have their wits about them."

Mornay wondered if DI Gordon was excluded from her father's definition of a member of the force; she didn't seem embarrassed by her father's pointed insult. Mornay didn't have that kind of control over his emotions.

"It's a pity I've been deprived of the opportunity to exercise those wits on an investigation that's far more urgent than this one, Lord Gordon. Yesterday you were on the verge of accusing our office of being incompetent. Today you've exerted your political influence to send us on an errand. Most stolen vehicles are never returned to their owners."

"They warned me you were blunt." Lord Gordon's expression was impossible to read, but he could not keep the anger out of his voice. "Let's hope for your sake that you're wrong. I will not accept anything less than the return of my car."

"I will speak with ACC Donaldson, my cousin, and make certain you and your colleagues will exhaust every resource you have to find my Jaguar. Roger Donaldson knows how dear that car is to me. He will be watching this investigation closely, that I can guarantee." Gordon turned to his daughter. "Laina, his point regarding this Harold Cosgrove could be a valid one."

"Mornay's already pointed out that it's a small country and the racing world makes up an even smaller fraction of it. I don't think it's odd in the least."

Gordon didn't caution her father that despite his role in the government, he was still only a civilian and had no authority. Instead, the moment her father left the room, she said to Mornay, "If you've the time to make additional inquiries, you should spend more time clearing out the paperwork on your desk. Or attempting to be punctual."

Mornay folded himself into one of the chip shop's tiny booths and breathed in the fragrant scent of curry and hot grease. It was nearly one-thirty, Friday morning. He and Claire were both exhausted and starving and had to report back for duty at seven.

Claire settled into the booth across from him.

"What's going on?" she asked quietly. She had an uncanny way of staring at him that made him want to flinch away from her gaze. It was as if she could lock in on something in his eyes and see all the things he hid so well from everyone else.

"The Dons had a terrible year."

Claire refused to drop her gaze.

Mornay looked away first and turned to stare out the window. The pavement was glossy from the rain, and light glinted off its oily surface. Beyond the wet pavement, hidden in the darkness, were the North Sea and a white crescent of sand that used to be one of his favorite places to visit when he was a child. The beach was too small to attract tourists or summer sunbathers. After his brother died, he used to spend hours on it, mucking around the clumps of kelp or in the trapped pools of water, trying to catch the tiny crabs that skittered beneath the rocks. Or he would just sit on the sand and gaze at the sea and wish for Robbie to be alive. When he was old enough to help his father on the fishing trawler, those quiet times on the beach became impossible to find. By the time he'd spent a year working the nets, he'd forgotten what he'd loved about the sea.

Their food was delivered by a boy who didn't look much older than Matthew Adair. Mornay started ripping apart his warm nan bread. "What was your childhood like?"

The question caught Claire off guard. She used her plastic fork to mix rice into her steaming curry before answering. "Mother. Father. House on the corner. Small garden. Cat. It was normal."

"When I was ten, normal was being rolled out of bed in the middle of the night and spending hours pulling at heavy nets. I would get so cold I couldn't feel my hands. Normal for Matthew Adair was eating take-away on Fridays and watching a movie his parents had rented. Normal for that wee bloke"— he jerked his thumb in the direction of the boy that'd delivered their food—"is dishing out curry to all the drunks in town. Normal for Lady Eilish Lockwood is raising sheep for fun and traipsing around a castle."

He pushed his plate away. His hunger had evaporated, as it often did lately.

Claire's gaze pierced him. "What's really wrong? You've lost weight. You've been snapping at everyone, including me. That scene with Teddy, then the way you spoke with DI Gordon and her father . . ." She shook her head, as if it were too much to take.

"I don't like being manipulated and insulted."

He avoided her gaze and tried to remember a time he'd been more exhausted. It wasn't the long hours he spent on the Adair investigation; long hours, he could manage. If anything, his work was what was keeping him sane.

"Pamela is having seizures." The words came out slowly. "The doctors haven't been able to control them. Some of the medications they want to use could hurt the baby, so they've been holding off. But the seizures are getting worse."

Only Claire and two other people from work knew that he was going to be a father: Constable Dunnholland and Detective Chief Inspector McNab, their boss. Claire was the only one who knew that Pamela had been a drug addict and that she was the younger sister of his best friend, Victoria.

"How far along is Pamela?" she asked.

"Twenty-four weeks. The baby is only half the size it should be, which the doctors attribute to the accident and to Pamela's drug use."

"What's going to happen to Pamela after the baby is born?"

"Her doctors aren't thinking that far ahead. They refuse to speculate about her condition beyond the end of the day."

Two drunks tottered through the door of the chip shop. They called out boisterously to the boy working behind the counter. He shouted something profane back, and the drunks started laughing.

Claire pushed her food away and leaned closer. "I'm sorry. You should've told me sooner instead of keeping it bottled up inside."

He slouched farther into the molded curves of the booth, still staring at the black street. "Victoria is trying to prove I won't be a proper father. I'm single. I work long hours, with no time for a child. She wants sole custody. She's been refusing to speak to me. She has her solicitor pass messages along."

The drunks began a loud conversation as they

stood in front of the menu board, deciding what they wanted to eat.

"How often do you go to hospital?" Claire asked, when the drunks had walked back outside without ordering.

"Nearly every day."

He was tired of questions and he half regretted telling Claire about Pamela's worsening condition. "Did you notice David Lockwood's reaction when Lord Gordon spoke?"

"I did. Eilish's was in a similar vein, only not as intense. Both seem to be genuinely fond of their step-mother. I don't like the coincidence that Lockwood knew Harold Cosgrove." She put her fork down. "I don't like that the accident happened so close to his property. A fifteen-minute drive, and you're there. Maybe less if you crossed the fields," she added thoughtfully. "Did you see the bandage on Lockwood's hand?"

"Hard to miss it."

Another long silence stretched between them. "Obviously we're going to need more information about the inhabitants of Finovar Castle," she said. "How will we manage that with Gordon around?"

He'd been expecting her to caution him from doing anything rash. Surprised, he liked that she'd already assumed he was going to ignore Gordon's orders to back off the connection between Harold Cosgrove and David Lockwood, and he smiled with a degree of satisfaction he hadn't felt in weeks. "We'll give her the illusion that we're doing what we're told with happy faces. And then we'll do a proper job."

\*        \*        \*

Mornay was up early enough to watch the sunrise over Banff Bay, had the sun been visible. A harbor was first built in Macduff in 1760, and fishing had always been central to the town's economic health. The harbor, which fronted the center part of the town, had been busier in past years, but the diminishing fish stocks and restrictions imposed by the European Union were taking their toll. There was less work and more idle men. If he were a cynical man, he could look on the changes in the local economy as job security: crime was on the rise.

Mornay's favorite view of the harbor was from the park near Doune Church. The church sat on a hill, one of the best vantage points in the area. A person could look down on the harbor and see the town in its entirety. But no force in this world or the next would ever get him to climb Doune Hill again.

Mornay lived in a modern housing estate off Gamrie Road. The drive to the harbor should've taken five minutes, but was stretched into a quarter of an hour because the roads were glazed with ice, and everyone was cautiously creeping along.

The three- and four-story granite buildings transformed Skene Street—one of the main streets in Macduff—into a wind tunnel. His car was buffeted by a wind that was less a force of nature and more a sharply biting entity that existed purely to torment those who found themselves scuttling onto their buses or away from their cars.

As he followed Market Street and turned right on High Shore, the scent of the harbor leached into his car. It was a mixture of petrol and the heavy oils used to lubricate the trawler engines, of algae on slick granite blocks. The scent was so ingrained into his psyche that he couldn't look at a body of water without smelling it, even if the body of water was a land-bound, spring-fed lake. The scent also brought memories he'd prefer remained crammed into the far reaches of his subconscious.

Mornay parked on the road and walked directly into the wind, barely feeling the cold because of the adrenaline coursing through his bloodstream as he headed for one particular building. He braced his feet and put his full weight behind opening the heavy door, knowing from long experience that rust had nearly solidified the hinges. As he entered the darkened building, his senses were assaulted with other, more noxious scents: paint stripper, varnish, and petrol, used to clean heavily oiled fittings. The fear of fire was so pervasive in the building that smoking was prohibited. The building's interior was poorly lit and nearly as cold inside as out. The heaters were only fired up when paint or varnish needed to be applied. He remembered how the cold used to eat into his fingers, stiffening them, turning the simplest of tasks into a torture.

A traditional open-deck Scottish trawler dominated the floor space. Behind it were massive doors that opened directly onto the water. The trawler was nearly twenty meters in length and her hull—painted a dark blue with two broad white stripes running the entire length—showed the usual scars. The *Bevin* sat on a bed of braces and rollers that lifted it nearly two meters off the stained concrete floor. It had the traditional tapered cruiser stern, which was far more graceful-looking than the square-cut transom sterns that had become common since the mid 1960s. Given the amount of misery he'd endured on the harsh open decks of his father's fishing trawlers, it was hard to believe he could find anything admirable about Scottish trawlers, with their tangle of lines and low, swooped-forward profiles.

The high-pitched ringing of a hammer against metal stopped as Mornay walked alongside the trawler, making for the offices at the back. He heard the scuffing clump of someone walking in thick-soled boots. This particular someone walked with a limp.

Angus rounded the bow. "The fuck you doing here?" Angus's words came out with a garbled lisp, because of the number of teeth he was missing from fighting: center four on the top, center four on the bottom. Square-shouldered, with hardly any neck, Angus probably wouldn't live to see his fourth decade.

Mornay sidestepped the smaller man to walk around him, but Angus moved to block him with surprising speed. Angus made a quick dash forward; Mornay sliced a leg out, kicking the shin of Angus's bad leg. The leg buckled, and the shorter, less dexterous man couldn't fight the pull of gravity. He toppled forward onto the stained concrete. Mornay stepped over the cursing man and veered toward his father's office.

Though it was still early, barely six in the morning, the scent of overcooked coffee assailed Mornay when he walked through the door. The office was a study in brown, with caramel-colored shag carpet— matted down from years of wear—and dark faux wood paneling, puckering where it was held against the wall with panel nails. Tobacco smoke had stained the ceiling panels a watery shade of tan. As a child, Mornay had always wondered how the tiles had come to be stained with tobacco smoke since smoking was prohibited.

There was only a single light to relieve the unrelenting darkness of the room; it stood behind Clyde's desk, casting dark shadows beneath the boat-builder's craggy cheeks.

Clyde's hostility was subtler than Angus's, which made it infinitely more menacing; he was a master of understatement. The older man interlinked his thick, scarred fingers and rested them on his flat abdomen, leaning back in his chair as if he hadn't a care in the world.

"I was wondering when you would come around."

The casualness was as calculated as the position of his lamp. If Clyde showed any sorrow over the death of his crew, he was keeping it buried deep inside his tall, muscular frame. The *Sunward*'s explosion had killed two men Clyde had known his entire life. The other he'd known for over half his life— thirty-odd years. He'd employed all of them on and off again through the years, their lives as intertwined as the knots on a fishing net.

Mornay wandered to the wall that held pictures of boats Clyde had built over the years. The *Sunward*'s photo was in the top right corner, its hull a bright, tropical blue, its red-and-yellow stripes crisp. There were perhaps thirty photos, a lifetime of work, assembled on the wall. There were times when Mornay had envied Clyde's tangible connection to his past, to be able to see something he'd created from planking and bits of metal. The ability to do something as useful as building a boat had made

Mornay envious through the years. Envious because Clyde knew his place in his world and the worth he brought to it, while Mornay was forever struggling with the minutiae.

"So hunting men is what you're good at now?" Clyde said in the manner of a man scoffing at the existence of UFOs. "Am I in your sights?"

Mornay's gaze remained blindly on the third picture from the left, his mind having zoomed instinctively to that protective zone where he kept his true feelings buried, safe from scrutiny and ridicule. "That comment was taken entirely out of context."

"Right," Clyde said, with a conspirator's hushed voice. "And I suppose it was just the angle of the camera that made you look like you were on the verge of strangling that reporter with his own microphone. How many sad bastards has the force recruited because of that bit of film?"

Mornay turned away from the photographs of the trawlers and faced his father. "Why would they tell me?"

Clyde lifted a shoulder dismissively, as if to say he'd tried to be polite, but his son wasn't playing along. "We both know why they sent you here, so let's just get on with it, eh?"

Mornay reached a hand into his pocket and pulled out the fragment he'd acquired the previous day. "What was your crew hauling in the *Sunward*?" Mornay held up the fragment. "This metal has been coated with a plastic."

"There's fish, and then there's fish," Clyde said, barely glancing at the bit of hull. Clyde had been questioned by too many cops to do something as amateurish as reveal what he was really thinking.

Silence spanned a handful of heartbeats while they stared at each other.

Then Clyde leaned farther back into his chair, relaxing. "So what's this I hear about you and Victoria's wee sister?"

"Do you believe everything you hear?" Mornay replied. "I'll send a constable around later to pick up the original plans for the *Sunward*. Make sure they're ready, or we might just have grounds to do a search."

Clyde's deep laugh filled the room. "Right. You lot would have been in here already if you could've. That's why they sent you fishing." He laughed even more heartily.

# Chapter Seven

The windowless blue van sat conspicuously on the other side of the road, opposite the sign that read MORNAY'S BOAT REPAIR. The van was forcing the oncoming traffic to drive around. Icy rain was slicing down at the perfect angle for slipping beneath collars, and Mornay tried to shrug down into his anorak as he trotted past his car to reach the van. The side door, which faced Clyde's boatyard, slid open.

He ducked and stepped inside the van, the door closing noisily behind him. The air was stale.

Two computer monitors lit the interior of the vehicle. DI Maggie Cray and DC Kathy Berra sat in front of the monitors.

Cray, who was running the *Sunward* inquiry for the Scottish Drug Enforcement Agency, chain-smoked, preferred straight whiskey to any other beverage, and the only thing that impressed her was seeing the baddies get locked up, by whatever means possible. Maggie was tall and thin in the sinewy way that distance runners or refugees from war-torn countries were. Her face was all angles, and her favorite expression was a scowl.

"Nice suit," Maggie said, when Mornay had squirmed out of his anorak inside the claustrophobic space. She reached out and touched his lapel, her fingers slipping beneath his jacket and sliding against his shirt. He'd ceased to be surprised by the blatant sexual nature of her gestures; she did it to shock her male counterparts. Keep the men uneasy, and they were more easily molded to her will.

"Very nice," Maggie murmured. "Someday you'll have to tell me how you can afford this kind of material with your pay."

"There's a reason they call it undercover surveillance. You're supposed to watch without being seen."

"Where's the fun in hiding down dark alleyways?" she asked. "I'm here to make him nervous."

"I'm sure you've got Clyde shivering in his fucking boots."

Kathy Berra stifled a giggle as she took his coat and put it out of the way on the bench next to her. Kathy Berra was a shy woman near Claire's age; she wore hideous polyester blends that always crackled with static electricity. But the SDEA hadn't recruited Berra for her fashion sense, she was brilliant with electronics, which were notoriously fickle in the field. Berra had a workbench set up next to Maggie's laptop. Screwed to the bench was a board that held a neatly arranged assortment of small tools—screwdrivers, pliers, various-sized tweezers—all with shadowed outlines to show where the tools were to be placed. The board also had a spongy rubber mat glued to it; this was where Berra did her repairs. Some of the parts were so small they could only be handled with the tweezers.

Mornay shrugged out of his suit jacket, aware of Maggie's frank stare. He kept his attention on Berra's hands and her long, elegant fingers.

"You were supposed to engage him in conversation, not start an argument."

Maggie's criticism was nearly conversational, and he was immediately on his guard.

Mornay pulled off his tie, added it to the pile of clothes, and started unbuttoning his shirt. "You're daft if you think Clyde would say anything to a cop. He'll say even less to me."

Maggie winked at Berra. "We've heard this tune before, haven't we, Kat? Getting fucking old, isn't it?"

Berra was concentrating on looking anywhere but at Mornay's bare chest, and Maggie seemed to find her embarrassment amusing. But after Berra fumbled twice with the wires taped to Mornay's chest, Maggie snapped, "Get on with it. We need to be ready to roll when Clyde leaves."

Berra pulled off the taped wire quickly, snagging some of Mornay's hair.

"Christ," he grumbled to Berra, "with your budget, you've got to have something in one of those drawers that would've been easier than this bloody thing." He tugged his shirt free of his trousers so she could reach the transmitter taped to the small of his back, just above his waistband.

"We've fantastic units," Berra said enthusiastically as she put the transmitter on the bench. "Their range—"

"Berra, there's no need to give him a lecture, right? Let him get dressed in peace."

Berra ducked her head, cowed by Maggie Cray's aggression. Mornay buttoned his shirt, shoved the tails back into his trousers, and pulled on his jacket, wondering what was going through Maggie Cray's mind. Did she really think Clyde was the mastermind behind the death of the *Sunward*'s crew? He knew he'd never get an answer out of her, or even a hint.

"Who's going around to pick up the plans? It should be someone local."

Maggie grinned, holding the tie Mornay had been searching for. She hooked it around his neck, pulling ever so slightly to get him to lean forward. He resisted, and she let the tie go, her grin widening. "I'll manage, so no worries, right? Don't forget about tomorrow. You're expected to make an appearance at the press briefing."

"I should start charging to make appearances at press briefings."

Maggie leaned forward, her voice low, almost breathless. "From what I've heard, you could start charging for lots of things." She slammed the door to the van closed, but Mornay could hear her deep, throaty laughter as he walked away.

Friday morning Eilish found David sequestered in the library, which served as his office when he was home. He was talking on the telephone and quickly wrapped up his call when she entered.

"Where's Deborah?" he asked.

"With you-know-who. She'll return sometime this afternoon." David and Eilish had decided they didn't care for Lord Gordon shortly after Deborah began dating him. She preferred calling him you-know-who, while David usually pretended he wasn't even in the room.

Eilish wandered to his desk, scrutinizing its surface, trying to discover a clue to the mysterious phone calls David had been making since his arrival. The desk was immaculately kept, as usual. She would have to snoop when he was away. "I wonder what she sees in him."

"Besides the fact he's tall, handsome, wealthy, and immensely influential?"

"I wouldn't put up with him. There's his temper, and he's postponed the wedding three times."

"Are you in that much hurry to be married, Lee?"

"Don't be ridiculous, and we're not talking about me. I wonder why you-know-who bothered with an engagement in the first place. I don't think he's really interested in getting married, only in how it influences the voting public."

"I need to come home more often and nip this budding cynical streak you're developing."

"Deborah would be better off with someone who can come home at night."

"Home to Finovar, or home to Deborah?"

"What's wrong with Finovar? What's wrong with Deborah living here with another husband?" Eilish knew her voice was growing defensive.

"Lee, have you ever considered how lonely it must be for her here?" His voice grew quieter. "Things change, and sometimes it's not bad."

"I know things change, but you didn't have to leave, you chose to leave. Now Deborah's going to leave." This was not the conversation she'd intended to have with David. Now she was near tears. "You hardly ever come to visit anymore. You spend more time with my bloody horse than you do here. Now Deborah wants to leave. What if you-know-who keeps Deborah too busy being the perfect politician's wife, and she can't come home to visit?"

"We'll have to worry about that when or if it happens. She won't abandon you, Eilish; she loves being your mother."

It was exactly what Eilish *didn't* want to hear. She adored Deborah, and the thought of not having her within walking distance was absolutely terrifying. Eilish started sniffling, despite her firm intentions absolutely *not* to cry. David gathered her into a hug, which only made the tears come faster.

"Better?" he asked, when the worst of her crying had passed.

"No." Her voice was muffled against his shoulder.

"I'll need my arm back soon, it's gone numb," he said, in shades of his old, mocking self.

She thumped him on the shoulder, then used his handkerchief to blow her nose.

"Have you talked about any of this to Calvin?" he asked, as she finished cleaning her face.

"No. I didn't want to sound silly."

He nodded. "How serious are you two?" The question was casual, but she saw how intently he was watching her.

"Serious enough, which is all you need to know."

"Then you should tell him what you're feeling. If

he's going to be a part of your life, it's time you started confiding in him."

"I'm part of your life, and you never confide in me."

"Our relationship doesn't fall under those sorts of rules."

"You're still angry I never told you about Calvin, but somehow I knew you'd act . . ." She waved her hand in the air, searching for the right word, and when it failed to materialize, she gave up. "I knew you'd act strange when you met him."

"There's nothing strange about wanting what's best for you. If it's Calvin Walsh, then I'm happy for you. But I think you're a bit young to become engrossed with one young man. Particularly one no one really knows anything about."

"Funny that you've never before used my age as an argument against anything else I've ever wanted to do. Why would my good sense evaporate because I'm interested in a male, rather than replacing the double glazing or buying a new loom? Why shouldn't I be interested in doing what every other female my age is doing?"

"You're right," he conceded. "But I can't help worrying that your Calvin has certain expectations."

"We've already discussed that, just last week, in fact. He doesn't care that I don't have loads of money."

"You do have everything sorted, then, don't you?"

Angus was absent the second time Mornay entered Clyde's boatyard that morning. The door to Clyde's office was open.

Mornay leaned against the doorframe. "We need to talk."

"I'm busy," Clyde said, without looking up from his computer screen. He appeared to be working on invoices.

"You're just going to have to squeeze me in. Let's get a coffee at the bakery. I hate this bloody place."

Clyde looked up, his gaze dark and impenetrable. "Just like your mother . . ." Clyde's voice faded away. He clamped his lips together, and after a moment he said gruffly, "Always have been." It sounded like an accusation—as if Clyde had been expecting some measure of approval from his wife and younger son, but the approval had never been given, only complaints.

Mornay could vaguely remember his parents arguing when he was a child, but in his child's mind, most of the arguments were about Robbie, not what his father did for a living. But perhaps that was just a twist his guilty conscience had put on the memories.

"I'll be at Nan's."

Mornay left the building, grateful for the blustery wind that blew away the clinging fumes. He hunched into his coat and walked up the hill on the edge of the street, since there were no sidewalks to Nan's.

Nanette Tucker was as integral a part of Mornay's childhood as the scent of the harbor. Her bakery was in a one-story building built shortly after the First World War, modern by Macduff standards. It faced the North Sea and was within spitting distance of the Macduff Marine Aquarium, which was said to have the deepest tanks in all of Britain. The aquarium was the principal tourist attraction for Macduff. Soon after the aquarium opened, Nan put in a small seating area with well-padded chairs and appealing watercolors of sea life on the walls. She'd left the view to the kitchen open so that customers could watch the bakers working.

" 'Lo, Nan," he said, after the door's bells stopped jangling. A heavy, sweet, yeasty scent drifted from the ovens, and he was transported back to the days when he'd sat on his stool in the back of the kitchen, stuffing himself with fresh rolls.

Nan looked up from the pad of paper she was jotting notes on, and smiled broadly. Though well into her sixties, Nan was exactly as he remembered as a child: thin, sleeves rolled past her elbows, spotless white apron, short silver hair tucked behind her small pink ears. "Seth, I've a fresh batch of rolls coming out in five minutes. Can you wait?"

"Sounds grand. Clyde will be here in a minute. Can I get a tea and a coffee?"

She rang up his order, and he took a seat while she waited on the next customer. Mornay sat at the table in front of the bay window, remembering all the times Nan had packed sweet rolls in a paper sack at no charge, so he'd be sure to get something to eat that day. That'd been the year his mother and Robbie had died. First Robbie, then Mum. His father had mourned by working from dawn until dark, and avoided speaking to his younger son by spending his off-hours in the pubs. He'd had no preference where he drank, as long as the bartender was attentive to his empty glass and didn't talk.

The door jangled, announcing Clyde's arrival.

"This better be worth my while, laddie," his father said, when he'd seated himself.

Mornay pitched his voice low so they wouldn't be

overheard. "The SDEA seems convinced you're their next Jimmy Fara, and they're salivating over the prospect of arresting you. If I don't offer them an explanation of why Scott Gray let the Paisley brothers blow up the *Sunward*, the SDEA will be tearing apart your boatyard, rivet by rivet."

Jimmy Fara, a long-distance driver for a top UK bakery, had been arrested six months earlier after the SDEA had confiscated heroin from his tractor-trailer. The heroin had been hidden, not so imaginatively, in flour bags. It was the SDEA's biggest drug bust to date, and they were eager for their next.

"Did you work the Fara case?"

"No." Mornay took a sip of his coffee and nodded his thanks to Nan when she delivered a steaming plate of rolls. He ate his first in two bites.

Clyde was looking out the window. All the tables were filled now, and the room hummed with low conversations. "I've seen them outside my house and the boatyard for the past two weeks. Well before the trawler was destroyed. I'd assumed you put them there." This was said as if Clyde was going to be skeptical of any denials Mornay might make.

Mornay hadn't known the surveillance had been going on that long. He'd assumed it began the day the wreckage of the *Sunward* was found. "I've already told you they're looking for their next big arrest. The *Sunward*'s explosion has given them the perfect excuse to get inside your boatyard."

"Why should you care what they do?" Clyde asked.

"Because I know the woman who's been put in charge of the investigation, Maggie Cray, and she's got no problem getting results any way it takes."

Clyde lifted a shoulder as if he didn't really care one way or the other. But he did care, or he wouldn't be sitting across the table talking to a son he'd barely spoken to in the past ten years.

"So why did you hire the Paisley brothers?" Mornay asked again, working on his third roll. His father had yet to eat one. "They're daft," Mornay continued. "Get a few drops of whiskey in them, and they'd tell you everything they know, which is precious little. They don't know how to run a proper trawler, and they rarely took anything to market, yet they went out regularly. We've determined that from the petrol logs."

"What did you think about the *Sunward*'s engines?" his father asked slyly.

His father didn't appear upset over the death of his crew or the loss of his trawler. Mornay had seen people show stronger reactions when they found themselves in a long queue. His father's utter lack of emotion was unsettling.

Mornay had gotten a good look at the remains of the engines the day before, because, oddly enough, they were intact. The explosion had occurred forward of the deck cabin, which was centered between stern and bow. The odd bit of metal Mornay carried in his pocket had come from the forward part of the trawler. "Oversized."

"Too bloody right. I had the best of everything on that boat. And hired one of the best men to run it, and the Paisley brothers still managed to muck things up. They didn't have enough brains between them to smuggle a tin of biscuits."

"So why were they running your trawler?"

"Because they needed the work."

The answer was too fast coming. Too pat. Mornay didn't imagine that his father was going soft in his old age; the *real* reason he'd hired the brothers had to lie in the job he'd hired them to do. Which obviously didn't have anything to do with fish.

His father drained his mug of tea. "I've got somewhere I need to be." He stood but then leaned over the table, his face a mask of barely controlled anger. "And another thing, laddie," he whispered. "Come on my property again, and I'll give you a fucking thrashing that will make your last stay in hospital seem like a holiday. No one touches any of my lads without paying the consequences." Then he walked out of the restaurant without a backward glance.

# Chapter Eight

"You're late." Claire was sprinkling a pinch of dry flakes into Willie's tank.

Willie was a pretentious goldfish who preferred crisps to the nutritionally balanced fish flakes Claire attempted to feed him twice daily. It was Sahotra and Mornay who kept the fish happily plump with his favorite salmon-flavored crisps. Willie's octagonal tank was displayed on the top of a filing cabinet that separated Mornay and Claire's communal CID desk from the other two desks in the small police office. The tank had been his welcome-back gift to Claire after she was released from hospital several months earlier after a gunshot wound.

"Maggie Cray was at my house at five this morning with more questions," Mornay said. "I need to grab some more coffee."

"Better not, they're waiting on you. Including Dr. Hall."

He and Claire were the last to walk into the inquiry room. DI Gordon was standing on the far side of the tables, arms crossed, staring distastefully at the state of the partially constructed room. There were eight CID personnel assembled, not counting Mornay, Claire, Byrne, or Chief Inspector McNab; the rest were from the Aberdeen Division. Though Matthew was abducted from Aberdeen, control of the investigation had been transferred to their office because of simple logistics. The Adairs lived closer to Macduff than Aberdeen. Dr. Hall and DCI McNab sat at the far end of the island of tables.

Mornay and Claire took their usual places, propped against a pair of filing cabinets at the other end of the room. As far away from Byrne as possible.

Byrne wore an older suit that hung loosely on his slimmed-down frame. The skin on his face was looser and more sallow beneath the blush of broken veins across his cheeks and nose. Byrne's gaze flicked in Mornay's direction, the bright blue eyes as sharp as ever. And his temper certainly wasn't softening as he grew thinner; if anything, it was getting worse. Mornay held the man's gaze.

Dr. Hall stood. He was as impeccably dressed as ever, and Mornay wondered how he managed to keep the construction dust off his dark gray suit. Every time Mornay sat in a chair, he came away looking as if he'd just zoomed down a chalk slide.

Claire made a low sound.

"What?" he asked, breaking his eye contact with Byrne to look down at her, but Claire was scanning the room, studying the other officers. Claire was keen to crack this case before anyone else, and not because finding Matthew's killer would obviously put her on a faster track for promotion. There was another, personal reason she'd yet to share: each time they had a case that dealt with abused or neglected children she seemed driven by a fierce determination.

"Don't goad Byrne," she whispered. "You'll only make it worse for both of us."

Dr. Hall's voice cut off any reply. "The press office has been receiving calls; there are people worried that Matthew Adair's death might be the work of a pedophile. There is no evidence at this point that suggests Matthew's death is the work of a pedophile. What is clear is that Matthew struggled with his assailant and was killed with a blow to his right temple. His clothes were removed and his body meticulously washed with a bleach water solution. All of which was clearly outlined in the PM report each of you should have read by now."

Mornay leaned closer to Claire and whispered, "I'll bet you a meal anywhere that someone from Lord Gordon's office has been spreading the pedophile rumors."

"He wouldn't be that stupid."

"Don't underestimate his political ambitions. He's always touting his involvement in creating the National Pedophile Task Force. He's after the First Minister's job, and he's just found the way to get it. Incite a nationwide panic, then be the man who restores order."

Laina Gordon's voice sliced across the room. "How did you determine his clothes were removed after death?"

"There are scuff patterns on his jeans from being

dragged. There was an orange stain on the front of his clothes. It was Irn-Bru laced with a sedative. The Irn-Bru was in his stomach contents. However, he died before the drug could enter his bloodstream, which is significant since this particular sedative starts to take effect within ten minutes of ingestion. The blow to his temple was massive, but he might not have died as quickly as I'd originally thought. It could have taken as long as a minute or more. It appears Matthew was dragged by his arms over a rough, jagged surface after the struggle that caused the blow to his temple. It is possible that he was still alive as he was being dragged; but, given the state of his body and the fight he'd put up, I think it's more probable that he was dead."

Gordon snapped, "You're surmising, Doctor. We can't rule out the possibility that he was kidnapped by a pedophile and died during transportation. And just because you can't find the evidence doesn't mean the pedophile didn't abuse him. By your own admission, Matthew's body was thoroughly washed."

"That also sounds remarkably like an assumption, Inspector."

McNab stepped in before the argument between Gordon and Dr. Hall could escalate. "Sergeants Spencer and Aiden," he said to Tracy Spencer and Nina Aiden. They were CID, senior to Mornay, and both women had been pursuing him for weeks. "I want you to tackle the known pedophiles. Get with the prison service officials in Peterhead; have them give you a list of any sexual offenders who have been released during the past year. We will not have any accusations of a lack of thoroughness on this matter. I want you to trace their movements back through the past six months. Is that understood?"

Nina and Tracy were conscientious police officers, and they were relentless—that, Mornay could attest to personally.

"Do you have any ideas on the weapon that killed Matthew?" McNab asked Dr. Hall.

In reply, Hall switched on his projector, which was connected to a laptop. The projector enlarged the image from the laptop's screen onto the wall; they were looking at a vividly colored close-up of Matthew Adair's temple.

"There's significant tissue damage in this area. Whatever object we're dealing with has a blunt surface. It has an unusual profile and is an oblong oval, not round. I think we can safely rule out most types of commercial hammers; however, there are oddly shaped upholstery hammers that we need to look at. What you don't see is that the object was tapered, wider at the base than at the front. It is 1.5 centimeters at its widest.

"Now"—Hall removed a pointer from his pocket—"notice this bruising here." The small bruise Hall pointed out was below and to the left of the wound. Mornay wouldn't have noticed the slightly darker spot amidst the ring of purplish red flesh had Hall not pointed it out. "We might be looking for a tool with some sort of knobbed edging protruding next to the hammer face."

Hall took a breath and spent a moment gathering his thoughts. Though he wasn't a cold man, his demeanor was usually one of clinical efficiency. A new photograph replaced the temple wound. It showed a close-up of Matthew's right hand.

"I would like you to notice his fingernails. See

how the nails are quite ragged, as if he gnawed the nail to the quick. I've already verified with his family that Matthew was not a nail biter. All of the nails on both hands were ragged, as if they'd been ripping frantically at something."

"But the fingertips aren't damaged," Claire pointed out. "Shouldn't they be raw if he was trying to claw his way out of something?"

Hall nodded. "They should show more damage than they do. I've provided blown-up copies of both of these photographs for reference."

"What day did he die?" McNab asked. "Any idea?"

"Matthew's body was frozen shortly after death, very little dessication to the tissue, less than thirty days is what I would have told if I didn't know the exact date of Matthew's disappearance. He still had the remains of his lunch in his stomach."

Byrne seemed the only person in the room unaffected by the news; he continued chewing his thumbnail.

Mornay raised a hand. "The blood found in the Nissan. Were you able to determine what type it is?"

"It's O negative."

"So now we've just got to go around sticking everyone with needles?" Byrne asked.

"Perhaps we should start with the inhabitants of Finovar Castle," Mornay suggested. "David Lockwood was apparently good friends with Harold Cosgrove, the owner of the trailer Matthew was found in. He had a plaster on his right hand when we saw him yesterday."

"Interesting," McNab said quietly, glancing in Laina Gordon's direction. "You're familiar with the residents of Finovar; what do you know about David Lockwood?"

"Sir, the horse racing world is very small. It would probably be more significant if David Lockwood *didn't* know Harold Cosgrove."

"That's not what I asked."

Laina Gordon hesitated for the briefest of moments before saying, "David Lockwood is twenty-eight and a successful businessman. He was adopted by Gerald Lockwood when he was a young child. They were very close. He moved to Australia ten or eleven years ago."

"How successful?" Mornay asked.

"He's quite wealthy. He owns two companies; one makes equipment for extreme sports enthusiasts, it's called Loc-Down Gear. David's other company arranges extreme vacations, it's called Loc-Down Adventures. David is also an amateur steeplechase jockey. Quite a good one."

McNab focused on Sahotra. "Have a look at Loc-Down's line of equipment, see if there's anything that could have been used to attack Matthew Adair."

"Sir," Laina Gordon protested.

McNab cut her off with a glance. "We're here to find Matthew Adair's killer, Inspector, not to give the appearance we're coddling old friends. If you've a problem with the direction this investigation is moving, you can remove yourself from the team. Is that what you want to do?"

Laina Gordon's jaw tensed. "No, sir."

Mornay leaned forward and whispered in Claire's ear, "Is it just me, or does it sound like when she says sir, she's really saying 'fuck off?' "

"You've something to add?" McNab asked Mornay.

"No, sir."

"I do," Claire said. "Perhaps we should pick up the rest of Matthew's journals and see if we can find any references to Loc-Down products or the adventure vacations. It's possible the Adairs were planning a holiday to Australia."

DCI McNab was nodding his approval. "Good point. We'll need to requestion Charles Adair's coworkers, as well. And Matthew's mates at school. School first, then his parents' house."

Mornay cursed when he saw the empty coffeepot. The person who poured the last cup hadn't bothered to put on a new pot.

Claire leaned against the doorframe, arms folded, watching him. "So what's Maggie Cray asking you questions about? Does she have her sights set on your father?"

"News certainly travels. My father was carrying something on his boat, and Maggie's made a deductive leap that defies logic. She's got him pegged for drug trafficking." Mornay dumped out the old grounds. The filter disintegrated in the free fall from the coffeepot basket to the bin, and half the grounds splattered on the floor. "Bollocks," he said, but there was little conviction in the curse; he was too intent on getting hot coffee into a cup as soon as possible. "Maggie's practically salivating over the possibility of arresting Clyde."

"And she needs you for what?"

"I believe my role in the farce is to deliver the ultimatums."

"Don't deliver them."

"It's not that simple." Mornay lost count of the scoops of grounds, so he added an extra one for good measure.

"You're not with their agency. You're on the top case in the country. Let them find someone else."

"Inspector McNab's made it clear that if I want to stay on the Adair case, I need to do what I'm told."

Claire moved closer as he searched for a clean cup. In the end, he had to wash one out. "You've a reputation for disregarding orders; why change now? And what could you possibly do for your father if you find something you wished you hadn't?"

"I don't know."

"Then why look?"

He didn't have an answer.

Claire stopped peppering him with questions while they watched the coffee drip into the pot and Mornay finally poured himself a cup.

Byrne sauntered into the small canteen, stained cup in hand. "Why were you late for the briefing?" he asked, with his usual aggression. Stale cigarette smoke drifted from the folds of his clothes, as did a faint, pungent fruity scent. Byrne's after-hours drinking was getting worse.

"The SDEA had me working on the *Sunward* investigation this morning."

"Did they?" Byrne feigned interest as he poured coffee into his cup. "You are a popular lad these days." Byrne grimaced as he took a sip of the hot liquid. "Though I doubt it will matter when your father's finally caught."

"Caught doing what?"

Byrne grinned. "Don't ask me, ask Saint McNab. He'll tell you anything you want to know. After all, you're the man who can do no wrong. They like you so much, they're plastering your face on bloody billboards now."

Mornay didn't want to discuss the new and humiliating direction Roger Donaldson was taking CID in a bid to rework their public image. His purpose for returning home two years ago had been to seek the anonymity of life in the country and a quiet job.

Mornay sipped scalding, overly strong coffee, affecting nonchalance. "Might as well paint a bull's-eye on my back, for all the good the publicity is doing me."

Byrne lifted his coffee mug in a mocking salute. "There's worse places to be than balancing on a pedestal, though I'm damned if I can think of one at the moment."

Claire eyed the overflowing rubbish bin next to the curb as Mornay pulled out of traffic. "I don't think you'll want to park here."

Mornay dismissed her warning by turning off the engine. "We'll only be a minute," he assured her.

They were parked in front of E's, a pub that catered to the rougher side of Macduff. Mornay pointed to a midnight blue BMW with a personalized tag that read MR. E. "Business is good."

"It's amazing what a drunk will pay for watered-down whiskey. Do you know what the E stands for?" Claire asked.

"Elrod." He opened the bar door, and they walked in, pausing on the other side for their eyes to adjust to the dim interior.

Claire didn't care for pub crawls or spending her off-hours choking on cigarette smoke in crowded rooms. So she'd never been inside E's. She found the bar surprisingly clean, if spare on the amenities. The floor was concrete, the walls were red brick. The furnishings were a mix of zinc-topped tables and wooden stools—short stools for the tables, tall ones for the bar. There was more dull zinc behind the bar. Centered on the wall behind the bar was a blue neon E. in a slanted script. The same logo was stenciled on the café doors that led to the bathrooms, and on every piece of furniture.

The sound of Claire's heels on the concrete floor reverberated around them, and a door behind the bar opened before they'd gotten halfway into the room.

"The prodigal son returns. I was wondering if I'd recognize you the next time you showed your scarred mug."

Mornay grinned; the transformation from his usual dour expression was startling. "Claire, this is Elrod, E. to the rough bastards that chuck their hard-earned money at him every night. Elrod, my colleague, Claire Gillespie."

Elrod was a slim man near Mornay's age. His skin was heavily scarred by acne; he wore a neatly trimmed beard to cover the majority of the scars. He had a smile that belonged on an altar boy, not a thirtysomething bar owner wearing tight jeans, thick-soled black boots, a football jersey, and a leather jacket. Elrod turned his brilliant grin on Claire, and she couldn't help but warm to him.

He put his arm around Mornay's shoulders. "Can you believe this ugly bastard is going to be my best man in a month's time?"

"Does your fiancée know?"

Elrod laughed and clapped Mornay heartily on the shoulder. "Did you hear that? Aye, Diane knows Seth is my best mate, and she still loves me anyway. I'm a blessed man. Christ, I can't believe you've stayed away so bloody long. Drink?" Elrod let his gaze slip sideways to the bar.

Mornay declined.

"Orange juice, if you have it," Claire said. They took seats at the bar while Elrod served Claire her drink, waving away her offer to pay.

Elrod's expression turned serious. "It must have been horrible finding that poor boy's body yesterday."

"It was," Mornay agreed. "I need your help, Elrod."

"You've got it."

Claire studied Mornay's features in the mirror behind the bar. Though he'd never been one to preen, she'd never seen him quite so disheveled. He needed a haircut; his dark hair was curling around his ears and at the back of his neck. His tie was on slightly crooked, as if he'd tugged it away from his neck. He'd worn the same tie the previous day. It matched his current suit better. The quality of his suits was enough to convince her he wasn't on a permanent downward spiral, but she was concerned about how long this temporary spiral would last. Oddly enough, his lack of care in his appearance had done little to stem the daily flirtations from women. They were as bold as ever, but, unusually, Mornay was completely ignoring them.

"Were the Paisley brothers or Scott Gray regulars here?"

"The Paisleys were as regular as they were anywhere, I suppose. Scott Gray didn't drink. Ulcers."

"Did they ever talk about what they did for my father?"

"And lose their jobs? They might be idiots, but they knew better than to cross Clyde Mornay."

"I need to know why they were working for him. What possible use could they have been to him? I can think of half a dozen more qualified men than the Paisleys."

"I agree, it seems strange to pass over better men to have the Paisleys, but Clyde must've had a good reason. I've heard the Paisleys were tops at their business on the oil rigs."

"Do you remember what their duties were on the oil rigs?" Claire asked Elrod.

"They worked with pumping stations," he answered. "I've no idea what that entailed: All I remember is that they were sacked because they wouldn't stop fighting on their off time."

To Mornay, she said, "Did your father's trawler have a pump?"

"As far as I know there was only a bilge pump, the sort of equipment a ten-year-old can run. So, my original question remains: What were they doing for my father?"

"Maybe he was smuggling petrol, Seth. If they knew their business from the oil platforms, they might have a few mates who were willing to work with them. Siphon off a few hundred liters from some oil platform's holding tanks. Who would miss it?"

Mornay reached into his pocket and pulled out a warped hunk of metal. "This was one of the remnants of the *Sunward*'s forward hold. See that coating?" Mornay asked, pointing out the lighter side of the metal. "That was on the inside."

Elrod turned the bit of metal over in his fingers and scratched the coated surface with a thumbnail. "Looks like some kind of plastic. Is that usually in hulls?"

"Never, that I've seen. It is possible Clyde could've been hauling petrol in a tank if he'd converted the forward part of the fish hold. I don't understand why he'd need the coating, but then, I've never smuggled petrol."

"He has the facility to make a special conversion."

"But petrol?" Mornay asked. "He'd have to haul thousands of liters to make it worth his while."

Elrod put both hands on the bar and leaned closer. "He'd make a fortune if he worked slow and steady. And if he were selling the petrol directly to the fishing fleet—not just the trawlers, but the creel boats, seine netters, and pursers—he wouldn't need to bring it to shore. Who'd be looking for black-market petrol? The police are hot for drug traffickers these days. Petrol would explain the massive explosion."

The door to the bar opened, and two men entered. They were young, maybe late teens or early twenties. One had multiple brow piercings; the other wore a leather coat full of metal studs. They both grinned when they saw Mornay.

"Kyle, it's him, it's that cop from the telly," the one with the piercings said.

Mornay slid off the stool. A fast retreat was his usual reaction when he was recognized. "We'll finish talking later, Elrod," he said in a low voice. "Thanks for Claire's drink."

# Chapter Nine

Deborah continued stirring her coffee, though she'd added the sugar several minutes earlier. The clinking sound was beginning to annoy David, but no more than the conversation, which had been spinning around in circles for the last quarter of an hour.

"You're going to have to give her a reason," she said at last.

"Deborah, I don't want to talk about it anymore."

"You've never been one to hide your head in the sand."

David pushed out of his seat, shoved his hands in his pockets, and started pacing in front of the fire. His body ached from the bruises. He'd been hoping to avoid Deborah since her return, but she'd been waiting to pounce.

"Why are you seeing a therapist?"

He stopped, turned. "None of your business?"

"Then why did you tell me yesterday?"

"I was drunk."

Hand beneath her chin, Deborah turned her amazing green eyes in his direction and deftly switched the conversation to another topic; it was Deborah's forte. "So what are you going to do about Lee?" Was she using *his* nickname for Eilish to manipulate him?

"Do? What *can* I do? She's going to marry a lumbering clod and produce her own clan of bonnie wee bairns who can milk with one hand and weave with the other."

"Just because she *says* she wants to marry him doesn't mean she *really* wants to marry him."

He loved Deborah, but the woman was maddening at times. Her logic made no sense to him. "Fortunately for Calvin the Magnificent, Eilish doesn't appear to use twisted logic to reason her way through life. When she says something, she means exactly what she says. She always has."

"A trait she certainly didn't learn from either of us. When was the last time you spoke frankly to her? Or to me, for that matter? There was a time when you trusted me completely."

He looked away. "I don't distrust you, Deborah."

"That's not quite the same, is it? Eilish doesn't trust me, either. She'd been carrying on with Calvin for nearly two months before I found out. So when will you tell her?"

"Tell her what? That I'm seeing a therapist?"

Deborah's voice softened. "No, David. When are you going to tell her that you're in love with her?"

*       *       *

Mornay and Claire arrived at Cordiff's Primary School at noon, and checked in at the reception desk inside the front entrance. The school's head teacher was away at a conference, and the deputy head teacher, Mrs. Haver, looked too young to attend university, let alone hold a job. She was a small woman with a serene, calming way about her. And she got right to the point by asking them the purpose of their visit.

"We need to know if Matthew worked on any projects about Australia during the past year?"

"I can check."

"Can you also ask his closest mates if he had a particular interest in Australia?"

If Mrs. Haver was curious about the nature of their questions, she hid it well. When she hurried off for her task, Mornay slid down in his chair and closed his eyes.

The office door opened, and an older man entered. He wore a blue Nike jogging suit and white trainers.

"I'm Mick Trenton, the school's P.E. instructor. Mrs. Haver said you might want to talk to me."

Mick Trenton was Australian.

Mornay stood and offered Mick the chair. The instructor declined. He was shorter than Mornay; his chest, neck, and arms bulged with muscles, an action-figure physique. Trenton staked out a patch of floor by Mrs. Haver's desk and waited with a patience that was probably honed by hours of dealing with overly energetic children.

"Why didn't we speak with you before?" Claire asked. "You weren't on our list of Matthew's instructors."

"I was out of the country when Matthew was taken, and I'm not assigned to a particular level."

Claire, notebook at the ready, asked, "Where?"

"Home. Australia."

"Visiting family?"

"I was on vacation. My family lives in America now." He seemed comfortable answering Claire's questions, so Mornay let her continue.

"Was it a planned vacation?" she asked.

"Yes."

"Can you give us the name of your travel agent and the flight numbers you were on?"

Mick's gaze swung in Mornay's direction. "What's this about?"

"This is about eliminating variables," Mornay said, trying to sound reasonable. "We're working methodically through a list. The quicker you can provide us the information, the quicker we can be on to the next item."

"Shouldn't be too hard, I suppose," Mick said. "I took one of those package vacations, a company that specializes in trips with a bit of risk. Didn't want to do the usual this year—visit old mates, clubbing, surfing. I like thrills." This was said with a look at Claire.

"Which company?" she asked.

"Loc-Down Adventures."

"Did you happen to discuss this vacation with any of your students?"

"I might've, can't really remember. But before I left I taught the younger levels a course in self-defense," he offered.

Mornay exchanged looks with Claire before asking, "What sort of self-defense?"

"I showed them some basic simple arts moves anyone can use to make someone let go of you if they grab you. I taught them how to pay more attention to their surroundings, and the first thing they should do if they are grabbed."

Claire had stopped taking notes. "And what would that be?"

"Scream their bloody heads off. Most attackers want passive victims. Then I showed them what to do if they were abducted."

"Was this course on the school's curriculum?"

"If I've finished with a particular section, I've got time to show the kids other things. Everyone should know a bit of self-defense these days. I was given permission."

Mick's condescending tone to Claire was beginning to annoy Mornay. "What else did you tell your students to do if they did happen to get abducted?" he asked.

"Leave behind fingerprints, hair, saliva, anything that would let someone else know where they were. That way their abductor or attacker could be convicted, no matter what sort of story they came up with." Mick Trenton grinned. "DNA evidence doesn't lie."

Mornay was revolted by Trenton's cavalier attitude; he seemed completely unmoved by the fact that one of his students had been abducted and murdered.

Claire seemed to sense Mornay's growing disgust, for she continued. "Mr. Trenton, is it possible you might have discussed your vacation with Matthew?"

"Like I said, I might've, but I don't really remember who I said what to."

Mornay's voice was frosty. "Do you even know the names of your students?"

"I don't need to know their names to teach them to play football, now do I?"

"Did any of the teachers, like Jonathan Cross, for instance, participate in the self-defense course?" Claire asked.

Mick laughed. "He's not that sort of lad, is he?"

She paused her note taking. "What do you mean by that?"

"Doesn't like to get his hair or his clothes mussed. You know the type."

"Mr. Trenton," Claire said, "were you surprised to hear Matthew had been abducted?" Mornay admired how Claire was keeping the conversation on track.

"I suppose I wondered how he could let it happen. He'd been taught better, hadn't he?"

School was dismissed by the time Mornay and Claire finished questioning other staff members. The most curious fact they discovered was that the staff unanimously supported Jonathan Cross.

"That Trenton was a cold bastard," Mornay said. "DNA trails? The things children are forced to worry about these days."

"At the risk of sounding insensitive," she said, "has anything really changed? A hundred years ago we had children living and dying in coal mines. The horrors just have new faces now." She opened the passenger door. "Didn't you think it was strange that most of the staff didn't have a bad word to say about Cross?"

"He has the personality of wet bread, yet everyone's falling over themselves to defend him. Is it his looks?"

"You're asking me? I don't notice those sorts of things."

Mornay chuckled at her haughty tone. "Claire. You're wired to notice certain things about the male species, just like I'm wired to notice things about women."

Mornay opened the door to his three-year-old Corsa and folded himself into the seat. When he'd had his motorbike, it didn't seem important to find a more comfortable car. Now he didn't have the time.

"It's nearly five, too late to drive to the Adairs' and fetch Matthew's journals," he said. "Let's park in front of Cross's house and see if we can make him nervous."


Victoria was waiting at the curb in front of Mornay's house when he finally got home at nine that evening. He hadn't stopped by Elrod's, as was his habit on Friday nights; he was too tired to bother. Victoria walked with him to the kitchen door, neither speaking. They hadn't spoken to each other face-to-face in over a month.

Pamela's prolonged hospital stay was taking its toll on Victoria, though sometimes he wondered if it was Fiona, her mother, who was really doing the damage. Fiona's drinking was steadily growing worse, and she was making increasing demands on her elder daughter, whom she couldn't forgive for being alive and well while her favorite daughter lay comatose in hospital.

There were dark circles under her eyes, and worry lines etched into the once-smooth skin of her forehead. She didn't smile anymore.

"Have you thought about what I asked, Seth?"

"Are you allowed to talk without your solicitor present?"

"I'm only doing what's best."

"For who?"

"For that poor baby."

"Aye," Mornay said slowly. "I've thought about it." He shrugged out of his jacket and pulled off his tie to stall for time. He didn't want a repeat of their last discussion, with both of them shouting at each other. He offered her a drink. She refused. She planted herself in the center of the kitchen and waited. He bought an extra minute by fetching a can of Tennent's and opening it.

"Why is raising this child so important to you?" he asked.

"I want it to have a better life growing up than we did. You're just not equipped to give a child that." She pointed in the direction of the lounge and the cardboard boxes stacked against the wall. "You've lived here two years, and you haven't bothered to unpack. I think you chose to come back not to start a life, but to delay living it. Which is why you're happy working here."

"What's wrong with my job?"

"You couldn't have picked a less-demanding area to be a police officer."

"You've obviously not been watching the news lately."

But Victoria was in the middle of a rant; nothing could stop her.

"Seth, you're refusing to face what happened to you when you were in service. How can you expect to be a proper parent if you can't even handle the problems in your own life? There are no dress rehearsals when it comes to raising children. You're either committed, or you're not. And you're firmly in the *not* category."

"I'm not my father, Tori."

She didn't flinch away from his gaze. "I never said you were. I know you're a better man, but that still doesn't mean you're prepared to be a father."

She pulled a large envelope out of her bag. "I want you to sign these papers; they'll begin the process that will give me full custody of your child. Ring me once you've done it. And in case you lose this set, I've had another set delivered to your office."

"What if we go through all this bother and it turns out I'm not the father at all?"

"Then take the test and put the issue to rest. But sign the papers either way. If you don't, I'll fight you for the child, and, believe me, I won't pull any punches. Your career is all you have, and if I start this fight, that will be the first thing I go after. Think about it before you decide to chuck those papers."

# Chapter Ten

News reporters had gathered in the Adairs' front garden—an impressive crowd, considering the frigid temperature and the fact it was eight o'clock on a Saturday morning. News vans stretched down the block, obscuring the large front gardens of the neighbors. The neighborhood was fairly new but had been designed to look like the older cottages nearer the center of the village. The large front gardens weren't fenced but left open, increasing the feeling of spaciousness.

A ring of barricades kept the reporters off the majority of the Adairs' garden. They were relegated to the farthest corner, where a microphone and a stand had been installed. Mornay and Claire flashed their IDs to the special constable manning the wooden barricade set up at the end of the drive. Special constables were generally retirees who were looking for a side job that would occasionally get them out of the house. This one—Terry Frett—was particularly good at crowd control; he had a massive neck and heavily muscled shoulders from his former trade as a stonemason. One look at Terry was enough to discourage the rowdiest of crowds.

They followed the dour Glaswegian down a stone path and through a wooden gate into an equally impressive back garden. A wooden fence surrounded the garden, providing a measure of privacy from the neighbors. The Adairs had landscaped the small space with fruit trees, curving paths, flower beds, and stone benches. In the back left corner was a small shed; its walls were harled the same color as the house. In front of the shed was a patch of bare ground: the remains of Matthew Adair's small vegetable garden.

Mornay and Claire followed Special Constable Frett to a back door that led into a glass-walled conservatory. Charles and Rita Adair sat on a wicker divan surrounded by sunlight and verdant green plants. Rita Adair's skin was so pale it almost seemed transparent, a network of blue veins clearly visible beneath the surface. She was absently petting a large gray cat that was draped across her lap. Charles Adair had missed several places shaving that morning; the hair that'd escaped the razor showed silver-gray in the sunlight. It was a stark contrast to the pale pink skin of his cheeks.

"Has Lord Gordon arrived?" Adair asked. "He was delayed in Aberdeen."

"Not that I'm aware," Mornay answered. "You're continuing with the press briefings?"

"It was Lord Gordon's suggestion." Adair spoke

as if by rote. "He said it was his duty to warn other families about pedophiles."

"He used the word *pedophile*?"

"Yes."

It appeared Lord Gordon was anxious to see his face on every telly from John o' Groat's to the borders. The politician was blatantly taking advantage of the Adairs' vulnerability.

"Mr. Adair, I can assure you that there's been no definitive proof discovered that this is the work of a pedophile. Do you mind my asking how Lord Gordon became acquainted with your family?"

"He's the chair of the Aberdeen Arts and Histories Council board. My wife has been the board's secretary for nearly ten years." Charles Adair's gaze traveled from Mornay to Claire, resignation stretching his features into a mask of weariness. "You're not here for the briefing?"

"We're here to pick up Matthew's journals. We're going back through them. We'll return them soon."

Time didn't have the same meaning for Charles Adair as it had two weeks ago. "Take as long as you need. We'll just stay here; Lord Gordon will be arriving at any moment. You know where Matthew's room is."

"Yes. But first I wanted to ask if you knew of the self-defense course Matthew took in school?"

"We did," Rita said. "Matthew loved it. He was always wanting to practice his release moves on my thumbs. He even had us come up with a family password."

"Password?"

"For emergencies," Rita Adair's voice cracked. "Or if a stranger tried to tell him his mum wanted him, and he needed to get in the car. If the stranger didn't know the family password, he wouldn't get in. I suppose it's silly, now, considering."

"Why didn't you tell us about the password before?" Claire asked. Her voice was gentle; she excelled at coaxing answers out of people who seemed incapable of talking.

"I'd forgotten about it until you mentioned the self-defense course," Rita replied.

"Did he mention anything about Australia to you while he was taking the defense course?"

"Australia?" the Adairs echoed in unison.

Charles answered, "I think we would've remembered if he had."

Mornay was thankful Charles Adair didn't follow them into his son's room; he wanted a private look around. Claire closed the door behind them.

Given the size of the house, the room was small. Bunk beds fashioned from white tubing were pushed against the far wall. A cluttered desk flanked the door to the left. Next to the desk was a floor-to-ceiling bookshelf, the wood painted a glossy white. A window seat and additional shelving had been built into the wall surrounding the room's only window, also painted glossy white. The cheerful room was completely opposite the dingy room he'd had as a child. Mornay shook off those memories and started methodically searching the room.

"The journal is on the desk, next to the computer," Claire pointed out.

"So it is." Mornay got on his back and squirmed under the lowest bunk bed, running his fingers along the metal railing supporting the mattress.

"What are you looking for, then?" Claire asked, when he emerged from beneath the bed, hair mussed and empty-handed.

"Matthew Adair was a clever boy. And clever boys have clever hiding places. Pull out the books and see if there's anything wedged in the bookshelves, particularly the upper ones."

"You think he was clever enough to hide something that escaped our other search?" She worked while she talked, her movements neat and precise.

"If you recall we barely spent a quarter of an hour in here, and Gordon did most of the searching." Mornay started searching the bookshelves surrounding the window.

He used a finger to open the slats of the miniblinds over the window, to look outside. The crowds had thickened in front of the Adair house. Still no sign of Lord Gordon. As Mornay dropped his hand, he noticed scuffmarks that stood out starkly black against the white windowsill.

"Claire, have a look."

She crossed the room and peered at the marks he pointed out. "The screen can't be opened from the inside," she said.

He peered through the window and studied the brick-edged windowsill outside. The mortared bricks were clean.

Mornay backed up and studied the top of the window frame. "Maybe Matthew wasn't opening the window. Maybe he was standing on his window ledge."

The ceilings in the house were high, and the windows were tall. The window was easily higher than Matthew had been tall, even if he'd been standing on the window seat. But standing on the ledge, he would've been able to reach the top of the window frame.

Claire was gazing at the top of the window. "Perhaps we should ask his parents."

"Did you tell your parents everything? Even good boys keep secrets." He winked at her. "And good girls."

He moved around her and stepped onto the window seat, his feet sinking into the thick cushion. He ran his hands along the molding at the top of the window. At the corner he dislodged a bit of molding, revealing a small opening.

"Told you he was a clever boy," he said. "What's inside? My hand won't fit." He reached down and helped Claire onto the cushioned seat. She tentatively reached inside the opening, her hand disappearing to the wrist.

She pulled out a long brass key. The brass was corroded a blackish green and was crusted with dirt. Claire rubbed off the dirt and held the key in her palm for him to see. "Now what? This could be for anything."

He took the key, but he was looking at Claire. Her suit was a dark spruce green. The color made the green of her eyes seem darker, nearly black. She was wearing a pale lipstick that was invisible from more than a few feet away, as were the sprinkling of freckles across her nose. "New scent?" he asked.

She ignored the question by stepping off the window seat.

Footsteps thumped in the hall outside the bedroom. Mornay pocketed the key with a deft movement and snapped the molding back in place, then stepped off the seat and crossed the room. He picked up the journal, opened it to a random page, and pretended to be deeply engrossed in the neatly written words Matthew had penned two months ago. Claire pried open a space between the plastic slats of the blinds and peered outside. Charles Adair opened the door to his son's room.

"I see you've found the journals. Is there anything else we can do for you?"

"No, sir," Mornay said. He snapped the journal closed, picked up its mates, and handed them to Claire. "We'll return them as soon as we can."

Charles Adair nodded absently. Mornay could only wonder what kept the man going.

Charles Adair let Claire past, then held up a hand to stop Mornay. "Do you have any idea who might have done this to our son? No one will tell us."

"You need to give us time to work through the facts we do know, sir. And whoever mentioned the word pedophile is getting ahead of himself."

"If that's true, then why was he taken?"

"I don't know."

Outside the Adairs' house, Claire seemed unaware of the stares she was receiving from the male journalists. "Look who's finally arrived." She pointed to Lord Gordon's Mercedes.

"And I was hoping we'd miss him."

Lord Gordon's driver walked around the Mercedes to open the back door.

"Think he'll come over?" Claire asked.

"He'd be foolish to throw away an opportunity to put us in our proper place in front of such an eager audience."

"Or maybe he'll glom on to the force's golden boy," she suggested.

Canting his head so he could more clearly read her expression, Mornay said, "You're starting to sound like Byrne. I'd mind that if I were you."

"Why do you think Inspector Gordon sent us here? If I were a gambler, I'd bet she wanted the cameras to catch you talking to her father. It'd make him look like a man of action."

He dismissed her theory. "A conversation is not action."

"Look where he's walking."

Lord Gordon was coming directly toward them. The politician was just tall enough to catch people's attention, but not so tall that everyone had to crane their necks up to talk to him. He exuded confidence. He'd never be mistaken for a people's man; but he always seemed to get the people, particularly the common ones, on his side with his chameleon expressions.

"DS Mornay, we meet again so soon." Though he was smiling, his overall expression was one of studied concern.

Mornay shook the proffered hand, noting how some of the reporters were edging closer; cameras were being turned, focusing on the impromptu meeting in the Adairs' drive. A knot of neighbors had gathered several yards away. He wondered if Claire had a point—the meeting did have a contrived feeling to it. Had DI Gordon set it up solely to provide a photo opportunity for her father?

"Another press briefing?" Mornay asked. If Lord Gordon noted the derisive tone in Mornay's voice, he ignored it.

"Your command area isn't the only one being affected by this tragedy. Command areas throughout Scotland are reporting more hostility from the public. It's important that we reassure the public at every opportunity."

"How very conscientious of you, sir." Mornay lowered his voice. "Did you tell the Adairs their son was killed by a pedophile?"

Several beats passed while Lord Gordon held Mornay's gaze, his expression still one of concern. It was only when one was as close as Mornay that the calculation in the man's eyes was apparent.

Mornay continued, his voice low and menacing. "You'll be as surprised to discover as we were that Matthew had taken a self-defense course just before his abduction. One of the things his instructor told the students was to create a family password to prevent abductions. Matthew created one, which means whoever took him did so by force. Another thing they learned was how not to be a passive victim. You should've seen the state of Matthew's hands when he was found. Every one of his fingernails had been ripped off; it's possible he left them behind as evidence. Clever boy, wasn't he?"

"He was a child, one can't expect him to have the capacity to be so aware of what was happening."

"I think he did. It'd be devastating to Matthew's parents if his inquiry was undermined by some thoughtless bastard making blatantly stupid assumptions about Matthew's attacker."

"You're quite right." Lord Gordon's voice was cold and unfriendly. "So you'll be wise not to make any missteps during the investigation. Roger Donaldson assures me that recruitment levels are rising for the

force. Apparently, replacements have never been easier to find for those officers who choose to leave."
The politician nodded politely, as if they'd just
reached an agreement, and walked up the drive to
greet the Adairs.

"Keep antagonizing the Gordons," Claire said, as
they walked toward his car, "and you'll end up like
Constable Walden, trapped in an office too far from
civilization for anyone to remember you even exist."

"Solitude is beginning to sound appealing these
days."

Harris Veterinary Clinic was more or less on the way
to Finovar Castle, if you didn't mind spending half
an hour backtracking down twisty roads. Ian Harris
lived in a stone cottage built around the same time
the American colonies were deciding to wriggle out
of King George's possessive grasp. There were four
outbuildings behind the cottage, all newer, all
immaculately kept. The state of the buildings was a
marked contrast to the state of the road leading to
the buildings. Mornay wondered if Harris kept the
approach to his property in such a disgraceful state
to avoid the casual drop-in. If he could get in and out
of Harris's place without stripping off some vital bit
of his undercarriage, it was going to be a miracle.

Harris came out of the cottage immediately, a
chipped blue mug in hand. He wore muddy
Wellingtons and had a scowl firmly in place.

"He's not happy to see us," Claire said. "You
should've been more empathetic when he wanted in
the horse box on Thursday."

"He's a big boy; he doesn't need me to hold his
hand."

"Are you here about my bill?" Harris called out. "I get paid for my time. I had five patients waiting on me while you lot had me wasting my day at that bloody wreck. And for what? Two rams not even worth the bother to butcher."

Mornay had been prepared to deal with a bad temper; he could soft talk with the best of them when he needed to. But Harris's utter callousness was beyond endurance. "And what worth do you place on the life of a child then, Mr. Harris?" Mornay asked. He heard Claire draw in a sharp breath, but he was not going to be warned off. Not today. "Matthew Adair didn't deserve to be tossed in a garbage bag like yesterday's peelings."

Harris's voice was as hard as the slate covering the roof of his cottage. "I'm not wasting any more of my time with you lot," he said, walking away.

"We're conducting a murder inquiry," Mornay called out. "You'll answer our questions at your convenience or ours."

Harris turned around. "You'd like that, eh? Bullying an old man?" Harris raised one of his hands, the skin around the knuckles red and raw-looking. He pointed at Mornay. "I'll tell you this, I'm sick to death of hearing the Adairs come on the telly when I'm trying to have my tea and go on and on about their Matthew, as if they're the only family in this country that's ever worried about their children. If they didn't have the money they did, you can be sure we wouldn't have seen them on the telly more than once. And even more sure that Lord Gordon wouldn't have noticed them, for all that he's acting like a long-lost uncle now."

"Granddad?" a young boy called from the doorway. He looked about ten. Matthew Adair's age. He had ginger-colored hair cropped very short, almost in a military style. "Do you want to keep playing?" the boy asked. "Your star bases are being attacked."

"Play for me, I'll be there in just a minute."

The boy spent several seconds eyeing Mornay and Claire, before saying, "All right." With a final glance in Mornay's direction, the boy closed the door.

From the angle of his shoulders and the cant of Harris's head, Mornay could tell his anger had evaporated. It'd been replaced with something akin to apprehension. "My grandson. What is it you want?" he asked, his voice gruff. "I've patients to see this afternoon."

Mornay glanced at Claire, letting her have a go at him.

"We want to know more about the sheep that were in the trailer," she said. "Did you recognize them?"

"Do you want to know what type they were, or what breed?"

"There's a difference?" Mornay asked.

"Oh, aye. You've five basic types of sheep. Your dead ones were the fat-tailed type."

"Fat-tailed?" Mornay wondered if Harris was toying with them.

"Aye, fat-tailed or broad-tailed."

Claire pulled out her notebook and pen and started taking notes. Mornay was amazed the ink in her pen was running, he was positive frostbite was setting in on his toes.

Harris picked up his narrative, counting out the types on his fingers. "You've got your fine-wooled, your mutton-type, the short-tailed variety, haired, then the fat-tailed." He showed them his open hand to emphasize that the number came to five. "Yours were fat-tailed. They're called fat-tailed because they can store large amounts of fat in the tail and the region of the rump."

"What breed are they, then?"

"They're a cross of two breeds. Awassi and Karakul."

"Those are odd names. Are they rare?" Claire asked.

"They're not rare if you live in Turkestan. But we don't have too many scampering about the mountains in Scotland."

"Do you know who might be raising them in this area?"

"There's only one place in this part of the country," Harris answered. "Finovar Castle. That young Eilish has been raising both breeds since her original herd was destroyed with the hoof-and-mouth breakouts a few years back. She uses their wool for the rugs and things she sells in her shop. There was a right fuss when she imported them; the local farmers were still reeling over the hoof-and-mouth herd destruction. They were worried the animals would bring new diseases into the country."

"Do you look after the Finovar animals?" Claire asked

"I do."

"Are the Lockwoods in the habit of transporting their livestock around the countryside?" he asked.

"Eilish wouldn't hear of it. She won't even put them in a trailer to bring them to me. They're too valuable."

"So she keeps close tabs on the herd?"

"As close as you can."

"What do you think about the Lockwoods in general?"

Harris's bushy brows pinched together. "I don't think about them at all. Eilish Lockwood makes an appointment. I keep it. They pay their bills on time, and they listen to what I tell them to do."

"What did you do with the carcasses that were in the trailer?" Mornay asked.

"They're buried in the back field."

"Did you look them over before burying them?"

Mornay was treated to another long and considering look before Harris replied. "I might have."

"What killed them?"

"One broke its neck. One was impaled on a pitchfork. Whoever put them in the trailer didn't bother tying them up—not that a rope would've saved them when the trailer flipped."

# Chapter Eleven

Eilish climbed into the passenger side of Calvin's car. As he reversed neatly, Eilish breathed a sigh of relief to be leaving the castle, even just for lunch at the pub.

"You're not sorry you refused it, are you?"

Eilish knew he wanted her to admit even a small fraction of regret, but she couldn't admit to something she didn't feel. "Why should I be? It was a ridiculous gift."

Eilish looked out across the familiar swells of ground, not really seeing anything.

"How is it your brother is so rich and you're not?"

Calvin had never been so blunt before. "He's rich because there are too many idiots in the world willing to pay lots of money to defy death. Do we really need to talk about this?"

"He was barely eighteen when he left home. Why would he move halfway around the world to start his company? What was so wrong with living here, close to home?" Calvin asked.

"You'll have to ask David. Can we talk about something else, please? I've a pounding headache."

"We don't have to talk at all."

Eilish found the silence just as annoying as Calvin's questions. "Have the police questioned you?" she asked.

"Were they going to?"

"I think so. There's a tall one. His name's Mornay. He seemed suspicious of David."

"For what?"

"For knowing someone else, I can't remember his name. Then Murdo's daughter was throwing herself at David again—she can't be in the same room he is without fondling him."

Calvin grinned at her. "Jealous?"

"Don't be ridiculous. A woman in her position should know how to act professionally."

"So you had two detectives? For a stolen car?"

"Three actually, and men looking for finger-prints." She debated telling Calvin what David had urged her to do. But Calvin never seemed to have the patience to listen.

"Your David wasn't like what I'd imagined he'd be."

"What did you think he would be like?"

"More interesting, I suppose, and more in con-trol. He seemed touchy when anyone spoke to him." He pulled into a parking spot in front of Fox's Pub. "So, are we still on for that trip to Edinburgh next weekend?"

She'd been dreading the question; he'd been pressuring her for weeks to spend a weekend with him in Edinburgh.

"I don't think everything will be sorted by then."

"It's only a car that you didn't own; what's there to sort?"

"It's not that simple. Give me a couple of days to work it out."

"I'm going. And if you don't give me an answer by tonight, I'll ask someone who doesn't mind being seen with me."

"Then you better take her. And don't bother coming around to see me when you get back." Eilish got out of the car and started walking toward the bus stop.

Mornay watched Claire sort the contents of her purse, pulling out old receipts and empty gum wrappers. They'd had a quick lunch after leaving Harris's cottage, and were on their way to Cordiff.

"So who's the lucky man?" he asked.

The contents of Claire's purse clattered to the floor. "What?"

"You're . . ." He looked at her hair and makeup, the more feminine clothes, and realized his blunder. If he told her how much more attractive she looked now than a few months ago, she'd probably take a swing at his head with her bag. "You look more content. I just thought it might've been because you've met someone."

Claire retrieved everything from the floorboard and stuffed it on her lap, then she began shoving things back inside her bag without any semblance of organization. "I don't need a man to feel happy with my life. And you're my ranking officer, not my father. The reason behind any changes you might notice these days is none of your business."

"Point taken. My apologies."

An uneasy silence settled between them until they arrived at Finovar Castle. The clouds seemed to be hovering just above the tree line; the dark, twisted oak and beech branches almost seemed to be holding up the cottony damp.

Constable Walden trotted down the broad front stairs, his thin chest heaving. There were patches of color high on his cheeks. Walden's gaze shifted from Claire to Mornay, then he squared his narrow shoulders and walked forward. He held out a piece of paper to Mornay. "This was faxed to my office this morning."

Mornay took the fax. SCRO, the Scottish Criminal Records Office, had come up with a match to fingerprints found in the entrance to Finovar Castle. The prints belonged to Michael O'Conner, Finovar's groundskeeper. The report was concise, listing three separate arrests for auto theft nearly nine years before.

Mornay passed the report to Claire, pointing to the list of recipients. Their office had been sent a copy the previous day, to Byrne's attention.

"Is there any hint in Cordiff that people know about O'Conner?" Mornay asked Walden.

"Something like that would've been talked about, wouldn't it?"

"Probably. Is he well liked, Michael O'Conner?"

"As well as anyone, I suppose."

"And David Lockwood?"

Walden shrugged. "He's hardly ever here, is he?"

"Where is O'Conner now?" Mornay asked.

"He left an hour ago," Walden replied promptly. "I didn't follow."

"And everyone else?"

"In the kitchen."

David Lockwood was at the fireplace, as he'd been the first day Mornay had visited the castle. He was dressed casually in faded jeans, a dark blue rugby shirt, and hiking boots. Deborah and Eilish Lockwood were also in the kitchen, near O'Conner's wife, Joan. She didn't have the look of a country-woman. She was thin, and her appearance was fastidiously maintained. Not too much makeup, but it was there, as was salon-styled hair and salon-maintained nails.

Mornay flipped some pages in his notebook. "Where's your husband, Mrs. O'Conner?"

"Mucking out the horse barn. Do you want him?" She nodded toward a window.

Mornay followed her gaze. The barn, built of the same roughly squared granite blocks as the castle, sat about fifty meters away. Its planked door, painted a dark shade of green, was open. There were two chimneys at either end of the well-maintained building. He could see a small diagonal portion of the interior. The walls were painted white and there were stalls lining the inside, painted the same dark green as the door and the shutters that flanked the windows. Beneath an overhang outside the barn, he could see the rear lights of a horse trailer. Just from the glimpse, he could see that it was in much better condition than the trailer involved in the wreck. "Not just yet. Where were you on the eleventh of this month, Mrs. O'Conner?"

Lockwood laughed. "How do you expect Joan to answer that? I'd have difficulty instantly recalling where I was two days ago, without consulting my appointment book."

"Do you or your husband keep an appointment book, Mrs. O'Conner?"

Joan O'Conner shook her head.

"What do you use to keep track of important dates then?"

"That calendar," Joan O'Conner's voice had lost all trace of friendliness, and she pointed to a calendar hanging on a post in the kitchen.

Everyone seemed on edge, most particularly David Lockwood.

Eilish Lockwood was so nervous, she was refusing to look in Mornay's direction.

"Can you check on the eleventh?"

Joan O'Conner did as she was asked. "There's nothing written there. Isn't that the day Matthew Adair went missing?"

"It is." Mornay let the confirmation sink in before continuing. "Can you remember what you were doing on the eleventh?"

"Same as usual. Deborah was returning from one of her buying trips, so we got her room ready. Did some tidying up."

Mornay's next question was directed at David Lockwood. "Did you know about Michael O'Conner's criminal background when you hired him?"

"Of course I knew," Lockwood replied as calmly as if he were being asked his opinion of the weather.

"Do the O'Conners work every day?"

"We have Tuesdays and Sundays off," Joan answered.

"The eleventh was a Sunday. Did you work on that particular day?"

"I must've gotten my days muddled. Deborah returned that Tuesday; I saw to her room on Monday."

"And where were you and your husband on Sunday?"

David Lockwood stepped forward. "Are you suggesting that Michael or Joan had something to do with that boy's disappearance? It's utterly ridiculous."

"The questions need to be asked, however unpleasant."

"But no one here knew him or his parents."

"But he lived in Cordiff and his body was discovered not too far from your property, with two rams that have been identified as belonging to Finovar. From the information we've gathered thus far, there's no possibility the animals belonged to someone else, as Finovar is the only farm in the area that raises these particular breeds. Do you take head counts of the herd every day?"

It was Eilish who spoke. "Michael counts them once a week or so. We've no predators, but sometimes one will wander off. When that happens we search for the animal on our ATVs."

"And none have gone missing, to the best of your knowledge?"

"No." But the answer was offered tentatively; he made a note to revisit the subject later.

His gaze returned to Joan O'Conner. "Back to the eleventh?"

"We were home all day."

Mornay turned to Eilish Lockwood. "And you."

"Home. Alone."

"I was in England," David said.

"France," was Deborah's succinct reply.

"What's your blood type?" Mornay asked David Lockwood.

"What relevance does that have to the missing Jaguar? Or are you using that as an opportunity to question us about a completely unrelated matter?"

"It's a simple question; what's your blood type?"

"B negative."

"I see you have a horse trailer. Does Michael O'Conner ever drive the trailer for you during the racing season?"

David Lockwood hesitated before replying, "Occasionally."

"Once a season, once a month, once a week?"

"Depends on which races I'm in the country for."

"When you're in the country, does he drive the trailer for every race you're in? It's a simple question that requires no more than a yes or no answer."

"I'm not following the logic of your questions, Sergeant. Michael O'Conner is an employee. He does what he's asked, within reason."

Mornay wondered about Lockwood's reluctance to answer the question directly. "Do you *ask* him to drive your trailer for every race you're in?"

Lockwood exchanged an enigmatic look with Joan O'Conner. "I suppose the answer is yes," he said carefully. "When it won't interfere with his duties here."

"Do you keep any sort of record of which races he would have driven you to?"

"No."

Mornay turned to Joan O'Conner. "Do you write them on the calendar?"

"I don't."

Back to Lockwood. "Can you recall your most recent races?"

Lockwood reeled off a few dates that had occurred several months earlier. Mornay wrote them down and snapped his notebook closed. "So the locals will be used to seeing Michael O'Conner driving a trailer. What sort of vehicle do you use to tow it?"

"We use the estate car, a Land Rover."

"Do *you* ever drive to the races?"

The pause before David Lockwood answered was minute, but unmistakable. "Occasionally."

"Have you driven recently?"

"There have been no recent races."

"You don't live here year-round?"

"I haven't for the past ten years. I've a home in Sydney."

"How long have you been in Scotland on this visit?"

Another slight pause. "Just a couple of days. I was in England for the past week. Australia before that."

"One last question. How did you hurt your hand?"

Lockwood glanced down to his wounded left hand, as if he'd forgotten all about it. "In a riding accident, a few days ago."

"I'll need you to jot down the name of the stable where the accident occurred. Please include it with the other information."


Outside, Mornay forestalled Claire's questions by pulling out his mobile and dialing Sahotra's desk directly. When Sahotra answered, Mornay's instructions were brief.

"I need you to try and find out how many times David Lockwood has traveled out of the country. Go back at least two months. Then I need you to find out everything you can about David and Eilish Lockwood's finances. Everything."

"How am I supposed to do that?"

"I think we both know the answer to that, don't we?"

Silence followed Mornay's question, so he thought some reassurance was in order. "We're keeping this between you and me. Quiet-like."

"I need to finish working on the horse trainer list."

"It'll take Claire and me three days to work the list you've put together so far. How many horse trainers do you think we can visit in one day?" Mornay asked. "Is Gordon there?"

"Queens Street. She'll be back for the briefing. Quiet-like?" Sahotra repeated, giving Mornay an opportunity to elaborate.

Mornay ignored the opening. "One last thing. Michael O'Conner, Finovar's groundskeeper, was a guest at Craiginches a few years ago." Mornay reeled off the dates to Sahotra. "Get a copy of his form. I want to know everything we've got on him."

"Ready for a word with Michael O'Conner?" Mornay asked Claire when he pocketed his mobile.

Claire wasn't to be put off. "What was going on in there?"

"Don't know. But it felt tense, so I'm curious."

A dramatic vista opened before them as they rounded the side of the castle. The rolling green grass stopped abruptly about a hundred yards ahead, and beyond the jagged cliff edge, the slate gray sea stretched away until it disappeared into the mist. The mists obscured the rest of the dramatic coastline and muted the sound of the waves breaking at the bottom of the cliffs. There were no fences or walls to stop anyone from catapulting themselves off the cliffs.

"Why did you go on about the dates?"

"I wanted to see what they would do. It made them nervous."

"They were afraid we'd find out about Michael O'Conner's criminal record and assume he was responsible for the Jaguar's theft."

They followed a path of crushed stone to the large barn that'd been constructed to look like a miniature castle. The horses at Finovar lived better than most people in third world countries.

"They knew about his record before hiring him. This is something else. Something I can't put my finger on, so I'll just keep poking about until I find out."

"Or until Gordon finds out and stops you."

Mornay grinned down at her. "With my luck, she already knows."

He let her walk through the open door first. It was a well-maintained building: The scent of straw was thick in the air, as was the pine scent of disinfectant. The four horses stabled inside stared at them curiously as they walked down the wide center aisle.

Michael O'Conner wasn't in the building.

They walked the length and exited through a door on the opposite end. Mornay walked around to the overhang that held the horse trailer he'd glimpsed from the kitchen window.

"Didn't Lockwood say he drove it a month ago?" Mornay asked Claire.

"So he said."

Mornay flicked off dried mud spatters from behind the wheel well with a finger. "Someone's had it out more recently."

He pulled down on the handle and opened the back door. It had a varnished wood interior. The wood was scarred from use, but otherwise the trailer was clean. Extremely clean. No straw. No tackle. Nothing.

"It's been scrubbed clean," Claire pointed out.

"So it has," he agreed quietly. "With bleach. That scent is enough to choke you."

# Chapter Twelve

Mornay and Claire returned to Macduff by seven. The mood in the inquiry room was the most lighthearted Mornay had seen in weeks, but a guilty silence fell the moment they walked into the room.

Propped on the end of a table was the *Zero Tolerance* poster. The lads were gathered around it, watching Dougie Brown carefully aim a plastic spoon loaded with a small white ball. Red rings had been drawn around Mornay's various body parts: five points for his head, ten for his chest, fifteen for his crotch.

"It was Byrne's idea," Sahotra said.

"When did he sprout a sense of humor?" Mornay picked up one of the small balls.

"Plumber's putty," Sahotra explained. "Dougie's ahead by twenty points."

"What's going on here?" Assistant Chief Constable Roger Donaldson asked.

"The lads were just having a laugh, sir," Mornay answered.

"The public's good opinion of the force is no laughing matter. We're under a microscope. Am I being perfectly clear?"

"Yes, sir."

Donaldson turned to McNab. "Chief Inspector, when you're ready."

McNab had Detective Sergeants Tracy Spencer and Nina Aiden go first. Nina passed around a photograph of a man with a shaven head while Tracy Spencer took the floor. "Our man's name is Gabriel Smith. He was one of the first long-term sexual offenders put into the Sex Offender National Induction Center at Peterhead. He's served his sentence and was released two months ago. According to his personal officer, his treatment was successful."

Dougie Brown, who'd been watching Jonathan Cross for nearly two weeks, said, "Give me a dull pair of pruning shears, and I'll show you how to successfully treat a man like that."

McNab squashed the rumble of approval that followed Brown's remark with a cold look. "I better not hear any of you repeat something like that in public. I expect professionalism from my officers, Constable Brown. Do you understand?"

Brown didn't look penitent, but said, "Yes, sir," meekly enough to appease McNab.

Tracy Spencer continued. "Smith is living with his sister. She works in the kitchen at Matthew's school. Smith has been driving his sister to and from work since his release."

"What were they doing the day Matthew was abducted?"

"Said they spent the day at home. No one can verify it, though. We've already spoken with the neighbors."

"Did you tell anyone he was recently released from Peterhead?"

Tina Spencer's expression was bland. "We might've told one or two of the neighbors, in the course of our conversations."

McNab's expression hardened. "What if those neighbors decide to make it known they don't want a convicted pedophile in their neighborhood, and our man disappears? Then what've we got? What were they doing on the day Matthew's body was found?"

"Smith's sister had the day off. She took the bus to see their mum. Smith stayed at home. Alone."

One of the other constables from Aberdeen Division asked, "What did Smith do to be put in the induction center?"

Roger Donaldson answered the question. "He kidnapped two young boys and kept them in his attic for a month. He was caught when he tried to have photographs he'd taken of the boys developed at the local chemist. Smith kept the boys, who were seven and nine, naked and tied to the rafters."

"And he was released?" the constable asked.

"He'd served his time," Donaldson said. "Let's move on."

McNab intervened. "Let's remember we might have had two people in the Nissan. What's his blood type?"

"A positive."

"So does a good portion of the population, it's not enough. Let's see what he does in the next few days. Since we've had to stop the Cross surveillance, Brown can help. But I want you to make sure this instructor, Mick Trenton, has been thoroughly checked first."

"You don't want to bring Smith in for questioning?" Mornay asked.

"Once we've got him, I want to keep him."

"What about Jonathan Cross?" Claire asked. "We're just to ignore him?"

McNab glanced Donaldson's way. The ACC had his arms crossed; his expression was dour. Donaldson nodded. "Our surveillance has been called off, but we can eat our lunch anywhere we please."

"Does Smith smoke?" Mornay asked Tracy Spencer.

"Kings."

"But Jonathan Cross doesn't smoke," Claire reminded them.

Brown spoke first. "Not that we've discovered, but he could be hiding it. We've never searched through his bins. I suppose if I happened to find them lying on the walk in the middle of the night, on my way home, I could kick the rubbish around, see what I find."

"Just mind you're quick and discreet," McNab warned.

"What about the Jaguar inquiry?" Laina Gordon asked. "We can't simply ignore it."

"A stolen vehicle is hardly a top priority, is it?" Mornay said. He was still stinging from the confrontation with Murdo Gordon that morning in the Adairs' front garden, and from his row with Victoria.

"Top priority is the Adair inquiry," Donaldson told Gordon. "You can assure your father that I will personally oversee his inquiry."

"Christ," Mornay whispered to Claire. "You watch, we'll be chauffeuring the bastard before the end of the week."

McNab held up a hand, asking for silence. "I want you to watch this." He walked to a television on a tall mobile stand, which put the television around shoulder level, easy for everyone to see. After the television and the VCR had been switched on, a hush fell across the room. McNab used the remote to turn up the volume of a newscast.

The dark-haired newswoman, who'd been smiling brightly a moment before, put on a serious expression. "And now for the latest on the Matthew Adair inquiry. Our Deputy Justice Minister, Lord Murdo Gordon, joins us from the Adairs' home for an exclusive interview."

The scene switched to the Adairs' drive. Lord Gordon was walking toward Claire and Mornay. The caption at the bottom of the screen read, *Lord Gordon consults with CID Sergeant Seth Mornay.* The camera was set at the wrong angle to catch Mornay's full expression, but at the perfect angle to capture Lord Gordon's face. Appearing concerned and worried, he nodded thoughtfully throughout the brief exchange. Mornay didn't remember seeing him nod; he only remembered trying to squelch his desire to launch himself at the interfering politician.

When seen from a distance, the conversation had a completely different look. At the conversation's conclusion, Lord Gordon strode purposefully away. It appeared as if he was propelled by what Mornay had told him.

The scene switched to Lord Gordon's news interview. He was answering a question that'd just been asked. "All avenues of investigation are being pursued by the police. If this is the work of a pedophile, I'm sure officials will inform the public immediately." Gordon made the police sound as if they were keeping secrets regarding the inquiry.

McNab switched off the television.

Nearly every head in the room swiveled in Mornay's direction. Donaldson spoke first. "DCI McNab has assured me that you didn't discuss particulars of the case with Lord Gordon."

"No, sir."

"I didn't expect that you had," Donaldson replied calmly. "Lord Gordon is as keen for us to have a quick result as we are, but cousin or not, his penchant for speaking to the press about police matters has gotten annoying."

A few nervous chuckles erupted around the room.

"The point we wanted to make," McNab said, "was that the most casual encounter can be spun into negative press, something the force doesn't need at this moment. Mornay, what else happened today?"

"We interviewed Ian Harris."

"The vet at the scene?"

"Yes, sir. He was surprisingly hostile, complaining that we wasted his time at the accident site."

"The man can't be blamed for having a bad temper."

"He told us about the sheep in the back of the trailer. Apparently they're imported from the Middle East."

"Christ in heaven," Byrne complained loudly. "Now we're tracking down sheep?"

McNab sent a warning look in Byrne's direction and motioned for Mornay to continue.

"Eilish Lockwood imported them after her herd was destroyed during the hoof-and-mouth epidemic. She's the only person in the country who has them."

"Do the Lockwoods have any idea how their sheep got in the back of the trailer?"

"None. They seem to keep close tabs on the herd, but that's directly from the man responsible for them, Michael O'Conner. Michael has an interesting history."

When Mornay finished relaying the particulars of Michael O'Conner's criminal activity at age sixteen, Byrne was the first to speak.

"But that still doesn't explain why anyone would want to bother sheep-napping."

"Maybe they wanted to have the blame for Matthew Adair's death laid on one of the inhabitants of Finovar Castle," Claire suggested.

Byrne barely glanced her way. "Why?" he demanded to know.

"Obviously we'll have to take a closer look at the inhabitants' lives to answer that."

"Did Ian Harris know Harold Cosgrove?" McNab asked.

"I didn't ask. Ian Harris has a large animal trailer of his own. It was at the accident site, but when we were there on his property I didn't see it. It must have been in one of the buildings." McNab looked impatient to be away, so Mornay hurried on. "Maybe it'd be worthwhile to inspect his property."

"Maybe," McNab said, not ready to commit to a full-blown search. "We'll keep that at the back of our minds."

McNab assigned a pair of officers each to focus on David Lockwood, Michael O'Conner, and Ian Harris.

After the briefing, McNab asked Mornay and Claire to wait in his office.

Mornay was expecting his quiet boss to launch into a disciplinary speech regarding the impromptu meeting with Lord Gordon.

"I want you two to drive to Harold Cosgrove's stable yard, and I want you to do it tonight. I've got a contact in the Durham Constabulary. He'll meet you there.

"I'm sure you noticed how quiet DI Gordon was during the briefing. She's already laying down plans to protect David Lockwood in case there's a connection between him, Matthew Adair, and Harold Cosgrove. If there is a connection, we're going to have to discover it in the next twelve hours or my hands will be officially tied. I'd underestimated her pull at headquarters and I've underestimated Roger Donaldson's eagerness to please his cousin."

"What if we don't find anything?"

"Then no one needs to know about your little excursion." McNab jotted a phone number on a memo pad and handed it to Mornay. "Let me know when you arrive."

Eilish couldn't sleep; she kept going over her argument with Calvin. Shortly after midnight she kicked off her comforter and blankets, too annoyed to feel the chill. She shoved her feet into her slippers and went searching for David, who was a notorious insomniac.

The air in the hall was so cold, it made her chest ache when she breathed. She rarely noticed the damp musty scent of the stone around her.

She went downstairs first to check the library, his usual haunt on his rare visits, but David wasn't there. Then she looked in the kitchen, the billiards room, and the lounge before going back upstairs to see if David was in his bedroom, which was just down the hall from hers.

She paused at the slightly open door, not knocking. What if he tried to kiss her again? Should she try to stop him? Or kiss him back? Pretend it didn't happen?

She heard David's voice. He wasn't talking to Deborah; there was no one else speaking. He must be on the telephone.

Curiosity kept her outside the door, listening.

"No, I haven't told either of them." David's voice was irritated.

"The accident wasn't my fault; the car was speeding."

What accident? She leaned closer, straining to hear. Suddenly, the door swung inward. She froze. David was sitting in the dark; she could just make out his silhouette on the edge of the bed. His back was to the door.

There was a fury in David's voice she'd never heard before. "No, it doesn't matter how long I was in the country." There was a long pause. "Just because I knew the man? Are they that desperate?"

When David next spoke, the fury had boiled down to a simmering rage that resonated from every syllable. "It's your job to see the police don't find out."

She reached forward to close the door, but the door handle slipped from her grasp and the door swung open even wider. She held her breath, prepared to run if he made any move to look her way.

"Let them bloody look, then." David stood, and Eilish flattened herself against the wall, not daring to try to close the door.

"No one knows anything," David insisted. "Of

course I'm sure. I might not be around much, but I'd at least know that."

Eilish made another grab for the door handle and caught it. Quickly, she pulled the door nearly closed and ran downstairs. She didn't stop running until she was in the library, the door locked behind her. The lamps behind the desk always remained lit; they provided a soft, comforting glow. The conversation she'd overheard frightened her. David was involved in something that he was afraid to tell his family and the police.

"You look like you've seen a ghost." Deborah's voice floated from the shadows of one of the massive wing chairs next to the fireplace.

"Deborah! The fright you've just given me!"

"Sorry, come here and sit with me; I'm cold."

Eilish crossed the room and settled into the wide chair, knees tucked close to her chest, her head on Deborah's shoulder.

"What's wrong?" Deborah asked soothingly.

"David. He's been acting so strangely lately."

"I hadn't noticed."

"How can you say that? He hasn't been normal in ages."

"I suppose that depends on your definition of normal. David has never been like other boys."

"At least he's usually friendly and more relaxed. He's so tense now, he makes me want to scream." Eilish didn't want to tell Deborah about the phone conversation, because she'd want to know what he'd said.

"Have you tried talking to him?"

"I haven't had the chance. Everything's been so strange and busy. And the wedding . . ."

"Is it so bad that I'm getting married?"

"No," Eilish answered reluctantly, "not if it makes you happy. I just can't imagine you married. Or me, for that matter."

"You've been talking about marriage with Calvin?"

Deborah's voice was lulling Eilish into a wonderfully relaxed state. She closed her eyes. "Calvin and I had a fight today. We're not talking at all."

"Do you love him?" Deborah asked gently.

"He can be a laugh when he's not moody. Do you love Murdo?"

Deborah laughed. "Of course I do."

"Why doesn't David like him?"

"I've no idea. Murdo was a friend of your father's; David never cared for him. I'd hoped that once David got to know him better, that would change. But it's not to be. You don't like him either, do you?"

"Not really, I've always thought there was something odd about him." Eilish gave Deborah's hand a squeeze. "But you love him, so I'll try harder to like him."

# Chapter Thirteen

Mornay and Claire hit sleet as they passed through Edinburgh. The sleet finally turned to rain shortly after crossing the border into England. The rain pounded the bonnet and the roof of the car, making conversation impossible and reducing visibility to practically nil. It was half past one in the morning when they arrived in Turnhill, a fair-sized village an hour south of the border.

Turnhill was located in a valley ringed with hills that were invisible in the darkness and rain. The village didn't have its own police office; it fell within the Durham Constabulary. Mornay rang the number McNab had given him, half-expecting the man on the other end to have given up his wait. But he spoke directly to McNab's contact, Inspector Kenneth Trotter, who provided directions and said he'd meet them in half an hour.

Harold Cosgrove's stable yard was at the end of a small lane just south of Turnhill. A drystone wall edged the property line along the road. Beyond the wall was a rectangular courtyard. Mornay turned into the drive, but was blocked by a broad wrought-iron gate secured with a massive padlock. At the courtyard's far side was a two-story cottage, but Mornay could only make out the barest of details through the rain. A large stable sat on the opposite side of the courtyard.

They waited less than half an hour before a dark blue Ford Mondeo pulled in behind them. There were two men in the car. The passenger got out, ducked his bare head against the rain, and ran to open the padlock. The gate swung easily, for all its mass, and soon everyone was parked at the far end of the rectangular courtyard.

Another gate, made of galvanized steel—much less ornate than the entrance gate—sat opposite the cottage. Beyond this gate Mornay couldn't see much; everything was shrouded in darkness.

Kenneth Trotter greeted them each with a firm handshake. He looked like he was in his mid to late forties, had thinning brown hair and wore a sport coat tailored for a thinner man. He was missing part of one of his top center teeth, and the ones that remained were badly stained with nicotine. Trotter introduced James Linley, the estate agent charged with maintaining the property. Linley had a limp handshake and a girlish aversion to the rain. Mornay wondered what lengths Trotter had to go to per-suade Linley that he needed to be there so early on a Sunday morning.

"Let's get on with it, shall we?" Trotter suggested. As Linley pulled out a heavy ring of keys from his coat pocket, Trotter continued speaking. "We had one of our lads pop over yesterday when we were given the call about the body, to see if anything was amiss."

"Have you done the inventory yet?" Mornay asked the estate agent.

Linley shook his head. "I phoned the heir's solicitors." Linley's voice was deep and resonant, at complete opposites with his effeminate appearance. "They're supposed to fax me a list, but this is Sunday. I don't expect it to arrive until tomorrow."

By rights, a scene-of-crime team should've been there to direct any search. Mornay found McNab's willingness to forgo proper procedure troubling. He was convinced that Cosgrove's yard was the most logical place to begin a search for answers to Matthew Adair's death, but not to the detriment of the inquiry. He hoped their efforts wouldn't be in vain.

Linley unlocked the second gate and ran awkwardly down the cobblestone drive, trying not to slip on the wet stones. He was making for a maintenance building behind the stables.

As Mornay's vision adjusted to the dim light, he noticed the maintenance building had a new roof. But, as with the rest of the property, the signs of neglect were evident; bundles of leaves had gathered in most of the doorways, and the walks needed edging and weeding.

"Who else has keys to the gates?" Claire asked. They were standing beneath the skimpy shelter provided by the overhang above the door.

"Hard to say, really," Linley answered. He fumbled with the heavy key ring, searching for the key that opened the wide double doors that led into the maintenance building. "Harold Cosgrove had two sons. One lives in America, the other in London. They're having a rather nasty battle over the estate. We've changed the locks twice, and they always manage to get copies of the keys."

"Do they come on the property regularly?"

"The sons don't come on at all. They'd be recognized in the village."

"There's no love lost for Harold's children in the village, then?"

"Right bastards, both of them. Give me no end of trouble when they call. They've got personal things in the house, paintings and what not, that they've been trying to steal from each other since the day their father died. I don't believe we've ever had a problem with them trying to gain access to the outbuildings. Selling off all the old equipment for as much as they can get is the one point they both seem to agree on. That and selling the property, if they can agree to a price."

"Has an interested buyer come forward and made an offer?"

Linley didn't immediately answer.

"There are other ways to find out if there's been one," Mornay said, hoping his tone of voice was sufficiently threatening to coax the information from the small man.

"Yes, there has been an offer recently."

"How recent?"

"Three days ago."

"Who?"

"He's not from the area."

"Who?" Mornay repeated.

"That's private information."

"No information's private, given enough time. You can tell me now, or you can tell me in six hours when I've got a search team going through the records in your office."

Linley considered the threat. "The offer was made by a man called David Lockwood."

"Did he have a look around the place?"

"Several looks," Linley admitted reluctantly. "He lives in Australia. He's flown over four times to inspect the property. The most recent inspection was three days ago, when he finally made an offer."

Mornay sent a look Claire's way. "Do you have records of the other visits?"

"At my office."

"You can fax them to this number." Mornay handed Linley his card.

They followed Linley into the musty confines of the maintenance building. The electricity was shut off, so they had to rely on the dim light coming through four dusty windows that lined the south wall, and on the torches Mornay and Claire had brought with them. The building was more cavernous than its exterior suggested. On the left wall were seven horse trailers of varying sizes. The largest was against the back wall, near a wide door that ran on tracks attached to the ceiling. To the right there was a Land Rover, black or dark green, the paint crisscrossed with scuffs and scratches. Next to it was a white, paneled van, and next to the van was a white Toyota four-by-four.

"Was Harold well liked in the village?" Claire asked.

Inspector Trotter said, "Oh, yes, Harry taught my

Sarah how to ride. Taught most of the children in the village how to ride. He kept ponies just for them. They had their own Pony Club and would meet every Saturday."

As Mornay walked forward, his gaze traveled to the concrete floor. There was a cigarette butt near Trotter's foot.

Mornay held up a hand to keep Claire from walking farther into the building, then he knelt and, after pulling on a latex glove, picked up the cigarette butt.

"Royals," he said. "Same brand as the one in the Nissan." Though it was a common brand and wasn't necessarily a link, he bagged the butt. Then he stood and slowly walked farther into the building.

Trotter held up his arm, preventing Linley from following. "What's this?" Linley asked.

"They've a job to do," Trotter said gruffly. "You can watch from here."

Mornay and Claire proceeded slowly. Ahead of them were two maintenance pits, rectangular holes in the floor perhaps two meters deep and completely barren. The scent of oil lingered in the air.

"How far into the building did you walk yesterday?" Mornay asked Linley over his shoulder.

"I didn't walk in at all. I just counted the vehicles. And they're all here, by the way."

"Did you check the registration numbers?"

"How would I be able to do that without the inventory?" Linley snapped.

"Has anyone from your firm borrowed equipment from the property?"

Even in the dim light, Mornay could see that the skin on Linley's face was glistening with moisture. However, his voice gave no hint at an underlying nervousness or tension, only anger at Mornay's accusation. "And why would we do that?"

"How many employees does your firm have?"

Linley's gaze darted furiously to each of them. "Four."

"Their names?"

Linley gave the names. Mornay asked him to repeat them slowly, so Trotter could write them down. Then he walked to the nearest vehicle, the Rover, and raised his flashlight. The interior was clean. The doors were unlocked. Mornay checked under the bonnet. There was no battery. He went to the van, which was essentially the same as the first, clean interior and no battery.

The Toyota had been used recently. There were food wrappers on the carpet and on the bench seat. The console had a thick coat of whitish dust, as if it'd been driven down a dirt road with the windows rolled down. The ashtray was overflowing with ashes and butts.

"Claire." He called her away from her inspection of the pits. "Have a look."

She leaned close to him to peer into the window, careful not to touch any part of the vehicle. He caught another faint hint of her scent.

"Cigarettes, Royals and Kings," she said softly. "They're common enough brands."

"Maybe. We'll have DNA tests run on the butts and see if they match the butts in our Nissan."

"But then we've still to find the people who left them."

"One step at a time." Mornay carefully opened the door and bagged several butts of each brand. Then he reached for a wadded-up ball of paper on the floor. It was a petrol receipt dated four weeks earlier; the petrol had been purchased in an Esso station in Banff, minutes down the coast from Cordiff.

"What now?" she asked.

"Time we called McNab."

Andy McNab and Laina Gordon arrived at Harold Cosgrove's property at half past five in the morning, bringing members of the Adair inquiry with them. It had taken McNab hours to work out the jurisdictional problems of the crime scene; English law was far different from Scottish law. In the end it was agreed that the Grampian CID would process the scene and maintain all evidence found, and that the Durham Constabulary would supervise. Meaning it would be like treading eggshells.

McNab brought a small army of police vehicles, the largest, two blue Technical Support Unit vans. Trotter whistled under his breath as the vehicles rolled into the courtyard. He slapped Linley on the back, and the smaller man winced.

"Time we opened the kitchen, little man, and get one of these plods"—Trotter pointed to some of the young constables who'd been assigned from Durham for search purposes—"to make tea all around. It's going to be a busy morning."

Mornay winked at his boss as he passed McNab's car to get to Gordon's Mercedes. He had an umbrella ready to shield her from the rain, which had lessened during the early-morning hours. Claire held an umbrella for McNab.

"Did you get the inventory list?" Gordon asked.

"About an hour ago. Claire and I have already made one inspection."

Gordon kept her body neatly under the umbrella without appearing overly concerned with the puddles she walked through with her sensible, thick-soled black loafers. "And?"

"Except for the Nissan and the trailer that was in the Cordiff accident, everything is accounted for. Someone's been using the Toyota."

"Does anyone have the legal authority to use any of the vehicles?"

"Not yet."

"So someone's been using them and returning them when they're finished?"

"Just the Toyota and Nissan."

"Are there any walk-in freezers on the premises?" she asked, as they entered the dark building. A pair of TSU technicians followed; she turned and ordered one of them to get the electric turned on.

"You might want to have a word with Inspector Trotter," Mornay said over his shoulder to the tech. "He's in the kitchen." Through the open door he saw Claire speaking with McNab in the courtyard and turned his attention back to Laina Gordon. The dim lighting suited her angled features; it made her look softer, younger. "There's a chest freezer in the house that would've been large enough to store a small body. However, there's been no electricity to keep it running."

"Then have one of the local constables do the rounds, see if any of the neighbors heard a generator running these last two weeks. See if they noticed any vehicles driving down the road toward the property these past several months. Should be easy enough to find out, since we're at the end of the road."

It was standing room only in Harold Cosgrove's kitchen. There were eleven other officers assembled, some cradling mugs of hot tea, some jotting notes in well-worn notebooks. Mornay and Claire's arrival made thirteen. The room smelled of wet wool. It wasn't much warmer inside than outside, but it did offer a respite from the wind.

He and Claire had spent the past two hours going door to door. All of Cosgrove's neighbors had been awake, many already tending their animals. But for all the surface cooperation, they'd learned very little. Mornay had gotten the feeling the neighbors were rationing out their information like they rationed out oats to their horses, fistfuls at a time.

McNab stood near the cooker, listening intently to a great hulking constable with ginger-colored hair and a dimple creasing his chin. McNab's gaze briefly flicked in their direction when a gust of wind slammed the door closed behind them.

With the exception of DI Gordon, who stood to McNab's immediate left, Claire was the only woman in the room. A tidal wave of attention swiveled in her direction when she arrived. As far as Mornay could discern, she seemed completely unconscious of the interest from the men. That couldn't be true; their attention was so focused, it made *him* feel uncomfortable.

Byrne was noticeably absent. But the majority of the team was there.

The northern command areas in Scotland were experiencing staff shortages for many reasons: Cops were overworked and underpaid; the growing arms problem—which seemed directly connected to the rise in drug crimes—was another massive deterrent to recruitment. No one wanted to take on hostile criminals who were armed with the latest high-tech assault weapons while they were only armed with pellet guns, batons, and inadequate body armor. The promise of better equipment was too far distant to be believed. All of these factors made Roger Donaldson's *Zero Tolerance* campaign laughable. Criminals didn't fear cops anymore.

Trotter walked into the kitchen, shaking snow off his shoulders and stamping his feet. The rain had turned to snow an hour earlier. He was followed by three men from the Durham Constabulary. The local force had been remarkably cooperative thus far. There were no disputes over jurisdiction, no wrangling over which agency would be credited with which jobs or which discoveries. The search for Matthew Adair's killer was doing what a thousand years of warfare had been unable to do; erase the border between England and Scotland. Mornay wondered how many of the men in the room were fathers; how many had families waiting for them at home.

"Ran into some reporters," Trotter said by way of explaining his delay. "I've left a man at the gate to keep them off the property."

They'd been free of reporters far longer than Mornay had anticipated. The discovery of Matthew Adair's body was the biggest news in the country.

"How many interviews did you conduct in the village?" McNab asked Trotter.

"A dozen at most," Trotter said. "We'll catch more at their breakfasts in an hour or so. Those we did talk to claim they would've remembered if someone had been driving around Harry's place. And they said they'd know if his trucks were on the roads."

There seemed to be some hesitation in Trotter's voice, prompting McNab to ask, "What do you think?"

"Harry's been dead and buried a year. His sons are fighting over who gets the chipped china. No one's expected to see one of Harry's trailers driving through town, because everyone knows they're locked away—and you don't see what you don't expect to see. We've so many of the ruddy things going past, they're practically invisible. It's that simple."

McNab's intense gaze swept the room. "We're going to continue with interviews until we find something." He paused, gathering his thoughts. "The Nissan used to transport Matthew Adair's body came from this yard. Someone's seen something. Perhaps they even saw the Nissan."

"The prints found in the Nissan, have we got anything on them yet?" Mornay asked.

"There were no hits in SCRO."

The Scottish Criminal Records office maintained the fingerprint records of everyone convicted in Scotland. "Maybe we should try England's database," Mornay suggested. Scotland had SCRO; England had FSS, the Forensic Science Service, its headquarters in Birmingham. It was the first and most comprehensive database of its kind in the world; they claimed to have over two million DNA samples and over five million sets of fingerprints on file. "We might get a faster reply if Inspector Trotter sends it out."

"It's worth a try."

"It doesn't appear from the evidence we've gathered thus far that Matthew's body was here. So what have we got that links this yard with Matthew Adair or any other place in Scotland, besides the Nissan? Are there any Scottish stable lads in the area? Or Scottish citizens, period?"

DS Taylor raised a hand. "Sir, we've found three Esso receipts in the Toyota that were from stations in northern Scotland. All dated earlier this month."

Gordon held up a hand to silence the sudden rumbling of whispered conversations in the room. "Which stations are the receipts from?"

"One from Banff, dated the sixth. We've one from Denmore, and the last, dated the twelfth, is from Stonehaven or Elgin. The receipt was torn, so we've only got a partial ID number to go from."

"Will you be able to determine which station?"

"Oh aye, it'll take a day or two, but I'll find out."

"We haven't got that long, Taylor. I want to know by tomorrow."

"Yes sir," Taylor said, but McNab wasn't through with him.

"What's the date on the receipt from Denmore?"

"The tenth."

"The day before Matthew disappeared," McNab said quietly.

McNab's hushed words reverberated through the room. Denmore was just outside of Aberdeen.

"It's the details that will be important in this case; the small, seemingly unimportant details. We can't make any assumptions; we've obviously got someone very clever out there. But we don't have a motive for Matthew's death. Why would someone need to beat a ten-year-old child to death?"

McNab laid out the assignments. A pair was assigned to conduct interviews at and around the

Esso stations. They were to also gather up security tapes, if the stations had them.

Then McNab said, "What was Matthew's abductor trying to accomplish? If this abduction was for money, why were there no ransom demands? If an accident happened to Matthew before the ransom note could be sent out, why was his body kept before disposing it?"

"What if this isn't about money?" Claire asked.

"We've already been through both his parents' backgrounds," Mornay said. "There was absolutely nothing that would lead us to believe a friend of the family or a business associate abducted Matthew as an act of revenge."

"So we've got a random act of violence?" McNab asked. "That won't do." He addressed the rest of the group. "The public will not accept ambiguity. Remember that. We need to discover the motivation behind this crime. This was carried out by someone who was methodical and resourceful. Matthew was abducted in broad daylight in Aberdeen, within a stone's throw of a CCTV camera. This is someone who isn't afraid to take chances but also smart enough to do everything in his power to cover his tracks." McNab paused, tenting his fingers. "We've never considered that Matthew might've been killed because he found out something about someone that he shouldn't have."

"How would that be possible?" Gordon demanded. "He was only ten."

"Anything is possible. Maybe he discovered an article about Gabriel Smith's original trial, and put it together that Gabriel Smith's sister worked for the school. I doubt very seriously that she disclosed to the school that her brother was a convicted pedophile. Who's reading through Matthew's journals?"

Two officers from Aberdeen Division raised their hands.

"Make sure you keep that possibility in mind. References to people must be checked out thoroughly."

When the briefing was over, McNab pulled Mornay and Claire aside. Across the courtyard, Trotter was directing some of his men where to carry gear. He'd become the unofficial coordinator between the different police units, and he was doing an admirable job of keeping things moving. In the east, the sky was growing paler. It was nearly half seven, but the thick layer of clouds was keeping the landscape dark and dreary. An occasional snowflake drifted by, the wind too restless to let it settle.

"I want you two to return to Finovar and have another go at David Lockwood," McNab said. "And we haven't had a look at Ms. Lockwood's boyfriend, Ian Harris's assistant. We need to make that happen today."

"How do you want us to handle the O'Conners?" Claire asked.

"Gently. We're going to need to establish the whereabouts of everyone in that household on the dates of these petrol receipts. And we need to do it before Lord Gordon outmaneuvers us."

# Chapter Fourteen

Mornay's mobile rang as he stood in the first-floor waiting room of the Royal Infirmary with Claire. He was blowing the surface of his watery coffee to cool it, and answered on the fourth ring.

"I've found some info on Ian Harris," Sahotra said. It was Sahotra's day off, but he'd agreed to Mornay's request for help without any grumbling. "He had a son, Fergus Harris. Persistent offender since the age of twelve. Was put into Craiginches for two years at the tender age of eighteen. Four months after his release he went on a spree robbing newsagent shops with an air pistol. He was sentenced to another four years in Craiginches, this time as a guest of long-term care. He died during the first year. He was barely twenty-one."

"Died of what?"

"Heroin overdose. His father got custody of

Fergus's son, who was only a few months old at the time. He's raised him ever since."

"How old is the boy now?" Mornay asked.

"Eight," Sahotra answered.

"What's your computer pal managed to dig up on the Lockwoods?"

"It's still in process," was Sahotra's evasive answer.

"We'll need something soon."

"Getting that kind of information isn't like going to the corner shop and fetching a paper."

"You'll manage."

Mornay pocketed his mobile and took a sip of scalding coffee. In the seating area, two children were arguing over who could push a toy lorry across the floor. A third child, much younger than the others, was crying. Her mother seemed to be stone-deaf as she flipped through an old copy of *That's Life* without a glance in the child's direction.

"Do you mind if I come up with you?" Claire asked quietly. "I can't wait here; those two will drive me mad in five minutes."

"You can get the doors." He grinned. "I've got coffee that might spill."

They took the stairs to the third floor. A female technician was seated behind a tall, narrow counter; she was filling out a report and barely glanced up when they entered the small, brightly lit lab.

"Seth Mornay," he said to the technician. "I was scheduled to come in today."

"Right," the technician said, "You can have a seat just there." She pointed to a row of three chairs against the wall, across from her counter. "I'll be with you soon." She walked into the small, glass-walled office.

Claire studied flyers pinned to a cork bulletin board. She'd changed into trousers while they waited for McNab to arrive at Cosgrove's farm; she also wore heeled boots. When had she started wearing heels? Claire always preferred sensible flats before. And she'd always preferred loose-fitting clothes, but her pale blue, finely knit sweater clung to the curves she'd always taken great pains to conceal.

"What?" she asked when she turned and found he was looking at her.

"Blue suits you."

Her chin lifted slightly. "Why haven't I ever heard you give Sahotra a compliment on his wardrobe?"

He held up his hands, surrendering. "Claire, it was a compliment, not a come-on."

"Mr. Mornay," the technician called. "I'm ready. I'll need you to remove your jacket and roll up your shirtsleeve."

He walked around the counter and sat in the chair the technician indicated. He put his arm on the broadened armrest, shoving up his sleeve to expose the vein in the crook of his arm.

"Make a fist," the technician ordered.

He could feel his pulse starting to race. Sweat was starting to prickle out along his hairline.

"Do you ever give Maggie Cray compliments?" Claire asked.

"I don't like Maggie Cray." He kept his attention focused on the technician, on the labels she was peeling off and sticking to small tubes. The labels had his name printed on them.

The technician unwrapped a long needle.

"Jesus," Mornay protested. "That's as big as a pencil."

"And you never compliment DI Gordon?" Claire asked.

The technician, unmoved by his protest, wrapped a rubber tube around his biceps. "Squeeze your fist, please."

"Gordon's wardrobe is probably worth more than my house," he said, tearing his gaze away from the needle the technician was holding. "I wouldn't give her a compliment if my next promotion depended on it."

His mouth was going dry. The technician was tapping the bulging blue vein. Then she raised the needle.

He stared at the wall above the technician's head as she steadied his arm on the table.

The next thing he heard was Claire, but he couldn't see her; the light was too bright.

"Seth? Can you hear me? Seth, look at me." She was slapping his cheek.

He blinked rapidly and the light focused. He was lying on the floor, staring at the ceiling light fixture.

"What happened?" he asked, trying to sit up. A wave of dizziness hit him, and he groaned and lay back down. Claire's face swam into view.

"You passed out when you saw the blood. You hit your head on a cabinet."

That explained the throbbing pain just behind his right ear.

Claire started tugging at his tie, loosening it.

"One compliment, and she can't get me out of my clothes fast enough."

"I'll never be that desperate." She unfastened the buttons at his neck. "Now shut up."

Her hands slid around his neck, and he flinched. "Jesus, your hands are cold."

"I thought Marines were supposed to be tough. Be still, I need to reach the gash behind your ear." She pressed a wad of tissues against his head and looked around. "Where *is* that woman?" She checked the blood-soaked tissues and reapplied pressure. "I've never seen you get squeamish over the sight of blood before."

"It's only the sight of my blood I can't stand. Help me up; this floor's freezing."

Pamela's doctor was off duty by the time Mornay got to the intensive care ward. He had four stitches behind his right ear, a shirt splotched with blood— probably ruined—and a massive headache. The nurse gave him the latest news regarding Pamela's medications—none of it good—while Claire waited discreetly across the ward.

"Who's that? Your new girlfriend?" It was Fiona, Pamela and Victoria's mother. Fiona wore a low-cut leopard-skin-patterned tunic dress over black tights. A wide, black, patent leather belt was cinched tightly around her waist; she balanced precariously on stiletto-heeled ankle boots. Her clothes reeked of stale cigarettes. He hadn't seen her in Pamela's room when he'd glanced inside; the curtain next to Pamela's bed must've shielded her from view.

Fiona turned her back to Mornay so she could study Claire. "She looks like a cop." Fiona's bleary gaze swiveled back in his direction. Her eyes were puffy from lack of sleep; they were outlined with black eyeliner, and her lashes were clotted with black mascara. "She know what you did to my Pammy?" Fiona's voice was rising above a normal speaking level. She'd already gotten the attention of two of the nurses at the station.

"She's my partner, Fiona."

"Partner? Can't see you with a partner—"

Mornay took her by the elbow and led her closer to Pamela's room. She wasn't tired; she was drunk. "Fiona, mind your manners."

"Or what? You'll arrest me?" She leaned into him, pressing her pendulous breasts against his arm. "Who knows what I might say if someone wanted to interrogate me."

"No one's going to interrogate you."

He backed up to escape the whiskey fumes on her breath. Then, before she could stop him, he pulled her large handbag off her shoulder and opened it up. Her protests died when he pulled out the nearly empty whiskey bottle.

"I'm going to call a cab, Fiona, and you're going to get in it and go home."

She tried to press close to him again, but he blocked her with the handbag.

She struck out with her voice, the words screeching out at an eardrum-splitting decibel. "Think just because you're on the telly now, you can make anyone do anything you want? Well, you can just fuck off!" Fiona spun around, but momentum and her heels conspired to fling her against the wall. She pushed away from the wall with another loud curse and began to wobble toward the doors that led out of the ward.

"Should I call security?" a nurse asked Mornay.

"I'll get her into a cab."

Claire followed him, walking up to Fiona's right side so that they neatly sandwiched the older woman. She cursed them all the way to the entrance and through the five-minute wait for the taxi.

"Now, there's a lady I could almost admire," said a familiar, unwelcome voice behind them. Byrne was leaning against the building, puffing a cigar. He looked like hell—skin pasty, eyes red-rimmed. "I'm glad I kept my consultation today, after my chat with Fiona. She can outcurse me, and she can damn near outdrink me." He pushed away from the building, walking slowly toward them. The breeze caught his mackintosh, causing it to billow out behind him. He pointed his half-smoked cigar at Mornay. "And she's not overly fond of you." Byrne grinned. "How was the weather down south?"

"Balmy," Mornay said.

Byrne didn't seem to notice the blood on Mornay's shirt. "Chief Inspector just told me you're on your way to Finovar."

"After I get a clean shirt," Mornay replied.

"I'll meet you there."


The temperature had risen ten degrees since the morning, melting much of the snow that had fallen the day before. The rise in temperature had caused a thick fog to hover at knee level, which caused the drive to take ages since Mornay could barely see the road.

Claire spent the drive rereading Matthew Adair's autopsy report, paying particular attention to the photographs of his hands.

"I think we're making a mistake focusing on David Lockwood so quickly." Her voice was pensive.

"Seems to me he's the one person that was in all the right places at all the right times." He cut her a look. "Now we know why he was so willing to be pinned down on dates."

She looked doubtful. "We've no link to him and Matthew Adair."

"Is it coincidence that Lockwood was in the vicinity of the Cosgrove property days before Matthew Adair's body was found? Or coincidence that he's got a gash on his hand? Or that sheep from his property were in the stolen trailer?"

"Coincidence isn't evidence. I think it's all a bit too convenient. The wreck, the subsequent discovery of the body, the dead rams. We don't have a single shred of evidence that firmly links Lockwood to Matthew Adair. If anything, we've got pointers to Finovar. We need to look at everyone at the castle. Both the O'Conners. The stepmother and Eilish Lockwood. Even Lord Gordon."

"Hard to imagine Deborah Lockwood manhandling full-grown rams into the back of a trailer."

"The same could be said for Jonathan Cross," she replied. "It doesn't take much exertion to mark papers. On the other hand, Gabriel Smith worked on a farm; he's had experience with animals. And Lord Gordon's another possibility; he wouldn't have had a problem with the animals."

"What were you saying before about antagonizing the Gordons?"

"You never listen to my advice; why should I listen to yours?"

"Claire, do you think Byrne really had a consultation today?"

"Maybe he's really ill. He's lost weight."

"Ill-tempered, more like. It's unbelievable that he would accidentally run into Fiona."

"She was probably smoking a ciggie and complaining loudly about what a bastard you are. How could Byrne resist?"

Mornay made a face.

"You have another theory?" she asked.

"I think he's following me."

Byrne strutted around the library, which also served as David Lockwood's office. He picked up a figurine displayed on a table by the fireplace, upended it as if he were in a shop looking for a price, then placed it back on its bit of lace. "That wasn't very bright, was it?" he said to Michael O'Conner.

"No," O'Conner answered. He was fidgeting in a chair next to David Lockwood's desk, refusing to make eye contact with either Byrne or Mornay. Claire had been dispatched to the kitchen for tea. "But I was only sixteen."

"You were old enough to know stealing your neighbor's car was a crime," Byrne replied. "How did you rationalize nicking the other three, after you wrecked the first one?"

Michael O'Conner made no reply.

From all accounts, O'Conner had been only too thankful to be arrested in Edinburgh a week after he'd stolen and subsequently wrecked his neighbor's car. He'd been with two other boys, both older; they were the ones who'd insisted on going to the city and creating a mini crime spree. O'Conner had found himself in a situation beyond his experience. He'd received leniency in the Sheriff's Court for his cooperation and his testimony against his friends.

"And your parents," Mornay said. "What did they do?"

"My mum stayed at home. My father worked for Deeside Oil."

"Does he still work there?"

"He retired a few months ago."

"What'd you think about Lady Lockwood's new Jag?" Byrne asked.

"I didn't think anything about it. Except I knew she wouldn't like it."

Byrne moved closer to O'Conner so he could peer down at the man. "Why's that?"

"She's practical, our Eilish. No airs. What would she do with a fancy sports car? Park it, that's what."

"Is that the only reason she didn't like the car?"

O'Conner's expression shifted slightly. "Dunno what you mean."

"I think you do," Byrne insisted.

"She doesn't care for Lord Gordon. Never has. And neither does David."

"Why were you let go early that night?" Mornay asked before Byrne could get in another question about the Jaguar.

"No reason. It's not unusual for him to give us early nights when he's back in town. The Lockwoods know how to do for themselves. It's Lord Gordon will have you fetching this and that. Run you fair ragged if he gets the chance."

"How many sheep are missing?" Mornay asked.

"Six."

"And the last time you counted them?"

"Last Wednesday."

Byrne interrupted. "What I'd like to know is how long you *knew* Lady Lockwood was going to get the Jaguar?"

"Lord Gordon told us last week," O'Conner said.

"Said it was in John Fox's garage. Wanted me to arrange to have it cleaned."

"Did you?"

"Cleaned it myself."

"Did you notice anything odd about the car?"

"Smelled a bit off. Musty-like. From sitting too long. Lord Gordon thought a mouse had died in the engine while it was parked. I couldn't find it."

"We're going to need to know your movements on the following dates." Mornay read the dates they'd taken from the petrol receipts.

"Joan and I were in Banff on the sixth. Her mother had a bad turn. We stayed two days."

"And on the other two dates?"

"Here, as usual. Working."

"The scent of bleach was overpowering in the trailer we examined yesterday. Why did you use bleach?"

"We're going to loan that trailer to Donald Williams. Doesn't care for our animals, he's afraid they might carry something that would damage his herd, but he needs the trailer. So we clean it out with bleach."

Byrne dismissed O'Conner when Claire brought in the teas. He sat in David Lockwood's chair, rubbing the leather arms appreciatively. "Gordon's keen on having me pass her any information you find out about Lockwood. Not that I will, mind you." Byrne plucked a biscuit from the tray Claire put on the desk. With a full mouth, he said, "She isn't exactly my sort of cop." He grinned. "No balls."

"You take male chauvinism to new lows," Mornay remarked.

Byrne's grin widened. "Someone's got to, laddie.

Now, tell me what you know about David Lockwood." He reached for another biscuit.

"Nothing we haven't shared at one of the briefings."

"I want to know why Laina Gordon is so eager to protect him." Byrne's voice was low, intense.

Mornay thought he had a good idea, considering how openly affectionate Gordon had been to David the night the Jaguar was stolen. "Afraid she might linger in Macduff after the Adair inquiry?"

"How long do you think someone like her will hang about our CID office? She's got plans, that one. I'm no worried."

Byrne reached into Lockwood's humidor and pulled out a cigar, then pointed it at Mornay. "Now, here's what's in it for you. You tell me what you find out about Lockwood first." Byrne was grinning, the expression feral. "And I'll make sure McNab doesn't find out about that wee problem you've got with Fiona's Pammy. Our chief inspector's gone right batty on religion. Attends church twice a week, kicked his daughter out of the house when she got pregnant at sixteen. And don't even ask about his son—as far as McNab's concerned, the boy's dead. Saint McNab's got some bloody strange views about people being responsible for their actions, if you get my meaning."

Byrne's gaze flicked to Claire. "Time to bring in Lockwood."

David Lockwood took the seat in front of his desk. Byrne was leaning against the desk, looking down at Lockwood.

"Any news about the car?" Lockwood asked. He appeared more at ease today.

"Not yet," Byrne replied, "but we have learned

some interesting things about you. For instance, we've learned you've made an offer to purchase a certain property in England. Those two"—Byrne nodded toward Mornay and Claire—"were there all night with the local plods, turning the place upside down. It appears the trailer that Matthew's body was discovered in was stolen from one of the storage buildings on that property."

There was no change in David Lockwood's expression, but he sat just a bit straighter than a moment earlier.

Byrne's voice lowered to a conspiratorial level. "Tell me about your weekly visits to Dr. Gayle Augustine."

"If you know about her, than there's very little to tell."

Byrne held up a hand and started ticking off thick, nicotine-stained fingers. "I've got a dead local boy, who was found on your door stoop and who only lived a five-minute drive away. This dead boy was found in a trailer that belongs to the estate of a man you knew. You've made an offer to buy this man's property. I've Lord Gordon giving daily press briefings, frightening every parent in the country about the pedophile who killed Matthew Adair. Then I've got you, who I've just discovered has been seeing a doctor who specializes in treating sexual dysfunction—including pedophilia—for nearly four years. You tell me what I should make of those facts."

"I don't have to tell you anything, Inspector. Not without my solicitor present."

David Lockwood stood and walked out of the room.

\* \* \*

Byrne chose to interview Deborah and Eilish Lockwood together. He was terse and all business, trying to learn something before Lord Gordon swooped down with an army of solicitors who'd make it impossible to get any unfiltered information from the women.

Byrne told them what the police had learned about David Lockwood—he seemed to relish reciting the extensive qualifications Lockwood's therapist had to deal with sexually dysfunctional patients. Then he asked if they knew how David hurt his hand.

"In a riding accident," Deborah offered. From the expression on her face, it was clear that Byrne had made a tactical error speaking to the women together. Not only was Eilish going to let Deborah take the lead, Deborah was clearly going to do everything in her power to take up David Lockwood's defense.

"What time did he arrive on Thursday?"

"He was here when I returned from my shop in the village. That would've been around one. He'd been here several hours."

"Do you just have his word on that or can someone else verify this?"

"There was no one here to verify it. Michael was running errands in Aberdeen. Joan was in Cordiff with her sister."

"I didn't see him until after three," Eilish offered. "I spent most of the day walking along the fences, looking for damaged sections."

"Why didn't you take one of the ATVs?" Claire asked. Byrne scowled at her for the intrusion, even though it was an excellent question. "You do have some, correct?"

"We have three ATVs, all in good working order. I just wanted to walk. I left after breakfast, after Deborah had gone to open her shop."

"Shop?" Byrne asked Deborah Lockwood.

"I sell antiques."

"What time did you leave?"

"Quarter to eight."

"Did you have any customers that morning?"

"Not a soul. It appears that we were all alone—with the exception of Joan—at the time of the accident. That is the purpose of these questions, I assume, to determine where we were at the crucial moment?"

"It's one of the things we'd like to determine."

To Eilish, Byrne said, "While you were walking the property, did you happen to see anyone?"

"I didn't see anyone except for Michael. That was around ten. He was driving from the direction of the village."

"Deborah said he was in Aberdeen," Mornay said.

"Are you sure it was Michael?" Deborah asked Eilish.

"Positive. He must've forgotten something because he did go to Aberdeen."

"Has anything strange happened at the castle in the past six months or so?" Mornay asked.

"There's been nothing except for the thefts," Deborah answered.

"Thefts?" Thefts should've been reported to Mornay immediately, not by the family, but by Constable Walden the evening the Jaguar was stolen.

"Someone's been stealing small things: trinkets, jewelry, some vases. Constable Walden suspects the thief is a child or a young teenager, because some of the things weren't very valuable."

"But some items were?"

"Yes, quite valuable."

"Do you have a security system?" Byrne asked.

"We had one installed to protect the rooms which house the most valuable family heirlooms. There are only five rooms wired."

"The rest of the house is wide open, then?"

"I wouldn't put it that way, Inspector."

"How would you put it?"

"Someone is obviously familiar with the building and our family habits, and they're using that knowledge to their benefit."

# Chapter Fifteen

To be a rural cop was to be a jack-of-all-trades. One had to be able to do minor investigative work, help stranded motorists change tires or open locked doors, track down poachers, answer traffic complaints, and a hundred other widely varied duties. Some people were suited to working in such a loosely structured environment, but it was Mornay's opinion that Police Constable Neal Walden wasn't such a person. Since he'd taken over this patch, the complaints about the level of service from the police office had risen. But the force was short-handed, and nobody else wanted the duty. And nobody wanted to work with Walden, so here he remained.

Walden answered his door after Claire rang the bell at least a dozen times. He wore dark corduroys and a blue acrylic cardigan covered with fuzz balls; his clothes were as ill-fitting as his uniform.

"Not answering your phone?" Mornay asked as he walked inside.

"I'm off duty," Walden stuttered.

The foyer was jammed with the sorts of things people put in their garages. A bicycle, a pair of sawhorses, a large rolling toolbox, and a phalanx of paint cans were just some of the items situated closest to the door. The jumble, which went nearly to the ceiling, filled the foyer to bursting.

A narrow path led to the hall. From where Mornay stood in the hall, the lounge wasn't much neater than the foyer. Walden, realizing he wasn't going to get rid of them easily, led them down the hall to the kitchen. A window in the kitchen looked into his office.

"Filthy bastard," Mornay whispered in Claire's ear when Walden went to plug in the electric kettle and search out some clean mugs. "I hope you're not seriously considering drinking the tea."

He wandered into Walden's office. There was also an outside door that opened directly into the office, sparing the public a view of Walden's slovenly housekeeping skills. A blackjack game was flashing on the computer screen.

"Now we know why he wasn't answering the door," Claire whispered.

"He was probably downloading porn. He's just put that up to throw you off."

Mornay went to the computer keyboard and pressed the Alt and Tab buttons to see what other programs Walden had open. "He's using the police office's Internet connection to play those online gambling sites. He's got four different games going." Mornay stood, whiping his fingers on his trouser leg. Walden's keyboard had been sticky.

"Have you talked to Mr. E about the Paisleys?"

"Not yet, I'll try to see him tonight."

"Tea's ready," Walden said from the door.

Mornay took a mug, but didn't sip. Claire followed suit. "Have you been in the village, asking if anyone had seen a stranger in town wearing plasters?"

"Oh, aye." Walden lit a cigarette. There were ashes littered across the counter and several over-flowing ashtrays. "No one remembers seeing anyone like that."

"And bandages?"

"Bandages or plasters, no one minds."

"Can *you* remember seeing anyone in the village with a bandage or a plaster on their hand or face or arm?"

"That sort of thing would get noticed, wouldn't it? Not much to talk about this time of year. Hardly any tourists."

"I imagine the thefts at Finovar provided some interesting topics of conversation at the pub," Mornay said.

"Aye." Walden's head was bobbing. "Still talking about it, aren't we?"

"Why didn't it occur to you to mention them to us?"

Walden shrugged.

"You didn't think that perhaps those early crimes could be connected to the theft of the Jaguar? Someone's obviously comfortable moving around the castle. Where are your reports and your call log?"

"I thought it might've been—"

Mornay interrupted. "We won't go into the flaws in your thought process. Show me the logs."

The reports were stacked in a folder sitting on top

of the filing cabinet's open drawer, beneath a stack of junk mail. The call log was on the floor, with the phone. Walden had moved everything from the desk so he had room for the computer and the printer and the fax machine.

"Make copies of the reports," Mornay ordered, when Walden had finally found them.

"Are there any other incidents at Finovar we should know about?" Mornay asked as he flipped pages in the log. "Prank calls? Peeping Toms? Missing pets? Arsons? UFO sightings?"

"There's been nothing else."

The log was uninformative. Mornay checked it for any unusual activity on the dates of the three petrol receipts. Walden was off duty on the first two dates. Nothing unusual was entered for the last date.

Mornay handed the log back. "What do you know about David Lockwood?"

"He's only at Finovar a few times a year."

"Does anyone at Finovar visit him in Australia?"

"Only his mother. Eilish Lockwood is afraid to fly."

"Has anyone ever cautioned you about this mini-malist approach you have to your job?"

Walden looked puzzled.

"Never mind." Mornay stood. "Anything else occurs to you, ring me immediately. I don't want any more surprises coming out of Finovar."

An outdoor stairway made of metal grating led up to Calvin Walsh's two-bedroom flat above a newsagents shop. Eilish Lockwood's boyfriend had yet to be seen, let alone interviewed.

The flat looked out onto a narrow dead-end alley with just enough room for two massive wheelie bins, brimming with trash. A pair of lights cast a dingy yellow glow that washed out Claire's fair skin and tinted her hair a mousy brown.

"That grate's going to murder the heels on your boots," Mornay pointed out.

"I'll manage."

Claire went up first, her weight on her toes. On the third step, the low tinkling of wind chimes started echoing off the walls of the darkened alley. Someone, probably Walsh, had rigged small wind chimes to hang below six of the stairs—two chimes per stair. The smallest vibration set them off.

"Not a bad warning."

"Warning for what?" she asked from the landing.

"To be ready to jump out the window?"

"Maybe he's dodging his boss. If Ian Harris is so unpleasant to strangers, can you imagine what he must be like to work for?" Mornay winked. "Just like working for Byrne."

He knocked loudly on the door, but there were no sounds from within the apartment. Since Walsh wasn't home, they went downstairs to talk to Walsh's landlord, Jin Jung Sul, the Korean owner of the newsagent shop. They discovered that Walsh had been renting the flat for six months, and, according to Sul, Walsh had an active nightlife.

"Lots of girls?" Mornay clarified. "Or just one? Pretty, this tall." He held his hand level with the top of Claire's head. "Dark hair, big gray eyes?"

"No, no. He brings lots of girls. Long hair, short hair, and fat." Sul shook a finger at them. "Only fat girls. Then bang, bang, bang." Because Sul couldn't pronounce G's well, the words sounded like *ban, ban, ban.* Sul stomped his foot to punctuate each

word. "Make my light swing, shake my cigarettes."
Sul pointed to the cigarette racks that were suspended from the ceiling above the cash register. "I
tell him no bang, bang till after closing the shop, but
he only laugh."

"Did he hang the wind chimes from the stairs?"
Mornay asked, trying not to laugh.

"Sure, sure."

"Do you know why?"

Sul shrugged his shoulders. He didn't know, and
he didn't care. But he did let them in the flat after he
carefully inspected their police identifications.

Except for the clothes in Walsh's cupboard, there
was nothing personal displayed in the flat. Mornay
got Claire to distract Sul in the lounge while he carefully fished an empty lager can out of the rubbish
and bagged it. Having Walsh's fingerprints was
going to make it much easier to determine if the
young man was who he claimed to be.

It was nearly nine when they returned to the office.
Byrne had not returned, leaving them free to work in
peace. Mornay made a brief stop at his desk to
search for phone messages and noticed that the
unfinished reports he'd shoved into one of his sorting bins had been neatly aligned.

Someone had straightened his desk.

Or searched it.

He noticed the envelope containing the papers
Victoria wanted him to sign at the bottom of the bin.
He pulled it out. The envelope was still sealed. He
put it back, still uneasy.

On the new side of the office, Claire was writing
out index cards that noted everyone's movements on

the petrol receipt dates. These were then taped to the wall—Claire's bold writing visible from the farthest seat. Mornay sank into a chair, put his feet on the table, and closed his eyes.

Sahotra startled him out of a slight doze. "Maggie Cray's left a message for you."

"Brilliant," Mornay grumbled. "SDEA must want me to fetch something." He cracked open an eye and took the slips of paper Sahotra passed along. Sahotra wore a Dons' jersey; the brilliant red material assaulted Mornay's tired eyes. "You get that meeting set up with your computer whiz?" he asked.

Sahotra's gaze shifted nervously to Claire. "I'm still working on it."

"How difficult can this be? Pick a day and a time, and call me."

"I will." Sahotra passed him a thick folder. "This is what I've found out about the Lockwoods so far. I've got more things coming, but I thought you'd want a look."

"Good man. Byrne seems to be nosing around more than usual," Mornay warned quietly. "Better make sure everything you've got is tucked away behind a locked drawer."

"Already is. I'm off." Sahotra held up a warning finger. "Don't muck up my desk with crumbs or wrappers."

"I'll try to restrain myself."

When Sahotra had gone, Claire asked, "What computer whiz?" She was slowly sorting through another pile of paperwork.

"Just one of his mates."

"What does he do that our information technology people couldn't do?"

"Claire, why do you always ask questions you really don't want to know the answer to?"

"Someone's got to watch after you." She held up a paper. "Constable Walden was working at Craiginches the same time Ian Harris's son, Fergus, was there. His signature is on the visitor forms."

"Is that Harris's dossier?"

"Aye."

"How many visitor forms did Walden sign?"

"Looks like the majority of them, up until Fergus's death."

Claire shuffled more papers, spreading them around the table. "They've given us a list of the inmates who were being held at the time of Harris's death. There's his counseling sheets. Some medical paperwork." She lifted one of the forms. "He was ill several times."

"Let me see the list of prisoners." Mornay scanned it for familiar names, and found Michael O'Conner's name.

"Are you going to return Maggie Cray's calls?" Claire asked.

"Not if my life depended on it. Time we went off duty. I'll buy you a drink at Elrod's."

"And choke on cigarette smoke while my bum goes numb on a hard stool? It's a tempting offer, but I'll pass."

"A simple no will do me." He stood. "It's Sunday, Elrod closes early. I've probably missed him."

"I want to finish the map and see what else has been turned up today."

Mornay sat back down and watched Claire. She was using blue pins to mark the locations on the map of the people who didn't have a satisfactory explanation of their whereabouts on one or more of the key dates: Matthew's favorite teacher, Jonathan Cross. Ian Harris. Michael O'Conner. David Lockwood. Gabriel Smith. Most of the pins were concentrated around Cordiff the day Matthew disappeared, not Aberdeen.

"I'm out of pins. Do you have any there?" Claire asked.

"There's some in Byrne's office. I'll get them."

Mornay pulled the pins off of Byrne's mysterious map. It was the first time he'd really looked at it, beyond noticing there were nearly two dozen pins stuck randomly over the northeast portion of the country. A closer inspection revealed that, beneath each pin, Byrne had lightly penciled in a pair of letters and a date. The dates weren't recent; they spanned over twenty years.

"Byrne's written dates on his map. Did you know?" he asked Claire.

Claire walked into Byrne's office, glanced at the dates. "Never looked. Maybe they're old cases, ones he never managed to solve."

While that wasn't uncommon among the more diligent, terrier-with-a-bone types of cops, Byrne had never seemed that dedicated. "He never had the map up when he worked here before. Perhaps it's a case he was assigned when he worked with the Scottish crime squad."

Claire wasn't interested. "Can I have the pins?"

He handed them over. "I'll be out in a minute. I want to see what else Byrne might have stashed away in here."

Mornay contemplated the significance of the map's dates as he drove home. His search of Byrne's desk had revealed little information. If Byrne kept notes, he either carried them with him or kept them at home. Mornay wondered if he was just trying to come up with an excuse not to think about the implications of Byrne's threat: cooperate, or have his personal life revealed. Knowing Byrne, it'd be done very publicly.

He was facing the same threat from Victoria, but coming from her it seemed less threatening. Particularly since he'd acquiesced to the blood test, which would prove without a doubt if he were the father of Pamela's child.

There were so many things he needed to do. Sleep, eat, pick up his cleaning, call the hospital and find out if they had the results from the blood work. Attempt to talk to Victoria. Find out what Maggie had on his father. That, he decided, was the easiest task to cross off the list.

He turned on Clergy Street so he could backtrack down Skene. It was late, but his father practically lived at his boatyard. Maggie would be outside, maintaining an undercover surveillance that bordered on harassment.

He spotted the SDEA's van in the exact spot it'd been parked the last time he was there.

Kathy Berra was in the van. Her face was a pale oval in the dim light. Maggie was in one of the front seats. Mornay closed the slider and sat on the bench seat next to Berra. "Gets a bit claustrophobic in here, don't you think?" he whispered to her.

"You get used to it," she whispered back. Berra seemed pleased to see him. He shouldn't wonder, after being cooped up with an ill-tempered Maggie Cray.

"You're supposed to be available when I need

assistance from the local forces," Maggie said. "You're a hard man to track down."

"It's part of my charm. Just ask Claire."

"I'll pass." She turned in her seat and smiled her feline smile when she saw that Mornay had purposely sat out of touching range.

"Aren't you curious why I need your assistance?"

"Not particularly. I'm here because I want to see what you've got on Clyde."

Maggie kept smiling. "Just like that?"

"Just like that."

"I don't think you're ready to see what we've got."

"Maybe you've nothing to show. That's why you've got me wearing wires under my clothes, wanting me to ask idiotic questions. You're trying to stir something up before you're shut down. Surveillance like this"—his gaze took in the computers and the electronics—"must cost a fortune. Someone's going to want results."

Wind was buffeting the van, making it sway back and forth.

"If that's what you really thought, you wouldn't be here," she said. "You're worried about what I might have on your father. Show him the pictures, Berra."

Berra tapped on one of the computer keyboards, and four photographs filled the screen. His father was featured in every one. Berra hit an arrow, bringing a new group of photographs up. One of these photographs had Elrod's pub in the background. This was the first time he'd been given a chance to see the true scope of their investigation. The images chilled him more than any wind. They featured his father with a variety of people, including the Paisley brothers.

"How long have you been watching him?" Mornay asked.

"You don't need to know," Maggie answered.

She left her seat and sat on the bench across from Mornay, her knees touching his. "Do you recognize him?" She pointed to one of the newest pictures Berra had brought up. The man she indicated had dark hair and dark skin; he looked Greek or Italian.

"I've never seen him before."

"His name is Antoni Cobaj. He's Albanian and his diverse business interests have attracted the attention of the NCIS."

Mornay studied the photograph. During the past eighteen months, Albanians had been rapidly and violently carving out a niche of the profitable heroin trade in Scandinavia and mainland Europe. Estimates from NCIS, the National Criminal Intelligence Service, said that approximately 70 percent of the UK's heroin trade was controlled by Turkish organized crime groups. A further 20 percent was controlled by South Asian, Indian, and Pakistani organized crime groups. The Albanians appeared keen on cashing into this lucrative business and were cutting their way into the South Asian groups, which depended on human couriers—the most vulnerable of delivery methods.

"What sort of business interests?" Mornay asked quietly.

"It would be easier to ask what Cobaj *isn't* interested in. He's dabbled in gambling, armed security, drug trafficking, and prostitution."

"God bless capitalism."

"We've had a report that your father's been meeting him the middle of every month like clockwork, for the past six months."

Mornay was fed up with her shock-factor approach. "What do they do, exchange holdalls?"

"They talk," she answered. "That's all."

"Where's the crime in that? Kathy, go back to that last set." He searched for other faces he didn't recognize. There were four. Could he talk Maggie Cray into giving him copies of the photographs?

"These men are no choirboys, Mornay. We might not know who they are, but one look is enough to tell they're up to something."

"Half the population in the country is up to something: You've got grannies buying from the black market to make their pensions go further and fourteen-year-olds breaking into cars so they can afford to buy the latest designer trainers. What crime has my father committed?"

Maggie just held his gaze with her cold blue stare.

"You don't have anything solid. You've only got suspicious pictures."

"When you smell smoke, you don't have to see the fire to know there is one."

This was a first: Maggie Cray on the defensive.

"So if the whizzes at NCIS are tracking Mr. Cobaj, there's more to him than you've told me. Is that why you were so insistent I was brought on board? Are you afraid one of the analysts in Glasgow will suggest someone else take over the case?"

Maggie didn't speak, which was as good as an admission.

"We've all got problems," he said. "I want copies of those pictures by tomorrow morning."

"Take it up with my chief superintendent."

"Then don't bother calling the next time you need someone to talk to Clyde."

"You might want to see what forensics discovered on the *Sunward* before you leave. They've found traces of heroin." She smiled. "It could've come from the Paisleys; they specialized in stupidity. Or it could be your father's."

Mornay leaned toward her. "I don't like you, Maggie. You're the sort of cop that takes the wrong kind of chances, and when you're wrong, it makes us all look bad. I'll only tell you this once: My father is not a drug user and he's not a supplier. That is an indisputable fact. So do yourself a favor and quit before you take some good cops down with you."

# Chapter Sixteen

At half past three in the morning, Mornay was startled out of fitful sleep by a loud knocking. He rolled himself out of bed and stumbled to his kitchen door as the knocking grew more incessant.

His stitches were making the entire right side of his head throb. Every step he took seemed to intensify the throbbing.

Claire was at the door. She pushed her way into the kitchen.

"You need to get dressed. Put on something warm."

She wore jeans, hiking boots, and a thick sweater beneath a zipped ski jacket. Her hair was held back from her face with a clip. She looked far more rested than he would have if he slept for an entire week.

"Claire, I've only just got to bed."

"This is about your friend Elrod." Claire's gaze skimmed across every bit of his kitchen except where he stood. "He was found about half an hour ago. He was attacked and severely beaten."

"Are you sure it's Elrod?"

"Yes." She pushed him down the hall, toward his bedroom.

"He's dead?"

"The coast guard has two crews at the lighthouse working to get him down."

"Down from what?"

"He's been pinned to the side of the lighthouse."

"Pinned with what?"

"Construction bolts."

Mornay pulled on his clothes while Claire waited in the kitchen.

Every move he made felt odd, as if he were still half-asleep.

"Do you want your door locked?" Claire asked, as he picked his way down the icy walk.

The chill air bit into his lungs, and his breath came out in silvery plumes. The familiar smoky scent of coal surrounded him. The hissing of a lorry's air brakes sounded in the distance. All of it seemed strange. Inconsequential.

"Don't bother."

His neighbor's front lights provided enough illumination to navigate the way to Claire's new black Peugeot.

It took only five minutes to make the drive to the harbor. There were two coast guard boats shining spotlights against the small, white lighthouse at the end of the granite block wall that framed the harbor. Elrod's body was suspended, spread-eagle, just below a curved guard that separated the light dome from the main tower. He was pinned to the lighthouse by his upper arms and at his thighs. Streaks of blood had streamed down the white wall.

"Christ."

No wonder Claire hadn't answered his question if Elrod was dead or alive. How could someone survive that?

He didn't wait for Claire to shift into neutral before he was out of the car and sprinting along the harbor wall as fast as he could in half-tied boots. He could see figures crowded inside the lighthouse dome, trying to reach Elrod from above—the likeliest way he was hung. There were others below with ladders too short to reach. Sirens were screaming down the road. A vicious wind ripped at his open coat, chilling his body, numbing his cheeks and nose.

McNab stopped him from going farther down the causeway. "He's alive," McNab shouted to be heard above the sirens, the droning boat motors, the howling wind and the waves crashing against the wall. The spray was being flung all the way into the calmer waters of the harbor. Everyone on the causeway was soaking wet. "But just." The shock of McNab's words made Mornay stop, and McNab walked him back toward Claire's car. "If you want to make yourself useful, have a look at his pub. I've got the forensics on their way, but it could take another hour for them to arrive. Secure the scene and wait for them. I know he was a mate, but you'll only be in the way here."

"Who found him?"

"A woman reported seeing two men running down the causeway, away from the lighthouse an hour ago. She watched them speed away in a blue delivery van. It was Mike Taylor who found him. God knows how Taylor recognized him, but he did. Mike called Claire."

"Two men did this?"

"They used rope and a pneumatic construction gun. We found them in the lighthouse."

"He closes at nine on Sundays, he should've been home. Has anyone checked on his fiancée?"

"Mike Taylor is on his way."

Elrod's pub was dark, but the door was unlocked and ajar. Mornay opened the door with the toe of his boot. Claire handed him a pair of latex gloves and a pair of blue booties. Once they'd donned booties and gloves, they slowly walked into the darkened bar.

Claire shined her torch on the walls flanking the door, looking for a light switch. "Any idea where the lights are?" she asked.

"In his office. Elrod doesn't come in or out this way. Let's walk around that way." He pointed to the right. "We'll be less likely to cross anything important."

He followed Claire, since she had the torch.

Tables and chairs were overturned. Broken glass glittered on the floor, and alcohol fumes filled the air. There was blood spattered on the floor, on one of the broken tables. Elrod had put up one hell of a fight.

"Take a right at the end of the bar, and we'll get the lights on."

After they walked through the doorway, there were three doors visible in the hall. The back entrance was hidden from sight around a corner. The door directly ahead of them led downstairs to the basement, where Elrod stored his liquor. The door to their right led to a small storage room. The door to their left, which led to Elrod's office, was splintered and hanging off two hinges.

The interior of the office was a disaster. Mornay reached around splinters and flipped up all the light switches. The radio, which suddenly started blaring out country and western tunes, was more startling than the sudden blaze of light.

"What was in there?" Claire asked, pointing to a door behind Elrod's desk. When closed, the door would look like a section of bookcase.

"Elrod had his security camera recorders in that closet. Someone must've known about the cameras and went after the tapes."

Elrod's office was carpeted and fitted with shelves surrounding a custom desk, all made from a pale blond maple. He had several prints on the walls, all tropical ocean scenes. The majority of the damage had been to the furniture. There was more blood in here, drops spattered on the wall and a dark stain in the carpet.

"We better leave this to the experts," Claire said. "Let's hope Gaither is on duty tonight."

Mornay nodded and walked out of the office.

DS Frank Gaither's work style was methodical and diligent. He had a patience that seemed unnatural and was, at times, maddening because you couldn't hurry the man, no matter what you did. He was the absolute best to have at a crime scene.

When forensics arrived a quarter of an hour later, Gaither was the first through the door. Byrne was on his heels.

"What've we got?" Gaither asked.

"He was surprised in his office. A struggle ensued and spilled out into the main bar."

Gaither wasted no time putting his team to work.

"Heard you were mates," Byrne said. "Poor bastard. He's being flown to the Royal Infirmary now."

It wasn't clear if Byrne felt sorry for Elrod because of the attack or for having Mornay as a friend.

"What's the E stand for?" Byrne asked.

His voice wooden, Mornay replied, "Elrod."

"Elrod?"

"His father was American." He didn't explain that Elrod's father had named his son after a character on a popular American television show. It was too personal a detail, and Byrne would only have made a crude joke about it.

Mornay vaguely wondered if this was how families rationalized their censorship of the details they told the police. Was it natural to hold back the details that were too personal to share with an uncaring stranger? It felt natural to him, and justified.

Byrne peered at him, his bushy eyebrows pulled together in a single line. "How long did you know him?"

"Fourteen years."

"When did you speak with him last?"

"I was here two days ago to question him about the Paisley brothers."

"The *Sunward* inquiry? What'd he tell you?"

"It was a shot in the dark. Nothing came of it."

"Obviously someone thinks otherwise," Byrne said, eyes narrowed, searching Mornay's body language for clues. "Did he know who the Paisleys were?" Byrne asked.

"Everyone knows them."

"Too right. Maybe your friend had other business interests."

Refusing to give him the opportunity, Mornay turned and walked through the door that led to Elrod's office. A place he'd whiled away many a pleasant evening, sipping Elrod's best whiskey and playing cards.

Claire followed; Byrne didn't.

Gaither was behind Elrod's desk. "Our man paranoid?" he asked, nodding toward the security equipment.

"He was cautious."

Gaither had been spreading dusting powder on all the spots most likely to be touched by someone opening the door.

"How many people knew about this room?" he asked.

"Three, that I'm aware of. Elrod, me, and his fiancée. The security firm he hired to install the system was from Aberdeen. I doubt very many people even knew he had hidden security cameras."

"Someone will need to call his fiancée," Claire said. "Where does she live?"

"Nine Willow Terrace. Her name's Diane. Diane Mull. Taylor was sent earlier, but I'd like to ask her some questions."

"Whoever did this wore gloves," Gaither said. "But maybe we'll get lucky and discover that not all of this blood is the victim's. Were you in the service together?"

The overly sweet aroma of cigar smoke drifted over as Byrne joined them in the office.

"Yes," Mornay answered, his brevity due to Byrne's proximity.

"With his training I'm surprised this happened,"

Byrne said. "He'd be a hard man to take down."

"Then he was surprised," Mornay said.

"Or he knew his attackers," Claire added. "Let them in, brought them to the office."

"That, I'd be willing to consider," Byrne said. "I'd wager he knew a few men tough enough to do this. But it's the details that are important. Like the detail Mornay here had a conversation with Elrod two days ago. And tonight Elrod was pegged to the lighthouse like a fucking bug with six-inch-long construction bolts. Not too subtle a detail, that one. The folks in casualty said if he hadn't been suffering from hypothermia, he'd have bled to death."

"Are you suggesting I should've been more cautious when I spoke to him?" Mornay asked.

"This isn't about blame," Byrne said smoothly. "It's about details."

"You keep saying that." Mornay's voice was low.

"You have a problem with how I'm conducting this investigation, laddie?" Byrne returned in a voice just as menacing. Mornay realized one of the reasons he disliked Byrne so much was the condescending way he said "laddie"—it was exactly the way his father had said it to him his entire life. Byrne also had the same habit as his father of discounting anything Mornay said before he'd even finished saying it.

"Is that what you call this? An investigation?"

"I think you'd better mind who you're talking to. This conversation is beginning to sound like contempt of a superior officer."

"You haven't lost your powers of deduction."

Byrne's gaze never left Mornay's face. "Someone used your mate to send you a message. It looks like your shot in the dark hit the target full on. If your mate dies, it's because of something you did, not me."

Mornay lunged forward and wrapped both of his hands around Byrne's neck, bending the shorter, stouter man backward over Elrod's desk.

The room exploded with noise.

Hands grabbed at Mornay while he struggled to force Byrne into a headlock. Byrne was huffing and wheezing and kicking out futilely. Somehow he managed to suck in enough oxygen to shout a string of blistering curses at Mornay. Three men pulled them apart.

DCI McNab's face loomed into Mornay's field of vision. "Gillespie, get him home, now!"

Mornay was pushed toward the entrance by Claire. He stumbled outside and walked to her car, using both hands to lean against it to try to slow his racing heart. The cold metal beneath his palms helped him focus, but he was still too keyed up to feel the frigid temperatures.

Claire hurried out of the bar, carrying both of their coats.

Once he was seated inside her car, he gave her the address of Diane Mull's house.

"Elrod never turned the security system off," Diane Mull repeated. Taylor had fortified her tea while she waited for her mother to arrive. They were going to drive to the Royal Infirmary together.

"What about the tapes?" Mornay asked. "How did he manage them?"

"He had two sets for every day of the week. An A.M. and a P.M. He had three cameras, so that was forty-two tapes."

"Was he diligent about switching the tapes?"

"Not always. He used to leave the tape in for the basement camera and just let it record over the previous day's recording. He did change the tapes for the bar camera and the outside camera."

"It's Monday morning now, so that means the oldest tape he had was from last Monday? Which he would've recorded over today?"

"Right."

"Did he tell anyone about the control room?"

Diane's eyes were red-rimmed, her lips so pale they could've been white. "You know he wouldn't."

"But someone's taken the tapes and destroyed the recording equipment. How would they get them if they didn't know where the control room was? He must've told someone else. You've got to think back. You've got to try and remember."

She looked away, her lips trembling.

Claire moved to sit next to her and handed Diane another tissue.

"If he did, I don't know who it was."

"Did he tell you he was worried about anything these last few days?"

"No. He was happy, planning the wedding."

Mornay knew Elrod; he wouldn't have wanted to worry Diane. What Elrod liked most about Diane was her domesticity. She was going to make a good mother, he always used to say. Diane liked to fuss over people; she liked keeping her house neat. Planning holidays to Spain was the most interested she got in the world beyond her terraced neighborhood. Mornay would have found a life with a woman like Diane suffocating; Elrod had found it so comforting, he made Mornay promise never to tell her about the things they'd done while in service, particularly the eighteen months they'd worked in Afghanistan. Diane wouldn't have understood.

"Did he seem worried? Did he mention needing to talk to me?"

His question brought a fresh wave of tears as she shook her head. Mornay wanted to shake the silly woman. He needed answers to his questions if he hoped to catch whoever had attacked Elrod.

When the tears subsided, Mornay prodded for more information as gently as he could manage. "Did he get any calls he didn't want to tell you about?"

Diane emphatically shook her head again.

Claire gave him a look, telling him no more questions.

So Mornay sat in an uncomfortable silence punctuated by Diane's sobs, until they were able to relinquish her to her mother's care. Elrod was still in surgery when the women left.

Mornay was restless when they walked outside. He paced on the road next to the Peugeot, images and sounds from the life he'd known before moving back to Scotland seizing his senses, as real and intense as the cold numbing his hands or the frost covering the car's bonnet. He saw Elrod, in desert-colored fatigues. Elrod with a bushy beard, the exposed skin on his face deeply tanned. Elrod in voluminous dark robes, laughing. Always laughing. The scent of heavily spiced lamb sizzling in a hand-beaten copper pot over a campfire. And the relentless sound of hissing sand at the back of so many of those memories.

Mornay stood in his lounge, staring at the boxes he'd never unpacked during the two years he'd lived in the house. Victoria had been dead-on when she accused him of avoiding the past. Seeing the things inside those boxes would force him to face certain events that he wanted to forget. He'd considered just chucking them dozens of times, but he'd never found the will to cut his past out that completely.

He should've gone to bed, like Claire ordered when she dropped him off. Instead he'd rummaged around his cupboards until he'd found an unopened bottle of whiskey, a housewarming gift. Since his surgeries, his body had little tolerance for hard liquor, so he rarely drank it. But whiskey was what he needed—he'd worry about the effects in the morning.

He opened the first box after he'd let the first swallow of whiskey burn its way into his stomach. The box contained athletic clothes he'd forgotten he owned. He put it to the side and opened another. Then another.

He found his childhood photographs in the fourth box, or what was left of them. His father had cleaned house not long after his mother's death, clearing out everything that had been hers or Robbie's: pictures, toys, and clothing. Mornay had managed to sneak out to the bin after his father had gone to bed and save a few items, which he'd hidden for years. He pushed that box away without touching the items inside. He might never find the courage to look at them again.

The bottle of whiskey was nearly half gone. His head was spinning and his gut was on fire.

He found the mementos of his military service in the sixth box: medals, uniforms, a prayer rug, photographs. And he found the picture he'd been searching for.

"Christ, Elrod," he said to his friend's image. "What have I done?"

# Chapter Seventeen

Kathy Berra shook Mornay awake.

"You were unpacking?" she asked, glancing around the piles cluttering the lounge.

Mornay had managed to empty nearly all of the boxes he'd had stored in his house. If he'd had a system of organization at the time he was unpacking, it wasn't apparent as he surveyed the disorganized piles.

He'd fallen asleep slouched against his settee. "What's the time?"

"Half eight."

"Why is it so dark?"

"It's Monday evening."

He groaned and sat up. His head ached from the whiskey, and his stitches were itchy as hell. He also needed to piss.

Berra didn't appear to have dropped by for a casual chat. She'd paid too much attention to her choice of clothes. No polyester. She wore tight jeans, a stretchy blouse beneath a black leather coat, and a new scent. She picked up the photographs that had fallen from his lap when he passed out.

He stood. "There's tea in the tin, if you want a cup."

In his bathroom, he stared into the mirror. Eyes bloodshot, underscored with dark circles, face unshaven, deep lines creasing his brow. He splashed water on his face, took some aspirin and the much-needed piss. A shower and a shave probably wouldn't prepare him for whatever it was that Berra wanted to talk about, not that he had the energy to bother.

"I've made you a cup," Berra told him.

She held out the photograph he'd searched his boxes for. It was of him and Elrod in light-colored robes and turbans, assault rifles slung over their shoulders. They both had heavy beards. Elrod's other arm was wrapped around a pregnant Muslim woman. All that could be seen of her face above a black veil were startling green eyes.

"I didn't think Muslim women were allowed to have their photographs taken."

"That's the daughter of an Afghan warlord. She did what she pleased." He took the photograph from her and turned it facedown on the table.

"I've brought copies of all the surveillance photographs."

"Maggie sent them?"

"She's not that generous, but what she doesn't know won't hurt her."

He took a sip of the tea she'd made him, then added three more spoons of sugar.

"Your pal Elrod made it out of surgery," she said.

He didn't know how to reply. The tea was too hot, so he stood and got a glass of water, drank it down, and filled his glass again. The aspirin were finally starting to work; the throbbing sensation at the back of his head was subsiding into a dull ache.

"The construction gun was part of a load of equipment stolen from a building site in England a month ago."

"Which doesn't help much. It could've changed hands three times since then. How'd you find this out?"

"I rang your partner. But it's been all over the news." She stared frankly at him. "I want to know why you don't think your father is smuggling drugs on his boats."

"You're an electronics expert, Berra. You don't need to know."

Her smile was enigmatic. "So tell me anyway."

Mornay stared at the unboxed piles of rubbish that represented a life's worth of memories. His memories. They were as necessary to his existence as breathing, and for far too long, he'd pretended they weren't. Maybe Berra could talk sense to Cray, if she knew.

"My brother Robbie ran away when I was seven. He was thirteen. He made me promise not to tell our mother where he'd gone."

"Only your mother?"

"He knew I wouldn't tell my father. He was not an easy man to live with; neither of us was close to him. But it was Robbie who took the brunt of my father's temper. I understood why he needed to leave. What Robbie didn't tell me was that, along with the money he'd found in my mother's bureau, he'd found her stash of heroin. I found that out years later. He took it with him."

"Did he tell you where he was going?"

The strength to tell Berra the story was literally coming a breath at a time. "Edinburgh. He'd heard there were jobs for anyone who knew how to work on the fishing boats, no questions asked. He was tall enough to pass for fifteen or sixteen, so he left. But he never made it out of Macduff. He hid behind the Doune Church and OD'd on my mother's heroin. He'd planned to hide out at the church until dark, then hitch a ride on a lorry that was going south."

"What did your father do when he found out Robbie had run away?"

"Broke my nose and two ribs because I wouldn't tell him where Robbie had gone. A tourist found Robbie's body around six that evening. He'd been dead for hours. My father was a hard man, but he adored Robbie more than anything else. I can see that now, looking back."

"But Robbie didn't know that," Berra said quietly. "Did your father know your mother was an addict?"

"He claims he didn't."

"What happened to your mother?"

"She killed herself a week after Robbie died. My father loathes drug users. All Maggie has to do is ask some of his former employees the things he's done to grown men who he discovered were users."

"Maybe Maggie will think he's using a lifetime of hatred as a cover."

"He's not that complex a man."

"Does he consider liquor a drug?"

"He likes his drink too much to apply his morals to his own vices."

"But if he's so dead set against drugs, why is he interacting with this Antoni Cobaj as if they were business partners?"

"If they're in business together, then it's for something else." Mornay went to his coat; he got the piece of hull he'd been carrying around. "See this, it's a piece of the *Sunward* hull, with a special coating on the interior. The Paisleys worked on the oil platforms before being laid off; I think my father might be smuggling petrol. He could sell it directly to the fishing fleet without bringing a drop into the harbor."

She seemed to be considering his theory. "Is this your idea?"

"Actually it was Elrod's."

"Did he tell you what gave him the idea?"

"He didn't get the chance. Our conversation was interrupted, and it looks as if someone was keen to see we never finish it."

His phone rang just then. He told Berra to hang on.

"Get over here, now," his father said.

"What's happened?"

"There was a package on my doorstep when I got home from work. I'm not going back inside until you get over here and get rid of the bloody thing." His father rang off.

"Bad news?" Berra asked.

"My father said there was a package on his steps. He sounded upset."

"Clyde Mornay upset? That's hard to picture. Was it through the post?"

"No. I'll need to go."

"You're in no shape to drive, so let me."

\*　　　\*　　　\*

Clyde was standing on the curb in front of his tiny house. His hands were shoved in his jean pockets to protect them from the bitter cold.

"Where's your coat?" Mornay asked.

"In there, with that fucking box."

Mornay walked inside, Berra close behind him.

"What a smell," Berra said.

"Now we know why he's in no hurry to come back inside."

Clyde's lounge was narrow and sparsely furnished: a chair, rug, and table were centered in front of the gas fireplace. The kitchen was through a glass-paneled door at the back of the room. The door was open.

On the small kitchen table was a large cube-shaped cardboard box. The sides were smeared with grime.

Berra handed Mornay a pen so he could open the cardboard flap. "Any idea what's inside?"

"Something that's decomposing nicely."

"I'll look, if you want."

"Hand me one of those spoons."

Mornay edged up to the box. Only sheer will kept his stomach from heaving its contents. He slipped the pen under the flap and used the spoon to open one of the interior flaps. The smell was appalling as he pushed the interior flap. Then he saw what was inside.

He dropped the spoon and pen and backed away from the box, cursing.

Berra wasn't eager to touch the box now. "That's a human head."

"It is."

"Any idea who?"

"Trevor Paisley."

Mornay walked out of the kitchen, joining his father on the curb. Clyde's eyes were bloodshot, his face ashen. "Why'd you open it?"

"That's what you do with packages, you open them. The bloody thing wasn't reeking like it is now. It's thawing."

"Is this Cobaj's work?"

"You'll have to ask him."

"Why's Cobaj after your business?"

"Because he's a canny bastard. I just want you to get rid of that bloody thing."

"What if Donald Paisley and Scott Gray are still alive?"

Clyde's expression hardened. "You don't think I haven't thought of that already? I've no clue how that happened to Trevor." Clyde pointed to his front door. "But you can be bloody damn sure that if this is Cobaj's doing, then they're all dead. And that Albanian bastard will be joining them as soon as I find him."

Mornay was standing in front of Andy McNab's desk at seven on Tuesday morning.

"No one saw the package delivered?" McNab asked.

"No one's admitting to it."

"You knew Trevor Paisley well?"

"He's worked on and off for my father all of my life."

"Forensics said he suffered no burns, which is going to change the direction of the SDEA's investigation. It'll give Maggie Cray a second wind."

"I know."

McNab sighed heavily. "You've been put on suspension." Before Mornay could protest, McNab said, "You struck a senior officer in front of nine witnesses. You're lucky Byrne didn't choose to pursue it further than an official reprimand. On top of that, Lord Gordon has filed an official complaint regarding the investigation of his stolen car. He's leveling negligence charges at our entire department, and he's leveled several serious charges at you in particular. I believe the charges are unwarranted and undeserved, and will do what I can to have them dropped. But these things take time. Officers have been assigned to review the inquiry, and it will be at least a week before they schedule a formal hearing. I realize the past few weeks have been stressful, and I'm not unsympathetic to the fact that a close friend of yours has been the victim of a particularly brutal attack—but there's no excuse for some of the behavior you displayed. If it were in my power to reduce your suspension, I wouldn't. I expect a higher level of conduct from my officers."

It was the harshest Andy McNab had ever spoken to him. Mornay's respect for his boss made the words all the more cutting. "I understand, sir."

"Let's hope you do. You've an appointment to see ACC Donaldson at three this afternoon. I'm advising you to be properly repentant, understood?"

"Yes, sir."

"I don't know what you've done to antagonize the man, Seth, but Lord Gordon wants you out of this department and of the force. He'll take any opportunity you give him to achieve his goal. You don't want that to happen, do you?"

"No, sir."

"Then there's nothing Lord Gordon could use against you?"

Mornay hesitated. "There is something."

McNab's expression was inscrutable as Mornay told him about his relationship with Pamela, the accident, and the aftermath. Partway through, McNab swiveled his chair around to face the wall behind his desk. Several shelves on that wall displayed photographs of his family. There was no picture of McNab's son, who Mornay hadn't even known existed until Byrne mentioned him. McNab picked up a picture of his daughter, and Mornay wondered if she was the one he'd put out of the house.

"Would you have married her had she not been in the accident?" McNab asked. He was still studying the picture of his daughter.

"No."

"And the child? Have you considered adoption?"

"I haven't thought that far ahead. I've just been concentrating on getting through each day."

"Her medical condition is that precarious?"

"It is, sir."

"I'm sorry to hear that. Children are precious. I've always believed that. So many people consider them to be a nuisance, a burden. I consider them our opportunity to better ourselves. They've got the benefit of our knowledge, of our experience." McNab took in a deep breath, as if to say more, then continued in a more reflective tone. "Inspector Byrne hasn't mentioned your dilemma to me yet. Which doesn't mean he won't; he's probably looking for a more opportune moment. You were right to tell me." McNab put the picture back and swiveled his chair around to face Mornay. "Personally, I find your actions repugnant, but I'm no lay minister, and I can't preach my morals to anyone, even my own

2 M.G. Kincaid

officers. So we'll deal with the problem whenever Inspector Byrne decides to make an issue of it, or if Lord Gordon should ever discover it."

Mornay had expected a more stringent tone, but McNab had larger problems. "Thank you, sir. Will I be able to run down some fringe jobs while the review is being conducted? It would save someone else legwork."

McNab smiled faintly. "I can't tell you what to do on your time off, can I? What did you have in mind?"

"Since I've got to go to Aberdeen today, I thought I could drop by Craiginches and find out more about Ian Harris's son."

"I've an old friend who works at the prison. I'll make sure he meets you at the Gate. His name is Harry Black."

McNab's introduction proved invaluable when Mornay arrived at HMP Craiginches. The prison was housed in a depressing building near the West Tullos Industrial Estate on the southern side of Aberdeen. The prison was near the River Dee and the A956, which paralleled the river. Craiginches served the northeast of Scotland, housing around 160 prisoners, from low-security fine defaulters up to long-term murderers. Harry Black was one of the senior officers at Craiginches. He met Mornay at the Gate, the prison's official entry point.

In Craiginches's case, the name was more impressive than the room. The office was poorly lit, the linoleum badly worn, and the dark counters were scarred from years of use and abuse. Behind the counter, desks were crowded with equipment, leaving little room for the officers to work comfortably.

"I've always wondered," Mornay said as Harry Black led him through a door, into a long hall, "do they keep the Gate grim-looking on purpose?"

"It's a matter of where priorities are placed," Black said. "And here, the prisoners are the top priority. If you think the Gate is grim, you should see the staff muster room and our locker area." He opened a door to a small, spartanly furnished office. Inside he offered Mornay some overcooked coffee, which Mornay declined.

"So, you're here about Fergus Harris's dossier?"

"I haven't had a chance to read it through," Mornay admitted. "I was interested in finding out what sort of inmate he was."

Harry Black held his gaze. "It was all in the dossier."

Mornay smiled blandly, not breaking the gaze. "We both know that sometimes things get left out. As you've probably heard, I'm working on the Matthew Adair inquiry, and one of the people we're taking a closer look at is Fergus Harris's father, Ian Harris. Did you ever meet him while his son was here?"

"No. As I recall, his girlfriend was his only visitor after he was sent to long-term. She came to tell him she was moving to London and leaving their baby with his father."

"You remember that after all these years?"

"I read the dossier."

Mornay grinned. "Point taken."

Harry returned the grin. "Ian Harris pitched a royal bloody fit after his son died. Claimed the prison service was negligent. As if he would've known—didn't come here once."

"What sort of negligence did he mean?"

"He claimed his son began using drugs because we housed him with hardened criminals."

"He wasn't before?"

"His father claimed he'd only done what other boys his age had done, experimentation." Harry Black's tone was derisive. "He claimed Fergus didn't hit the hard stuff until he was forced to live with the hard criminals."

"Heroin?"

"That's right. He overdosed. I suspect he started hitting it after his girlfriend ran out on him."

"How'd he get the drugs?"

"They've got their ways. He went to CAT B status after he started taking them, meaning we had to be wary of escape attempts."

"Did he try to escape?"

"Three times. Claimed he was going to be killed."

"Was he part of any prisoner-on-prisoner assaults?"

"No, never a mark on him. But he was bloody adamant about escaping. This first two attempts had no finesse—he went straight for the wall, silly bugger. No idea where he thought he'd go if he actually made it past the guards, through the locked gates, and over the top."

"Did he have a personal officer assigned to him?"

"We weren't assigning personal officers at that time."

"Did anyone look into his claim?"

"We tried to get him to fill out a complaint, but he refused. And at the time, we were experiencing a massive overcrowding problem and staff shortages." Harry Black shrugged. "Everyone thought he was mad."

"PC Neal Walden was assigned here during that time; do you recall him?"

"I do. I always wondered why he wanted to be a cop. Didn't seem to have the proper personality for it. He worked at the long-term offenders visitor center for the better part of a year. Surprisingly, he got on with the prisoners well enough."

"Why's that?"

"Ran their betting pools. He loved to gamble even though he never won."

Unfortunately, Harry Black's impressive memory didn't extend to Michael O'Conner. But Mornay had learned enough to suspect that Neal Walden was purposely trying to hide how much he knew about Michael O'Conner. Why?

At force headquarters, Mornay opted to take the stairs to reach Donaldson's office.

Roger Donaldson was not smiling. It was the first time Mornay could recall seeing anything but a pleasant expression on his face.

"Sir," Mornay said in greeting.

"Have a look." Donaldson tossed a newspaper across the desk. The headline read: MENACE OR MODEL CITIZEN? WELL-KNOWN POLICEMAN STRIKES SENIOR OFFICER. There were two color photographs of Mornay below the sensational headline. One was taken outside of Elrod's bar sometime yesterday morning; it showed him looking grimly into the distance. The other was the familiar still shot of Mornay pointing his finger at the journalist who'd been hounding Claire all those weeks ago. "That will be going out this evening. Not the sort of publicity we need right now, is it?" Donaldson asked quietly.

"No, sir."

"DI Cray's also sent in a formal complaint. Apparently you're not cooperating with her investigation. I thought Chief Inspector McNab made it clear about the level of cooperation he expected from you."

"Sir, she's—"

Donaldson smacked a flat palm on his desk. "Inspector Cray is a senior officer, who, at the very least, should be given the deference of her rank—something you've forgotten to do quite frequently."

How did he know that? Had Maggie taped their conversations? With Kathy Berra's electronic expertise at her fingertips, how difficult could that have been?

"Inspector Cray's interest in my father borders on extreme, sir."

"I don't care if it borders on suicidal; she's got a job to do, and you were there to help her do it. We can't afford the appearance of partiality in these troubled times."

Mornay nodded slowly, realizing the mistake he'd made by taking Roger Donaldson at face value: he was just as politically motivated as all the rest. He was just better at finessing what he wanted out of his subordinates without making them feel like they'd been bent over the desk.

"Aren't you a grim lad today." Sergeant Rory Williams was seated at the top of a ladder in the basement records room. Rory had seen Mornay the moment he'd walked through door, but the high metal-shelving units that ran the length of the room had hidden Rory from view.

"Anyone else here?" Mornay asked.

"And a cautious lad. No, there's no one else here."

"I've just come from the ACC's office." Mornay negotiated around the shelves, which held evidence from open cases, sometimes for years. There was everything from bed linens to athletic equipment on the shelves, making it look like the back room of a church rummage sale.

Rory had risen to the rank of sergeant years ago, then his career had flatlined, a fact that never made him bitter. He'd had a massive heart attack a year ago. Since then, he'd given up drinking alcohol and smoking. He'd slimmed down dramatically and even started jogging. He was due to retire in two months and was in better shape than when he'd originally pinned on his sergeant stripes. Yet the force still considered Rory a medical liability and was pushing for his retirement.

Rory was replacing a broken ceiling tile.

"Why didn't you have maintenance do that?"

"And have to look at it for the next year while they work their way through the mountain of work requests before mine? No thanks. Just as easy to steal a tile and fix it myself."

Rory made his descent. "I heard about what happened to your mate. Some brutal bastards in this world."

"Did you hear I've been suspended for punching Byrne?"

"Aye, but it's a miracle you didn't do it sooner. I'm assuming you've said fuck-all to your suspension. What is it you need me to do?"

Mornay grinned. "You'll be sorry you asked."

Rory shook his head, completely serious. "Not if it helps find who killed poor wee Matthew Adair."

Mornay passed across a copy of the list of dates he'd taken from the map in Byrne's office, without the corresponding initials. "I need you to put these numbers into your magic box and see what you come up with."

"Are they child abductions?"

Mornay would've liked to tell Rory the truth, but his old friend might not be so eager to do the research if he knew the source of the dates. "We're not sure what they pertain to; we've just discovered them in the course of the Adair investigation."

"Anything else?" Rory asked.

"It's possible they're linked to old cases from our command area. Maybe cases that are still open."

He nodded. "How soon do you need to know something?"

"As soon as you can manage."

"I'll have to borrow Arthur's computer if you want it by tomorrow."

Arthur was Dr. Hall's overweight assistant whom Mornay called Lothario. "Why his computer?"

"Some silly bugger in IT gave him full access. How do you think I can find what I do? Couldn't find my socks with what I've been authorized to access."

"How do you work it with Arthur?"

"The lads in the lab are right fond of my wife's baking. Arthur's given me his log-in and password, and he'll let me in the office at shift change."

# Chapter Eighteen

It was after eight that night when Claire rang Mornay. He was at the Royal Infirmary getting an update on Elrod's condition. She told him Sahotra had finally arranged the meeting with his computer expert, and asked him to meet her in front of the Saltoun Arms Hotel in Fraserburgh, a small fishing village forty-five minutes east of Macduff.

"I'm in Aberdeen. Why don't you just give me the directions to the spot, and I'll meet you there?"

"Sahotra's mate was adamant about us coming in a single car. I've found out some things today. I can tell you on the way."

"Then you can drive, as well."

Despite the late hour, traffic was heavy coming out of Aberdeen, so Claire arrived well ahead of him. She was waiting for him in the square dominated by views of the harbor and presided over in grand fashion by the historic Saltoun Arms. Streetlamps were lit around the square, casting meager pools of light. A sharp wind blew off the sea.

"Had a busy day?" he asked once inside her car.

"Very, you?"

"Busy enough for a man on suspension. What've you got?"

"More on David Lockwood. I found confirmations of his flights; all were correct. But he neglected to tell us that he'd only been in Australia one day before his last departure. He'd spent the previous two weeks in the UK."

"He wasn't in Australia the day Matthew Adair was abducted?"

"He arrived in Heathrow on the ninth, two days before. I don't know where he went from there. I've only got his arrivals and departures."

"Things are not looking good for Mr. Lockwood."

"How is Elrod doing?"

Mornay had spent an hour with Elrod after leaving Rory's basement office. "He's still in a coma. He was given quite a beating before he was taken to the lighthouse. But he's a tough bastard; he'll come through."

Claire flipped up her turn signal and turned into a housing estate on the outskirts of Fraserburgh. The houses had large front gardens—large in his mind was any garden wide enough to park his car with room to spare. Claire crept across her third traffic calmer and eased in front of the last house on the road.

Sahotra opened the front door before Claire even knocked. One look at Mornay's face kept him from asking what took them so long. He held a finger to his lips and hurried inside.

They followed him through the hall, past an

expensively furnished lounge—big-screen television, saltwater fish tank, overstuffed furniture, crystal knickknacks—into a bedroom whose door was set beneath the stairs.

The room would've been overcrowded with just one adult body; three made it claustrophobic. A narrow bed, neatly made, ran along the sidewall. There were no posters of musicians or football teams pinned up on the pale yellow walls.

A boy of twelve or thirteen sat in a padded leather computer chair that would've been the envy of any corporate executive.

Mornay took in the impressive array of computer equipment and studied the boy. He had sandy hair, apple cheeks, and massive blue eyes. He was so intent on the computer game he was playing that he'd tuned out the adults.

"Who is this?" Mornay asked Sahotra.

"My name's Paul," the boy said without looking up.

"If this is your *expert* I'm going to wring your neck."

The door behind Sahotra opened. A young woman, no older than twenty, walked into the room cradling a mug in one hand and holding a roll in the other.

"Paul," she said to the boy, "it's way past your bedtime. Get lost. And if you wake Mum, *I'll* wring your neck." She glanced back to Mornay when she said this, winking. "I'm Mary. Mum broke her leg last week," she said. "She's on painkillers. Did anyone see you drive up?"

"Why does it matter?" Mornay said.

"Some of my clients wouldn't like it if they knew I was associating with the police."

"Tell them you're doing consulting work for the

force." Mornay turned and sent a hard look in Sahotra's direction. This was *not* what he had in mind when he asked Sahotra to set up this meeting.

Mary's fingers were flying over the keyboard. "Right," she said sarcastically. "As if you could afford my fees. I'm doing this as a favor to a friend."

Was Sahotra blushing?

"What are your fees?"

"Depends on what you want me to do." Mary glanced his way. "There aren't fifteen people in the country that could do what I do."

"You should be working for the government."

"Who'd want the bother?"

The screen blinked, and suddenly they were treated to a view of the Bank of Scotland's logo. This wasn't the public access Web site, this was an internal system program that was demanding Mary put in the correct password. The screen changed again.

David Lockwood's financial transactions for the past year appeared. Sahotra wore a smug expression when Mornay glanced his way again.

Claire, of the straight and narrow, was completely absorbed by what Mary was doing. "How could you know which bank to access?" she asked.

"I looked up one of his companies and worked back from there."

"Funny he doesn't have his money in Australia, since that's where he lives."

"His father was on the board of directors for this particular bank. Family ties and all that rubbish."

Mary's fingers were flying over the keyboard, punching the keys forcefully. Screens flicked past faster than Mornay could read.

"From what I've discovered, David Lockwood appears to be liquidating his assets."

"Why would he do that?" Claire asked.

"The obvious answer is that he's got something big to purchase. However, for this amount of money, that would be a small- to medium-sized country. He's sold his shares in both companies and has converted quite a sizable chunk of his portfolio. He'd never go hungry if he lost every penny he's liquidized, but if he did lose it all, he'd no longer be disgustingly wealthy—he'd only be modestly wealthy."

Suddenly, Mary stopped typing, and the printer started whirring.

The summation from a quarterly statement showed that David Lockwood's net worth was in the millions. More screens flicked past. Mary had found a listing of transactions in David Lockwood's personal account. There were dozens of deposits, mostly from dividends, but what caught Mornay's attention were three transfers that had occurred in the past six months. One was a transfer of four hundred thousand pounds in May, and a transfer in July for a quarter of a million pounds. The last large transfer had happened four weeks earlier, four hundred thousand pounds. Though there were many deposits during the past twelve months, none came close to matching the outgoing transfers.

"He's got a considerable amount of free cash available, though he took some massive losses to free it up."

"What's massive?"

"Thousands and thousands. But when you've got millions, I suppose it's not much of a loss."

"Can you tell where he transferred the funds to?" Mornay asked.

"It's encrypted."

"And all this other information isn't? It's just out there for anyone to stumble across?"

Mary leaned back in her chair. "There's encryption, and then there's encryption. I could find out where the money went, but I don't think I'd be able to do it before the watchdogs at the other end found out I was poking around their systems. It's not worth the risk. Not for a freebie."

"What about his sister, Eilish Lockwood?"

Mary hit a couple of keys, typing fewer characters than Mornay did to access his e-mail address, and Eilish Lockwood's financial history was revealed. It was far less impressive than her stepbrother's. Though she'd been left a permanent trust, it appeared that all of it was used to maintain her property. Her accounts frequently went into overdraft.

Mary brought up a new screen. "When Kashik first called two days ago, he got me curious. I decided to do some searching into Lord Gordon."

Sahotra was immediately defensive. "I never asked you to do that."

Calmly, Mary said, "I know."

More lines of meaningless characters streamed into view. Mornay had no idea what he was looking at; there was only a jumble of letters and symbols.

"Why were you curious about Murdo Gordon?" he asked.

"Because I've always thought he was too arrogant. And his behavior toward the police since Matthew Adair's disappearance has been dreadful. I'd be delighted to find something that would knock him off that Waterford crystal pedestal he's put himself on." Another blinding grin. "And I think I've found it."

The screen flashed blue and faded to a silvery gray. Lines of text—numbers, letters, and symbols—began appearing. Mary explained, "I had to get creative. I found a way into his lordship's personal computer and put a lock on his keystrokes."

"What's that mean in language I'll understand?"

"Anytime he presses a key on his keyboard or clicks his mouse, the command is sent to one of my computers. Sounds clever, but it's actually a restrictive program. I made some modifications to it, but I can't resolve the strokes into regular text immediately—I've got to run every stroke through another program to clean up all the extraneous commands." She typed for a few keystrokes and a white screen appeared with black text. "Ta da. Here are the e-mails Lord Gordon has sent out during the past week. Mind, you're only seeing what he's typed. If he's added attachments of some sort, they would show up as extra key commands. Which I've dumped."

"How are you able to do that?" Claire asked.

"I'm a clever lass."

"Not overly modest either," Mornay remarked dryly.

"That's how I get away with charging the fees that I do without a bit of guilt. Back to the e-mails, they've made some interesting reading. I've got the times they were sent, because of one of the additions I made to the program, as well as the IP address the messages were sent to. This one should interest you." She tapped the screen with a finger. "It's straight to your police office in Macduff. I've just the IP address to work from—"

"What's an IP address?" Mornay asked.

"It's a numerical signature. Sometimes local area

networks randomly assign IPs to their workstation computers for security reasons, but I suspect each of the computers in your office will have a unique IP address. You'll have to go through your system administrator to discover which computer in your office has that particular address."

"Why can't you just read to whom he addressed the e-mail?"

"He didn't type it out. He probably chose it from his address book, which means it's likely someone he e-mails frequently."

Mornay passed the note to Claire. "I can guess which one: His daughter works in our building. Have you read through the information you've gleaned from his computer?" he asked Mary.

"I've skimmed some, but I didn't know what you were looking for. I've printed out everything. What we're looking at now is activity since I printed those copies. Last evening he was quite busy." She sent an inscrutable look in Mornay's direction. "And he's not particularly fond of you."

"He's mentioned my name?"

"Several times, very unflatteringly." Mary shuffled through some papers, pulled a sheet out, and passed it to him. "Don't worry, the page numbers are marked, so you won't lose your place. This is one of the more curious messages came through early Monday morning."

*The SDEA assignment isn't as distracting as I would have hoped. He's too close. Talk to Donaldson and get rid of him now, or I will.*

Claire spoke first. "That was sent around one, an hour or so before your friend Elrod was attacked."

"Was Inspector Gordon in the office that night?" he asked her.

"I don't know. Byrne and McNab were there quite late."

"Together?"

"That's what Taylor said—they were in McNab's office for over an hour."

If Byrne was Murdo Gordon's contact in the office, that would explain why Byrne was brought back to their office. Did Byrne have information he was using to blackmail Gordon's cooperation? Mornay had no problem believing Byrne would stoop to using blackmail. And he could easily believe Lord Gordon putting pressure on his cousin to get Byrne placed back in CID. If this were all true, then Byrne's behavior the morning Elrod was attacked had been a calculated attempt to provoke Mornay. And it'd worked beautifully.

"Does Gordon mention anyone else in his e-mails?" Mornay was searching the screen, using a finger to keep track of which line he'd scanned.

"Not that I've seen."

"Once you close out of this, can you get back in?"

"Anytime I feel like it."

"What if I needed to prove where this information came from? Would that be possible, even if he's already deleted the original e-mail from his computer?"

"Nothing's ever permanently deleted from a hard drive," Mary said. "But if you had to work backward from my system, that'd be possible." She held up a warning finger. "*If* I were willing to let you. And since you've exhausted my generosity for one week, that won't be possible. I've university fees to earn; I haven't the time to be wasting on free work."

"How about forwarding the keystrokes to another server?" Sahotra asked.

"Do you have one in mind?"

As Sahotra and Mary's discussion turned technical, Mornay whispered to Claire, "Did you understand any of what she said?"

"About every fifth word. But we've the printouts; those shouldn't be too difficult to work out. Hang on, it's my mobile." She pulled the mobile off of her waistband and listened. "It's Dunnholland," she whispered. "Says he's got something important to show us; he's wanting to meet you somewhere away from the office."

Mornay considered for a moment. "It will be nearly midnight by the time we return. We'll talk to him in the morning, at Nan's."

Joan O'Conner was shivering when she returned from the kitchen door. "Eilish, Calvin said he won't leave until you've talked to him."

Eilish sighed. "There's no point putting it off."

"Do you want me to stay?" Joan asked.

"Thanks, but I've got to do this myself."

"When do you want to start sorting through the new gift shop shipment tomorrow?"

"We could both do with a lie-in; let's start at nine."

Joan let Calvin in, then left.

Calvin's face was flushed from the cold, and he walked to the fireplace. "I said some stupid things, Eilish."

"Too right."

"But it's because I'm climbing the walls. We've been seeing each other for nearly six months. It's time we started treating this relationship more seriously."

"Is this conversation about sex?"

"It's not just sex. I want to marry you, but you're always keeping me away. And then anytime your David is around, you can't be bothered with me."

"David isn't the reason we're having this argument. You're angry because I won't sleep with you."

"It's *not* just that." Calvin's voice was growing increasingly frustrated. "It's this heap of stones. What happens two years from now, when one of the boilers breaks? I won't be able to fix it on what Harris pays me. David has the money; he should be helping you make repairs before the place falls down around you."

"What David does for the estate is between him and me. And so we're clear on this point, I don't like him helping. I want Finovar to be self-sustaining."

"He *should* help, after your father took him in and raised him like his own. The man gave him a home. Gave him a proper name. Gave him a start at a proper life. Your David should be grateful every day he's alive for what your father did, and he should be respectful enough to your father's memory to show it by helping you."

Eilish shook her head. "This isn't about me at all. Or the sex. It's about money. You thought I had money, and now you know I don't."

"There's nothing wrong with wanting a bit of security, Eilish. That doesn't make me a bad person."

"But you're not the person I thought you were. You're someone I don't care to be around any longer. Lock the door behind you and don't come back."

She walked out of the kitchen.

Eilish went to the chapel. She wasn't a devout

anything, but the small room was comforting to be in. The chapel was dark, except for two small spotlights aimed at the altar. It smelled of beeswax and lavender. There were five pews on either side of the wide aisle, with red velvet cushions and tartan throws woven on the estate. The tall, narrow windows made it a chilly room, even on the warmest of days.

She walked to her favorite spot, a deep alcove to the left of the altar. Carved out of the stone formation that the chapel was built against, the alcove faced a beautiful arched window that looked down on the sea.

"What a fool I've been!"

"You're talking to yourself again." David was sitting at the back of the cushioned alcove, hidden in shadow.

Eilish joined him, pulling one of the wool throws around her shoulders.

"Did I give you a fright?"

"No, actually."

He didn't look right, somehow. "What's wrong?" she asked.

"Eilish, you may be very capable, but there are some things that even you can't sort out."

She scooted closer till their shoulders were touching. This was the way they used to sit when she was a child. "But you could tell me anyway."

"Not right now."

She noticed the bottle of wine in his hand. "You've been drinking again."

"Liquid courage, my dear."

She couldn't remember seeing him so unsure of himself.

He lifted the bottle and took a swig. "It's been ages since I was here. It was my safe place. He never found me here."

"He?"

"I'm not ready to tell you. I thought I was—but I'm just . . . not ready."

He wouldn't look at her.

"David, what accident don't you want the police to find out about?"

"Listening at doors, are we?" He sounded hollow.

"I haven't told anyone. I won't, either."

"Not even Calvin?"

"I've chucked him, but I wouldn't have told him anyway. And I know that whatever has happened has nothing to do with Matthew Adair."

"How can you be so sure?" His voice was low.

"Because I know you."

"It's that simple?"

"For me, it is. Now, please pass the wine."

He was looking her way. "I don't think I want you drunk just yet." A slow grin appeared. "I'm not sober enough to undo those tiny buttons on your blouse."

She returned the smile. "If you're too drunk to unbutton my blouse, you're too drunk to do anything else."

He hooked an arm around her waist and pulled her closer. "Don't you believe that for a second."

# Chapter Nineteen

Mornay and Claire arrived at Nan's at six. Nan let them in through the back door. Mornay kissed her cheek. "Thanks for opening up for us, Nan."

"Your man is already here and he has a right healthy appetite." She brought out a plate of sausage rolls, a pot of tea, and mugs.

Dunnholland eyed the new plate of food with delight. His cheeks were rosy, and he had crumbs down his black uniform sweater. He reached under the table and got a large photo mailer from the seat next to him. "This came for you yesterday. Inspector Byrne left orders for anything that was delivered to you be forwarded to his office, but I got to this before it could be passed on." Dunnholland handed across the envelope.

There were copies of photographs inside the mailer. Mornay had requested speeding violations that had been issued to Jonathan Cross, David Lockwood, Michael O'Conner, Ian Harris, or Gabriel Smith during the past two months. He'd asked in particular about violations caught on surveillance cameras, as there were two near Matthew Adair's home. He'd added Ian Harris's name as an afterthought. It was Harris's photographs they were looking at.

The date of the photograph was November 11. Ian Harris was caught speeding by a stationary speed camera the day Matthew disappeared.

The photograph showed Ian Harris's veterinary truck and trailer. What made the photo significant was the view; it wasn't of the rear of Harris's vehicle, but of the front.

There were over ten thousand speed cameras in the UK, which used radar technology and a "flash" to capture the image required for prosecution. Since the flash would distract a driver if forward-facing, the great majority were rear-facing, only capturing an image of the car's registration. Consequently, the owners of the vehicles could claim they weren't driving the vehicle at the time of the incident.

Recently the Grampian Police started testing a speed camera popular in Switzerland and Germany, where driver recognition was a required factor for successful prosecution. Six forward-facing cameras, nicknamed "pink eyes" because of the infrared flash lens at the front of the unit, had been installed around the region. Four were around Aberdeen, the remaining two were on the A97. One of the Aberdeen cameras captured Ian Harris's image.

"He saw the camera." Mornay passed the photo to Claire.

As she studied it, Mornay pulled out the accompanying list of all known driving violations.

"How many speeding violations has Harris had?" Claire asked.

"One."

She glanced up. "Since when?"

"Harris had a perfect record up until two weeks ago, when that photograph was taken."

"What would make a careful driver suddenly drive nineteen kilometers over the speed limit?" she asked.

"Has anyone thought to search the surveillance photographs *only* for vehicles pulling trailers?" Sahotra asked.

"If a rear-facing camera captured the image, the photographs will be of the rear of the vehicle and will do us little good trying to identify the driver." Mornay tapped the photograph. "This explains Harris's aggressiveness when we questioned him. He knew he'd been caught on camera; he must've thought that's why we were there."

They finished their meals, and Mornay paid the bill, then because he didn't have to report to work, he hung back to speak with Nan alone.

"You've had some rough days." Nan nodded to the stand where the newspapers were kept; the "menace" story held center stage. "How are you doing?" she asked.

"I'm managing. I need to ask you some questions."

"Mind if I work while we talk? I'm opening soon."

He followed her into the kitchen. "I need to know what you've heard about Clyde recently."

Nan put dirty dishes into a slotted rack. "That covers a lot of ground," she said, her voice mild.

She might not care for his father, but Mornay

knew that she wasn't going to tell him any details without a compelling reason. Their mutual history held a certain weight, but when it came down to it, he was still a police officer.

"This is important, Nan. The SDEA has been investigating Clyde, and they've been very thorough. I had no idea how thorough until yesterday. Now that they've got evidence that Trevor Paisley was murdered, they're going to find a way to use it against him."

Still considering. "What do you want to know?"

"Anything you've heard about him and the Paisley brothers or his boatyard?"

She looked away. She knew something.

Mornay waited, afraid that urging her to tell him would accomplish exactly the opposite reaction.

"You've barely spoken to him in years. Why would you care what the SDEA does to him?"

She was testing his sincerity, his motivation.

"If he's done what they think he's done, I would have no problem seeing him arrested. But the woman that's running the investigation only sees him as her ticket to her next promotion. The truth is irrelevant to her."

"What does she think he's done?"

"It's the SDEA, Nan. They think he's distributing drugs."

"He could be," she said. "People change."

Mornay shook his head, adamant. "Not my father."

"Too right," she agreed in a quiet voice. "But you still haven't told me why you want to help him."

"It's the one thing I admire about him," he said, his gaze never leaving her face. "And the single thing I hate most about him, his intolerance to someone else's weakness."

She nodded slowly. "He hired the Paisleys over a year ago."

"So I'd heard."

"Everyone knew they weren't using the boat for fish. I couldn't tell you what they were really doing, but it wasn't any nonsense like drug smuggling. Whatever he's doing has attracted what my dad used to call the wrong sort of attention. Someone's been after him to sell his business," Nan said after an excruciating sixty seconds. "I've only seen the man once. Your father brought him here."

"Dark hair, close-set eyes, gold chains around his neck?"

"That's him."

Antoni Cobaj.

"Is Clyde going to sell?"

"Do you really care?"

"I care that the SDEA does their job right—and at the moment that doesn't seem possible, with their lead investigator blinded by ambition. Did you hear any of their conversation?"

"No, but I can tell you this: Whatever your father said to the man made him furious."

"When did this conversation take place?"

"Around the same time Matthew Adair went missing."

Mornay used a booth at Nan's bakery as his office. He was avoiding his house, which still needed cleaning. He checked with Trotter regarding the lab work FSS was doing. No results. Trotter warned him it might take another two weeks.

He rang DS Gaither next; no results on the samples gathered from Elrod's office, but Gaither was optimistic he'd have something by the end of the week. He also promised to forward the results to FSS in Birmingham to cross-reference.

And so Mornay's morning went. He had lunch at Nan's, then decided it was time to face his house. He spent three hours cleaning. Some items he repacked, but most of it was thrown away. He kept out a photograph of him and Robbie, taken when they were very young. He also kept out the photograph of him, Elrod, and the Muslim woman.

Mornay had told Elrod about Robbie when they were hiding in the desert, when they both thought they weren't going to survive that brutal landscape and the even more brutal people who hid in the hills and mountains, only coming out at night, like ghosts. While telling Elrod about his brother didn't relieve Mornay of the guilt he carried, it had lessened the sharp grief.

But with Elrod's attack, another noose of grief and guilt had been lowered around his neck.

The sun had gone down while he cleaned. He went for a drive to clear his thoughts. He drove on instinct, without really seeing what he was driving past. Familiar images blurred until he parked.

He found himself on the curb outside of Clyde's boatyard.

The realization gave him a strange sense of calm. As if he'd set out all along to come there and confront his father, something he'd avoided doing for nearly twenty-five years.

Mornay walked purposely along the road toward the building. If the SDEA was keeping surveillance, they were doing it more covertly than in the past.

Though every light was lit inside the building, no

one was in sight. The building was marginally warmer than it had been during his last visit. It appeared as if Clyde was preparing to remove the trawler's engine but had stepped away for a moment.

Mornay walked around the trawler, searching.

Angus limped into view; he held a spanner with a handle as long as Mornay's forearm. Angus pointed the spanner at Mornay. "Hoof it. Now."

Angus was all talk, had been since the age of seven. Mornay glanced at the office, wondering who was hidden behind the closed door to suddenly give Angus such courage.

"So you're back," Clyde said from behind him. Angus was grinning. Clyde's voice was low and menacing. Mornay had heard that tone often enough to know that Clyde was in the mood for a fight.

Slowly, Mornay turned around, not liking the fact that Angus was now out of sight—but there was little he could about it.

Clyde also held a spanner.

Antoni Cobaj stood behind Clyde, a mobile up to his ear.

"Is he going to be a problem, Clyde?" Cobaj asked in a thick accent. "I don't need no more fucking problems."

"Don't bother me, Cobaj," Clyde said, without taking his gaze off Mornay.

"Were you at Elrod's early Monday morning?" Mornay asked.

Clyde's smile was cold, his voice low and vicious. "It's Wednesday, what took you so long to come over and lay the blame?" Clyde's gaze slid beyond Mornay's left shoulder. "Hold him for me, Angus."

Before anyone could move, the front and back

doors to the building flew open and SDEA officers stormed inside.

Antoni Cobaj took off with the inherent ability of a rat or a cockroach to elude capture. He slid past three officers, barely avoiding getting tackled, and was out the side door. Two officers chased him, but then returned almost immediately. Cobaj had escaped.

As Maggie Cray approached Mornay, Clyde made no attempt to run. Instead he turned quickly and rammed Mornay with his shoulder, taking them both to the ground. Mornay's head hit the concrete so hard, his vision was blurred by bursts of white and blue sparks.

"You're no fucking son of mine." Clyde gave Mornay a vicious punch to the kidney, then pulled him by the hair, ripping out the stitches behind Mornay's ear. He barely tried to protect himself against the brutal punches his father was throwing. "Fight back, you bastard!" Clyde screamed at him.

It took three men to get Clyde under control. Mornay lay on the cold floor, panting, until Maggie came into view. She gave him a hand up. When he stood, his legs were too wobbly to support him properly.

Clyde's voice was thick with anger. "Looks like you've finally gotten your revenge."

"I've no idea what you're talking about," Mornay replied.

If Clyde's hand had been free, it would've been stabbing angrily in Mornay's direction. "What happened to Robbie, that's on your head, not mine."

Mornay leaned against the sloped side of the trawler for support. "I think I'm going to need a lift home," he muttered to Maggie. He used his cuff to dab at the blood on his bottom lip. He could feel blood from the pulled stitches trickling down his neck. The trek to her car took ages because he couldn't seem to walk in a straight line.

He leaned against her car for support while he caught his breath. Mornay glanced back and saw Angus being loaded into the rear of a van farther up the street. "What's changed today?" he asked.

"We found your father's fingerprints on Trevor Paisley's neck, on his windpipe, like he was choking Trevor." She caught his skeptical glance. "It's enough to get him off the street. We'll come up with the rest."

"I'm not the one you'll have to convince."

"Who's Robbie?" she asked.

"Go to hell, Maggie."

On Wednesday evening, DS Rory Williams waited until the shift change to cross the hall to forensics. He and Arthur had an information-sharing arrangement. Arthur would leave the lab unlocked on the nights Rory needed to do research. In turn, Rory would tell Arthur when Constable Claire Gillespie was in his office. Not that Arthur did anything when Claire was there, except watch her from behind the door.

Rory had already called his wife to tell her he'd be late coming home. He'd give himself three hours to search out the information Mornay had asked for, but it was where to look that was the problem.

He latched the door behind him, not minding the empty offices or darkened halls. He didn't even mind the smells. He walked into Arthur's small cubicle, which was decorated with pictures of dragons breathing fire and scorched castles. Instead of clubbing on the weekends, Arthur spent hours on role-playing computer games.

Rory sat, logged on, and began typing. He'd eliminate the most obvious variable first: that the sequence of numbers weren't dates at all, but report numbers. A digitization project was in progress within the command area, so that eventually all paper records would be accessible via computer. It took an hour for him to determine that the numbers did not belong to any reports that had been put into the system since the digitization project began. So if they were dates, what were they dates of?

Using a trick he'd learned a few months previously, he put in the day and the month variable and not the year, and asked for a list of every report associated with those numbers. The list this method produced was enormous, but it came out chronologically, so he could go directly to the time frame Seth needed. The problem was the list would take two hours to print. He went upstairs to the microfiche room to search the often-neglected records stored on the microfiche.

Bone-chilling air was blowing through Mornay's bedroom, as Claire entered. Mornay was lying on his back, eyes closed, a duvet pulled over his body. She woke him by slamming the window closed.

He sat up, groaned, and fell back against his pillow. There was a watery bloodstain on the pillow where his head had been resting. There were cuts on his face and red welts and bruises across his chest.

"Christ, Claire," he rasped, eyes still closed. "I've only just gotten to sleep."

"McNab is searching Ian Harris's property this morning, as soon as it's light enough to see. Byrne has him convinced to arrest him for Matthew Adair's abduction and murder because of the traffic camera. But he wants to bring in Lockwood as well."

He used his hand to shield his eyes from the dim light. The clothes he'd worn yesterday were at the foot of the bed, heavily bloodstained.

"Inspector Cray said you were at your father's boatyard last night when he was arrested."

He rolled onto his side and pushed himself up on an elbow, groaning with each shift of position. "She showed up just as Clyde and I were settling down to have a long chat."

"Does your father always hold a spanner when you chat with him?"

Mornay didn't answer because he was grimacing in pain from the effort of sitting up. Though the duvet slid off of his bare shoulders, he didn't seem to notice how cold the room was. Claire was shivering and she wore a jacket.

"What's the push for Lockwood?" he asked.

"The owner of the stable Lockwood claims to have been riding for when he was hurt last week got back with me yesterday. David Lockwood hasn't ridden for them since September, and he hasn't visited the stable since mid-October. We've no idea how he hurt his hand. So he had opportunity, he was in the country, and in the near vicinity when Matthew Adair was taken. Byrne's convinced they were working together; he says we'll discover the motive as soon as we arrest him. McNab is holding off on the arrest till late this afternoon or perhaps early evening, pending the results of what we find at Harris's property."

"Does DI Gordon know McNab's plans?"

"She was at the briefing this morning. She didn't say anything."

"Lockwood and Harris? Did they even know Matthew Adair?"

"Byrne doesn't seem to think that's relevant."

Claire watched him struggling to stand. His movements were slow, as if every shift in position was carefully thought out before he made it. He wore only a dark pair of boxers. His body was lean, not as heavily muscled as she would've guessed. The scars on his abdomen were startling; the scars on his back were horrific. He reached to a pile of clothes on the floor by the bed and picked out a shirt, wincing from the effort of pulling it over his head.

"How does Ian Harris work into the equation?" he asked.

"An accomplice? A driver? He's being brought in for a formal interview while his property is searched. I'm here to pick you up if you're fit for it."

"Just give me a minute." Mornay slowly walked out of the bedroom, his hands out to each side as if he were balancing on a high wire.

Claire took the opportunity to study the room, hoping it would give her some insight into the man she needed to trust.

The furniture was cheap birch veneer: one bureau and a small table he was using as a bedside stand. His closet door was open. The clothes that weren't in dry-cleaning bags were hung on wooden hangers. The bedroom was neat; it just had an uncared-for, temporary air about it. Like a hotel room.

There was a framed picture on the stand next to the bed, laid flat so the photograph it contained couldn't be seen. Claire walked around the bed and picked it up. The frame was heavy silver. The photo was of two boys standing on Doune Hill, Banff Bay glistening behind them. The older boy had his arm around the younger one.

"That's my brother Robbie," Mornay said from the doorway. "The snotty boy next to him is me."

Guiltily, she put the frame down, but properly, so the picture could be seen.

She'd picked up only bits and pieces about Mornay's family through the years. Curiosity made her ask, "Is he the reason you hate your father?"

"It's a little more complicated than that, Claire." A tone in his voice warned her not to ask any more questions. He had the ends of a linen towel bundled in his hand. The towel was bulging and lumpy, probably filled with ice cubes. He pressed it against the back of his head. Slowly he walked to the far side of the bed, picked up the photograph, and put it inside the top drawer of his bureau. Facedown.

He turned around, his expression impossible to read. Had she pushed too far by asking about the photograph? He didn't seem as weak as he had a moment before, but he seemed just as vulnerable. She wondered if that was what attracted the women. Could they somehow detect the vulnerability that lay just beneath the hard facade he presented to the world? It was most visible at times like this, when he was exhausted.

"Two wake-up visits in as many days. A bloke could read all this attention the wrong way, Claire."

"You're not answering your phone, your mobile, or your pager. And Inspector McNab wants you at the office as soon as possible."

"I'm suspended, remember? Is there another

reason you're here? Or did you want to ask more questions about my family?"

She knew him too well to be bullied. "Maggie Cray thinks you were at the boatyard to warn your father about her investigation."

"I wasn't," he said flatly.

Mornay had a foul temper and could be a moody bastard; but he was smart and thorough and, at times, startlingly compassionate. She hadn't realized how much she valued working with him until early that morning, when she'd overheard Maggie Cray ranting in McNab's office.

"Did McNab send you on a recon, Claire?" Now he was the one who was quietly assessing, wondering if he should trust her.

"McNab wanted me to warn you that Maggie Cray is pushing for you to be put on medical leave, pending an evaluation."

"Everyone's doing their best to see the back of me—Byrne, Lord Gordon, and now Maggie. She wants me out of the way so she can button up the investigation around my father."

"You think he's innocent?"

"Only of the drug charges."

Sahotra did a double take when Mornay walked into the office.

"I thought you were suspended."

"I'm here to renegotiate my sentence."

"Harris brought his solicitor."

"Not the action of an innocent man, is it?"

Ian Harris's solicitor, Harold Adiz—a tall young black man who didn't look a day over twenty, but who had an impressive grasp of the proceedings—

was literally standing guard over his client when Mornay walked into the interview room. What made the sight even more impressive was the fact that Mornay had to look up at Harold Adiz. The man was impeccably dressed and extraordinarily handsome. He was also massive.

Mornay usually enjoyed the psychological effect of looming over the occupant of the interview chair, even though it meant he stood for most of the interview. Adiz's presence was spoiling the effect.

DCI McNab was conducting Harris's interview. DI Gordon had requested to be present, but he'd chosen to have his own core officers present: Byrne and Mornay. Mornay was shocked by how gaunt McNab had become during the past couple of days; his skin had a sickly gray pallor to it.

Adiz clearly wasn't pleased with the crowded conditions of the interview room, but he had no grounds to complain.

"So what is it you think I've done?" Harris demanded, and was immediately silenced by Adiz.

"We'd like to discuss this." McNab slid across the photograph taken by the traffic camera.

"You're joking," Harris stated. "You've put me through all this bother for a speeding ticket?"

McNab didn't speak.

Harold Adiz leaned forward and whispered to his client. Ian Harris sat back in his chair, lips pressed together, the color leaving his features.

"Why were you traveling so fast?" Byrne asked.

"I was late."

"For what?" Byrne was slowly rolling an unsmoked cigar between his fingers, supremely uninterested in whatever it was that Harris would have to say. It was one of the only things Mornay actually admired about Byrne, this affected disinterest. He'd yet to master the ability to appear so totally disconnected emotionally.

"For an appointment."

"To the dentist? Your podiatrist? Your GP? What sort of appointment?"

"To my dentist."

"Really?" Byrne asked, "On a Sunday?"

Harris blinked. "I must've muddled the days."

Andy McNab tapped the photograph. "This was taken at 14:37 on the eleventh. A Sunday, as my inspector has just informed you. This is very clearly you. And you're very clearly driving. Why were you speeding?"

"I had an appointment."

"I'm beginning to think he really doesn't want to answer the question, sir," Byrne muttered.

"Is the nature of his appointment relevant?" Harold Adiz asked.

"Of course it is," McNab assured him. "But we'll get back to it in a minute. How many stock trailers do you own?"

"Trailers?" Harris echoed, the switch in topics clearly puzzling him. "I've four."

"There are only three on your property. Where's the fourth?"

"My assistant is using it."

"For what?"

"Whatever he needs. Sometimes we've got to transport a sick animal, and you can't always count on your clients to have the proper equipment."

"How long has he had this particular trailer?"

"He's been using it for over a month."

Harold Adiz said, "It sounds as if you're not exactly sure what information you're seeking. What is it you need from my client?"

McNab smiled as if he'd been waiting for that exact question. "We need to establish what your client was doing before and after this photograph was taken. As you might recall, Sunday the eleventh was the same day Matthew Adair was abducted around one P.M., which just happens to be a short drive distance away from where this particular camera is situated."

"You're going to have to come up with something more compelling to link my client to the Adair incident. Proximity isn't a valid argument."

Mornay wondered what would faze Harold Adiz. The revelation that the police were building a case against his client for child abduction and murder didn't seem to daunt him. Of course, anyone who could reduce the abduction of a child to a mere "incident" was probably missing the gene that made a human feel empathy.

"Why don't I do you one better?" McNab said quietly. "I can link your client directly to Matthew Adair's abduction and murder."

Harris watched the exchange in openmouthed shock. He turned to his solicitor. "They think I took that boy?"

"They're saying they've got proof you took him." Adiz was facing McNab as he spoke to his client. "However, as they've only just collected their alleged 'proof' this morning, I find it difficult to believe a thorough analysis could have been conducted on whatever this mysterious proof could be. That would indicate a degree of efficiency that seems quite out of character for this particular police force."

Adiz knew all the right buttons to push, but he was finding McNab difficult to intimidate. McNab might look ill and weak, but his steely determination came out in every word he spoke. "We've got a child's killer to catch, Mr. Adiz. We've got people working around the clock."

"I've never seen that boy," Harris insisted.

Adiz shushed his client with a look that would've made anyone else duck under the table in fear. "Are you going to charge my client formally?"

In answer, McNab pulled something out of his pocket. It was a small, oddly shaped tool inside an evidence bag. At first glance the tool looked like a hammer, but its head was narrower and oddly elongated. And it had a stouter handle than most hammers its size. On either side of the hammer's head, set slightly back, were two rounded spikes. They were what got Mornay's attention, because below the wound that had killed Matthew was a small, odd-shaped bruise. No wonder McNab had been so confident.

"Do you recognize this?" McNab asked Harris.

Harris had gone pale. He nodded.

"What do you use it for?"

"Cleaning hooves."

"Do you usually draw blood when you're cleaning hooves?" McNab used two hands to hold up the bag so Adiz could see the hammer more clearly. "Because this hammer is completely covered in blood. So in answer to your question, Mr. Adiz, yes, we are going to charge your client with the abduction and murder of Matthew Adair."

McNab stood and nodded to Byrne to take over, then he motioned to Mornay to follow him out of the room.

"I want you and Claire in Cordiff immediately. I want you to talk to people in the village and find out anything you can on Harris."

"What about Lockwood?"

"We'll bring him in later today. I want Byrne to have a go at Harris first."

"You think they're working together?"

"Did that trailer Harris was driving the day Matthew was abducted look similar to the one you found at Finovar that had the bleach scent in it?"

"Very similar," Mornay admitted.

"Until it's proven otherwise, we'll assume they're the same trailer."

# Chapter Twenty

Mornay's headache wasn't responding to the aspirin. He was suffering from too little sleep and too much caffeine. He was glad Claire was driving; he could keep his eyes closed.

"We should've told McNab about Lord Gordon's e-mails to Inspector Gordon," she said.

"Maybe, but I was hoping Sahotra's pal could come up with something more concrete than a menacing e-mail. The first thing McNab will want to know is why someone of Gordon's status thinks a CID cop could be any sort of a threat."

"Do you think it's possible Lord Gordon was sending the e-mail to Byrne and not his daughter?"

"Walter Byrne and Lord Gordon, now there's a pair; somehow I doubt they wander in the same circles. What's more believable is Byrne knowing something damaging about the man, and using it to get what he wants."

"What do you know about Gordon?"

"What everyone else does. His father got him started in the family business of running other peoples lives, and he's been working in progressively larger offices ever since."

"You've never met him before the Adair case?"

"Never met him. Never saw him in person. Never voted for him."

"Maybe his e-mails had to do with another inquiry."

"What have we got open? Two runaways who probably won't be coming home, our car park vandal, Matthew Adair, and the Finovar Jaguar that's gone forever."

"What if it isn't a case? What if he's afraid of something you might do?"

"We could speculate for the next month, Claire. What we need to do is concentrate on Ian Harris."

Cordiff was a small village. Working their way down Cordiff's narrow High Street, they weren't on the job a quarter of an hour before they found someone who was less than fond of Ian Harris.

Tom Merkle was the village butcher, as was his father before him, and his father's father. Rab Merkle had retired twenty years earlier, but he still worked five days a week behind the counter, measuring out sausage links and counting out meat pies. Father and son looked nearly identical, except Rab Merkle still had a full head of wavy hair, while his son was nearly bald. They both had slender builds, dark, close-set eyes, and narrow noses.

Rab Merkle wiped his scrupulously clean hands on

a white towel. "Ian Harris?" he repeated slowly. "Aye, we know him well enough. What are you asking for?"

Tom Merkle put down his knife. He'd been efficiently dismantling a joint of beef on a massive table that took up most of the floor space behind the counter, and now stood behind his father like a full color shadow, slightly taller, slightly heavier built.

Mornay showed his police ID. "An ongoing investigation."

"What do you want to know?" Rab Merkle asked.

"Does Ian Harris get on well with people?"

"Well enough," was Rab Merkle's cautious reply.

"Why'd you say you knew him well enough and sound like you wished you didn't?" Claire asked.

"I said that before I knew you were cops."

"Then you're the only person north of the Borders that hasn't seen his face on the telly." She nodded in Mornay's direction. "Hard to ignore a face like that, I'd think."

Rab's glance slid to Mornay, assessing. "Maybe I have seen you once or twice. Don't watch much television, mind you. Waste of time." He nodded toward Claire, his gaze still on Mornay. "She talk like that all the time?"

"Only when she's right."

"Tom, go and put the kettle on. I'll lock up." To Mornay, he said, "We won't want to be interrupted."

The back room of the butcher shop was warm and well lit. Mornay had been expecting something that looked like the inside of a cooler or a horror movie. There was a stainless-steel worktable in the center of the room, a counter along the right wall that held an assortment of supplies in clear plastic bins, and two walk-in coolers. The floors were covered in white tile.

Every surface gleamed, and there was a fresh, pleasant scent to the air. Off to one side, tucked against the wall between the door and the counter, was a small wooden table with four chairs. It was covered with a red-and-white-checked tablecloth and appeared to be where father and son took their meals.

An electric kettle was humming on the counter. Tom Merkle opened the small refrigerator under the counter and took out milk.

In minutes they were seated, a plate of biscuits within reach. Tom Merkle dunked his biscuits in his tea as Claire pulled out her notebook.

"How much time do you have?" Rab Merkle asked.

"As long as we need. Have you known Ian Harris long?"

"All my life. We were at school together."

"You were mates?"

"Never. But that didn't stop him coming around the shop when we were small. That was when the animals were in pens out back. There was a shed my father butchered them in. Ian Harris was always hanging about."

"To help your father?"

Rab Merkle shook his head. "It was the animals he was there to see. Gave him a thrill, watching them killed."

Mornay, leery of Rab Merkle's assumptions, asked, "Couldn't it have been curiosity?"

"Maybe the first or second time. But he was always hanging about. We eat meat, and there's only one way to get the meat, and that's that. You shouldn't enjoy the killing; it's just a necessary step in the process. Harris enjoyed watching the killing. And he did enough of it himself when he got the chance."

"How do you know?"

"He showed me what was left of one of the animals, once. A cat, poor thing. I told my father. My father told his father. After that he stopped coming around, but animals in the area kept disappearing."

"How old were you when he showed you the cat?"

"Seven."

"Odd career choice he made, don't you think?"

"I don't think so," Rab Merkle said. "I'd say it was perfect. It's a bloody shame for any animal that's put in his care. Now, his son wasn't like him one bit, which probably explains why he lost himself in the drugs. He was trying to escape. But that grandson, he's the worst yet. You mark my words, that boy will kill someone one of these days. Torturing animals is just the first step, they say."

"Some people might find your empathy toward animals hard to believe."

"They would be people that didn't know me," Rab Merkle answered. "We've a living to make, and you can do it without being cruel. And that's what Ian Harris is—a cruel bastard."

Mornay bought Claire a late lunch at the local pub. They'd spent another hour talking to shop owners, a waste of time. The Merkles had been the only ones willing to tell the police what they thought of Ian Harris. However, since the Merkles were well regarded by the other shop owners, Mornay thought what they'd been told was probably correct.

They'd taken a back booth, away from the other diners. "What's the chances Matthew Adair knew Harris's grandson?" he asked Claire.

"Slim. I think it's a better chance that his parents took the family cat to see Ian Harris."

"We should've already known who they took their cat to."

"We were concentrating on the parents' work and Matthew's school. We haven't had time to deconstruct every aspect of their lives."

"But we should've," Mornay insisted irritably. "I'm fed up with being told there's no money for overtime or more officers, and in the same breath, having the piss taken out of me because of my lack of results. And then having to see those bloody stupid recruitment adverts. I'd like to know what they cost."

Their waitress arrived. Mornay ordered whiskey; Claire ordered a salad. When she gave him a look that he interpreted as disapproving, he added pizza and chips to his order. Before Claire could caution him about drinking during lunch, he asked, "So how did Harris get Matthew away from his parents? They said he was only outside the shop a moment, before they came outside. But he was already gone. The family cat?"

"It's hard to believe no one remembered seeing an animal trailer."

"Maybe that's where David Lockwood comes in, if he's involved. He drove, got Matthew in a car, and switched off with Harris."

"But we're back to the question," he said. "How would Matthew be lured into a stranger's car?"

"We've forgotten about the key we found," Claire said. "It might help us answer that question."

"The Adairs' house isn't far; it wouldn't take long

to show the key to his parents, ask if they know what it belongs to."

They arrived at the Adairs' house an hour later. Rita Adair examined the key and told them it belonged to a small lockbox Matthew had been given. He used it as his treasure chest, burying it in the veg patch in the back garden.

Special Constable Terry Frett was still on duty, and he accompanied them outside. "Rough night?" he asked Mornay.

"They don't get much rougher."

The big Glaswegian pulled two spades out of the shed. Then he leaned forward, lowering his voice. "Mind you, they'll be watching from the windows." The warning was for the Adairs' benefit, motivated by Terry's desire to protect them. He'd been at the Adairs' house every day since Matthew's disappearance and could've requested another assignment, or even time off, as he was a special constable and not expected to put in the long hours required from full-time police officers. He'd stayed because he wanted to. "I'll put the kettle on for you." Terry walked into the house through the conservatory door.

"He's gotten too close to them," Claire said.

"They could've done worse than have Terry as their watchdog."

"Let's get this over with before my ears splinter from the cold."

They split the veg patch in half. It measured five-by-eight paces; Mornay traced a rough grid onto the soil with the end of the spade. Then, he and Claire methodically pushed their spades into their grid square for half an hour before going inside to have a cup of tea and thaw their hands and feet.

Neither spoke when they returned to their task. Mornay paused to watch Claire. She didn't have the strength to push the spade in the ground with her arms; she was hopping on the spade. He couldn't help grinning. "Claire, if your mummy could only see you now."

"You're welcome to finish—"

There was a distinct clunk below Claire's spade.

Claire flashed him a brilliant smile. "Look who's actually found something."

The box was shallowly buried in the far left corner of the patch. Claire carried it to the garden bench, fished the key out of her pocket, and opened the box.

It was crammed full of torn magazine pages and pictures printed off the Internet.

If Mornay's head hadn't been pounding and his ribs aching with each breath, he might've laughed aloud. Every picture in the box featured a Jaguar. Matthew wasn't very discriminating; he liked all body styles, all colors.

"All this for photos of cars?" Claire asked in disgust.

"Everyone fantasizes about something; even you." Mornay took the box and closed the lid. "At least it's a collection we won't be embarrassed to give his mum."

It was early evening when Mornay and Claire arrived at Finovar. The first stars Mornay had seen in days, maybe weeks, were twinkling overhead.

No one answered when he rang the front doorbell.

"Maybe it's not working," Claire suggested.

They got back in her car and she drove through an archway into a cobblestone courtyard. The kitchen door was open.

Eilish, Joan O'Conner, and Deborah Lockwood were standing in the center of the kitchen wearing their coats. Their cheeks and noses were red, as if they'd all just come from outside.

"No one answered the door," Mornay said to the women. They jumped with fright at the sound of his voice.

"I've only just made the call," Eilish said. "How could you be here so soon?" Her face was pale and she was clutching her coat close to her body.

"We're not here about a call. What happened?"

"David's missing," Deborah Lockwood said. "He went for a walk this morning and never returned. We've been searching for hours on the ATVs."

"Perhaps he's farther away than you thought."

"We found his mobile near the bridge." Eilish held up a mobile with a crushed LCD screen.

The drop was at least a hundred feet to the jagged fingers of granite at the base of the cliff; a stomach-jarring distance when viewed from above.

"Did you check the cliffs beneath the bridge?"

"He did not fall over the side," Eilish said. "He's been climbing these cliffs since he was a child."

Mornay negotiated the narrow path through Walden's foyer. His coat snagged on the handlebars of a rusted bicycle, tipping it over. A precarious pile of shoe boxes and old trainers came toppling down into the aisle, narrowly missing Mornay's head. "This place is a fire hazard."

As before, when they'd found Walden off duty, he

was wearing worn corduroys and an old cardigan. Both looked like rejects from a rummage sale.

"Are you sure David Lockwood's really missing?" Walden asked. "Has anyone thought to check the pub?"

"That's your job." Mornay grinned at Walden's crestfallen expression as he realized he was back on duty. "And I'm sure you'll be working tirelessly through the night, rounding up local volunteers for the search party you'll be leading in the morning. The more you muster, the faster the search will go."

"But you've got a helicopter on the way."

"To check below the cliffs. Lockwood won't last the night if he's fallen over the edge and is clinging to the cliff face." Mornay shrugged out of his anorak and put it on a chair in Walden's kitchen. "Now, point us in the direction of Kierson's files."

"What files?"

"Copies of reports from past years. And the logbooks. Where are they? Somewhere in this house are years of reports and logbooks, and God only knows what else." Mornay knew the paperwork hadn't been sent to Macduff; he'd already asked.

Walden didn't answer.

"I'm not asking permission. Show me the records."

Walden's gaze darted nervously to Claire, then back to Mornay. He glanced to the computer screen, then to the kitchen. Realizing he had no choice, he turned, mumbling, "They're upstairs. All of them. The older ones are mixed together."

"Ladies first," Mornay said, allowing Claire to follow Walden up the stairs.

Walden had used each of the stair treads up to the landing as a shelf for books, cardboard boxes, more shoe boxes, kitchen pans, old newspapers, and crockery. Once they made it past the landing, the stair treads were clear.

The upstairs hall was completely free of rubbish. The wooden floors gleamed, and a faint scent of lemon polish was in the air. The patterned runner that was centered down the hall was clean and showed the lines from recently being vacuumed.

Walden opened the first door to the left. "Everything's in here."

The room had angled ceilings and a naked bulb overhead.

"We'll manage on our own," Mornay said, pushing Walden out of the room.

Claire ran her finger across the top of one of the eight filing cabinets that lined the far wall. "This is the cleanest room in the house."

"You haven't checked his bedroom. Or the toilet."

Claire shuddered.

Mornay started pulling open drawers. The first had dates from 1989 through 1991. "Look for anything with Fergus Harris's name. Start around 1989 and work your way forward."

Mornay went further back, all the way to the fifties, looking for Ian Harris's name. "Christ, some of these forms should be in a museum. You sure you don't want to peek into Walden's bedroom?"

"Dead sure," Claire shot back. She was kneeling in front of one of the lower drawers, fingers quickly flipping through tabs and papers.

Mornay spotted Ian Harris's name midway through the 1954 drawer. He pulled the report—a complaint—and looked for more.

"What do we do with these reports?"

"Give them to McNab so he can use them to cor- roborate the Merkles' story."

After finding half a dozen reports that detailed Ian Harris's cruelty to animals, it became readily appar- ent that the police officer—Ernie Browne—was either exceptionally thick, or else Harris's parents had somehow coerced him into ignoring the com- plaints, because the reports abruptly stopped four years after they began. Mornay spent the next quar- ter of an hour searching through five more years of documents, but there wasn't a single complaint.

He stood, knees creaking, lower back aching from stooping over. The stooping had made the dull throb behind his right ear grow into another full-blown headache.

"Are you nearly through?" he asked.

"Can't really say. I've only found two early reports that have to do with vandalisms. There's nothing about animals."

"Was it Ernie Browne that wrote them?"

"Aye. There's nothing for years, then, when Paul Kierson takes the post, that's when Fergus starts making his appearances."

"Ernie Browne must've been on the job for thirty years or more, quietly shelving every incident involv- ing a Harris."

It took three calls on his mobile for Mornay to discover that Ernie Browne had been the nephew of Ian Harris's mother. They pulled all the relevant reports out of the files to take back to the office.

"Did the search helicopter find anything?" Mornay asked Walden, who was at his desk, staring morosely at the telephone that had been ringing continually while they were searching through the records.

"The helicopter's been called off because of high winds."

"You'll be going down to Finovar, then?"

Walden's expression was blank.

"You've a search to prepare for. We've a briefing to attend, but we'll be back."

Byrne read from his notes where he sat with his feet on one of the inquiry room tables. He explained how David Lockwood had systematically been selling his assets for the past four months, selling the controlling interest in his businesses and liquidating property into cash.

"What for?" McNab asked.

"I made a dozen calls trying to find out. I eventually found someone at the Loc-Down factory who had half a brain. Lockwood's reason for the sales had to do with spending the rest of his life doing what he loved."

"And what's that?" McNab asked.

"Working with horses, of all things. He gave an interview in a magazine a few months ago and explained he was in the process of buying property. I spoke with an editor at the magazine, and he filled in a few more details. Lockwood has spent hundreds of thousands on breeding stock from two farms. I called the farms and discovered Lockwood was a guest at one of them last week for three days. During his stay he had a nasty spill, gashing his hand badly enough to require stitches. Apparently a teenager was speeding and spooked the horse he was riding. I've got a police report, if you're interested."

"Then we've wasted our time on Lockwood. Why didn't he simply come out and tell us?"

"He didn't want anyone knowing he was shopping for breeding stock."

"Have you confirmed this information with anyone at Finovar?"

"That's next on my list."

Claire leaned closer to Mornay. "Did Lockwood strike you as the sort that would chuck it all for a life in the country?"

"Anyone who gets their thrills rappelling off cliffs or barreling around on horses needs their head examined."

"Maybe he's matured, decided to settle down."

"He's certainly got the money to do as he pleases."

McNab called on Mornay next. He shared what they'd learned about Ian Harris and his penchant for killing animals.

"Looks like we'll be having another round with Mr. Adiz," Byrne said with a grin.

"Aye," McNab agreed. "Only this time we've got better gloves." To Mornay he said, "I want you to talk to Harris's staff, starting with young Calvin Walsh. The staff might shed some light on Harris's activities." He turned toward Tracy Spencer and continued, "Have you and Sergeant Aiden made any progress?"

"We have, but not in a way that will help with the Matthew Adair inquiry. Gabriel Smith was home alone on the dates listed on the petrol receipts. He was on the computer, downloading child pornography. I've gotten that directly from a pornography task force member. They've already issued a warrant for Smith's arrest, and he'll be behind bars this time tomorrow."

"If your efforts get him off the streets before he can hurt another child, you've done an admirable job. That's another suspect off our list." McNab crossed his arms, his expression grim.

"Sir," Mornay said, "since Inspector Bryne has provided an explanation for Lockwood's actions, where's he gone?"

"Who cares?" Byrne retorted.

"I do," Mornay returned. "That first night, the night that Lord Gordon's Jaguar was stolen, David Lockwood was on edge. He was worse the next day. He might not be our man, but I wonder what he knows. And who's worried because of it."

"Are you saying he's someone's loose end?" Laina Gordon asked.

"I am. Your father was there that first night. Does he visit the Lockwoods often?"

"He became close to Gerald Lockwood when he was first elected as MP for the area over twenty years ago. He's stayed in contact with the family ever since."

"And now he's going to marry Gerald's widow."

"You have a point, I assume. Or are you simply thinking aloud?"

"Inspector Gordon," Mornay said, "how long has your father dated Deborah Lockwood?"

"If you think you're going to deflect any attention away from the charges my father leveled—"

"That's enough!" McNab said. "Mornay's asked a legitimate question. Please answer it."

"Sir, he's still officially on suspension."

"I've asked him to assist me!" McNab's voice boomed. "If you've a problem with my decision, Inspector, there's the door."

DI Gordon did not move.

"Answer the question if you're not leaving."

"I believe my father has been dating Deborah Lockwood for over a year. He's known her for nearly fifteen years."

"Inspector Gordon," Mornay said, "if your father was close friends with the man that raised David Lockwood, maybe he could offer us insight into David's behavior on those days, and provide us a direction to look."

Mornay glanced at Byrne, who'd gone uncharacteristically silent. He was staring intently toward his office at the back of the room. Byrne's mysterious map was visible through the open door. Gordon had been elected over twenty years ago. The dates on Byrne's map went back that far. Was there a connection?

McNab agreed. "I'm sure Inspector Gordon will accompany you to her father's office for the interview."

# Chapter Twenty-one

Even though Eilish had locked the door to the library, every sound made her jump. The police were assuming they were looking for a corpse, but she wasn't ready to give David up for dead just yet.

She searched through David's desk for Alec Thompson's phone number, and found his card tucked at the back of a drawer. There was no business listed, nor an address, just a phone number. An Edinburgh phone number. Alec Thompson was David's security consultant. He answered the phone, sounding fully awake though it was just after midnight. His Australian accent had mellowed during his years in Scotland.

"Alec, it's Eilish. I'm calling because David went missing nearly sixteen hours ago. The police aren't being very helpful, so I'm trying to find out if there's somewhere he might've gone. I'm asking you this

because David told me about the job he asked you
to do."

"When did he tell you?"

"Last night. He also told me about his doctor and
what you worked out with him. The police know
about the doctor."

"Are there police officers present?" Alec asked.

"They're downstairs in the kitchen."

"Do they know you're speaking with me?"

"No."

"Sixteen hours?" Alec repeated. "Was he dressed
for a night outside?"

"No."

"I'll be there in two hours."


"Dunnholland," Mornay shouted across the office
to get the constable's attention.

"Sir?"

"How's the search for Lockwood going?" It was
nearly two; they should've heard something by now.
Mornay's gaze shifted to just beyond Dunnholland's
right shoulder; Victoria was standing in the doorway.

"Can we talk?" Victoria mouthed.

"Save that thought," Mornay said to Dunnholland.
He pointed toward McNab's office. Victoria met
him at the door. Interruptions would be less likely in
there. Their conversation would also be less likely to
be overheard. He closed the door behind him.

"Why are there reporters outside at this time of
the morning?"

"The Adair case has had some recent develop-
ments."

She started pacing in front of McNab's desk.

"I've been cooped up in the hospital all night," she explained. "I'm too stiff to sit."

He leaned against the front of McNab's desk.

"I heard about your father," she said. "You should've said something about him and about Elrod."

"I didn't think it was appropriate, considering what you've been going through with Pamela."

"I've never liked your father, but I still care about you."

That caught him unawares.

"Will your father be charged?"

"The SDEA has convinced themselves they've got a strong enough case against him."

"Have you been working hard?"

His last few exchanges with Victoria hadn't prepared him for the unexpected tone of sympathy in her voice. "Everyone's been working hard."

"But it's not everyone in the news. It's you."

"Have the doctors decided to give Pamela the medicine for her seizures?"

She stopped pacing and stood in front of him. "I was so wrong," she whispered.

"About what?"

"About everything. I was so angry with you. I wanted Pamela to live to punish you, and look what I've done. She's suffered horribly. You've suffered. I've suffered, even Fiona's suffered, and all because I was angry."

The constriction in Mornay's chest increased. "What are you saying, Tori?"

"I've asked the doctors not to administer the medicine, but to give me an evaluation. Pamela is never going to wake up; her condition is only going to worsen. And it's most likely her baby hasn't developed properly. A neonatal specialist is being brought in to help with their evaluation."

"Why didn't they bring one in before?"

"They didn't expect Pamela to survive this long." Her soft words fell like hammer blows.

"When will their evaluation be complete?"

"Tomorrow."

"Have you told Fiona?"

"She still thinks her Pammy is going to wake up and waltz out of the hospital."

Another person would've thought Victoria cold, but the bitterness in Victoria's voice came from years of disappointment and the frustration because she knew her mother would never change.

There was a knock on the door, then Sahotra opened it and leaned into the office.

"This better be good," Mornay barked harshly without taking his gaze off of Victoria.

"David Lockwood's coat has been found."

"I need to go," Victoria said. Her nose was red, and tears were falling down her cheeks. "I'll call you later."

Sahotra opened the door wider so she could leave, and Mornay watched her walk quickly away.

"Have you let Byrne and McNab know?" Mornay asked when Victoria was gone.

"I'm to go round now and fetch DCI McNab. Inspector Byrne is on his way."


Alec Thompson arrived at a quarter past two. He had one of the policemen milling around in the kitchen escort him to the library. Thompson was tall and older than his voice sounded; Eilish guessed midforties. Deborah's age. The constable who escorted him looked ready to settle in until Thompson shot him a look, and said, "Your services won't be required."

The constable looked prepared to argue, so Thompson pointed to the door. "Out. I'm not asking you again."

Alec Thompson looked the same, though it had been ten years since she'd last seen him. He had sandy hair with streaks of gray at the temples and a sunburned nose. He was dressed in jeans, a heavy military-style pullover, and worn hiking boots. He shifted the holdall he was carrying to his other hand. "What's the ruckus downstairs?"

"They found David's coat just outside of Cordiff." Eilish had been watching the police activity from one of the library windows.

"I remember when you used to work for my father. You liked to walk along the cliffs. You were here almost every weekend."

He smiled. "And you used to follow me. Is your stepmother around?"

"Yes," she said, walking toward the door. "And David and I prefer to call her Mother, without the prefix."

Alec Thompson nodded. "Right. You always have. I'll need to talk to her, as well."

Deborah was in the library within five minutes. "Eilish," Deborah said, her gaze on Thompson, "why didn't you tell me it was Alec?" She walked forward and shook his hand. "It's been a long time; you're looking well."

"So are you."

Deborah sat in one of the chairs across from David's desk. "Why are you here?" she asked Thompson.

"Eilish called."

Deborah turned to Eilish for an explanation.

"David did not wander off this morning or leave on an unexpected errand, like the police think. Something has happened to him, and we're going to need Alec's help to find him."

"Eilish, how can you be so sure he's not rushed off on another of his jaunts? You know what he's like, always looking for something to climb. And you've pointed out numerous times this week that he's not been acting himself."

"I just know," Eilish insisted.

"That's not good enough, Eilish. You've told the police he went on a walk this morning. You've dragged Alec here on a whim, when we've got a dozen policemen downstairs searching for him as we speak."

"I lied," Eilish admitted. "This morning David didn't go for a walk; he went to the kitchen to fetch us rolls and juice around half seven. I fell back asleep. When I woke, it was almost nine. David hadn't returned. Deborah, he wouldn't have gone for a walk. Not this morning."

Deborah held Eilish's gaze for several long moments. "I see," she said quietly, then she turned to Thompson. "And here you are, just like old times, rescuing the Lockwoods. Gerald always claimed you were indispensable. He was heartbroken when you resigned." She sighed. "I think he'd be pleased to know David thinks as highly of you as he did."

"Alec," Eilish said, "we need to show her the photographs."

Thompson put his holdall on David's desk and unzipped one of the compartments. "David hired me for a particular job six months ago." He pulled out a package of photographs.

"Anything important?" Deborah asked.

"He wanted me to have a look at Murdo Gordon. A close look."

Eilish could see the jolt of Deborah's body, but Deborah's shock wasn't reflected in her expression. Eilish envied her that gift.

"Murdo must have one of the most public lives of anyone I know. What an utterly ridiculous assignment."

In reply, Thompson handed Deborah the packet of photographs. "These have been taken during the past four months."

Deborah started to shuffle through them quickly. "Have you seen these?" she asked Eilish.

"No, David just told me about them."

"Most of them were taken while you were on trips," Thompson said.

"You've been following us the past six months?"

"Yes."

She handed the photographs back. "You appear to have been thorough with your job. In the right light, anyone can look suspicious."

Thompson reached back into the holdall and withdrew another packet. "I took this set during your last trip to France."

Deborah reluctantly took the photographs, glanced only at the one on top, then handed the packet back and looked away, her hand at her mouth.

"Did David see those?" Deborah asked.

"Yes," Thompson replied.

"Do you know if he showed them to Murdo?"

"It's what he originally intended to do this weekend, but when I called on Thursday, after the car was stolen, he said he'd changed his mind."

"Deborah," Eilish said, "where was Murdo this morning?"

"I don't know."

It was the cold that woke David Lockwood. A bitter, musty-scented cold that punctured his bones, burrowing into the very marrow. He was shivering so hard every muscle in his body ached, leaving him little energy to suck in each breath and blow it out again. He opened his eyes and saw nothing, only blackness. He was lying on a gritty, hard stone surface, his shoulders pressed against more cold stone. He lifted his head, and his forehead struck a hard surface almost immediately. The blow was followed by a sharp pain; something had scratched his temple. He shifted his arm, the space so narrow he could barely move it. He flattened his palm, moving slowly. Testing, searching. His fingers touched wood. And nails. The nails were protruding through the wood. There appeared to be no pattern, just a random scattering.

He was beneath the floor of a building.

He couldn't remember how he'd gotten where he was. The last thing he remembered was parking his ATV.

The air stirred slightly around his head. Was there an opening nearby? He was wedged so tightly he had to raise his knees as high as he could, barely a handswidth, and use his heels to push. He propelled his body forward, barely. The consequence was a rip in his jeans at the knee, and another cut from another nail. But the alternative was lying still and doing nothing. And possibly dying of hypothermia. He lifted his right shoulder slightly to ease the pressure of the tight space. Then he lifted his knees and pushed again. He moved farther this time. His shoulder caught a protruding nail, but he ignored the sharp pain and pushed yet again.

# Chapter Twenty-two

"Did Constable Walden say where he was going?"
Mornay asked the constable sitting in Finovar's
kitchen.

"No, sir."

"Did he say when he'd return?"

"No, sir."

Discovering that Constable Walden had disappeared was not improving Mornay's mood.

"Claire, I want you to fetch him. Try his house;
it's too early for him to be anywhere else. If I've got
to be awake at this time of the morning, then so does
he."

Mornay drove to the site where Lockwood's coat
had been found, in front of a small grocer just outside of Cordiff. The scent of onions was overpowering when Mr. Gormon opened the front door to
his shop and let Mornay inside. Mornay had to

squeeze past two stands of vegetables to follow the small man into the long, narrow shop.

"I wheel those out to the sidewalk when we're open," Gormon explained.

Three constables were at the back of the store, being puttered over by Mrs. Gormon. They had mugs of tea in their hands. David Lockwood's coat was on the counter beside a half-empty box of Lee's Scottish Tablet.

"Did anyone touch the bin this was found near?" Mornay's voice was harsh. These men should've been outside, ensuring nothing happened to the bin or anything immediately around it. It was the most basic step in securing a scene.

"No, sir," the burliest of the constables replied. He didn't like Mornay's tone and didn't mind showing his displeasure at being shouted at.

"Good. How many people touched the coat?"

"I brought it inside," Mr. Gormon said. "And Mrs. Gormon went through the pockets to find the name of the owner."

"Did anyone else go through the pockets?" His question was directed at the three constables.

"I did," the smallest of them said.

"You three get back out there and wait until someone from forensics arrives." He pointed to the burly constable who had spoken earlier. "It's your job to make sure no one else traipses around the sidewalk and ruins whatever's out there for forensics to find."

Mornay ignored the glowering constable when he exited the building. He'd already memorized his badge number.

Claire peered through Walden's front windows. There

were no lamps visible behind the drawn curtains. She was hoping to peek through the narrow gap, but she couldn't see into the interior. She'd parked in front of the detached storage building, which joined the house by a narrow, covered passageway. The building looked barely large enough for a wheelbarrow, let alone any kind of motorized vehicle. She'd already knocked on the front door and rung the bell, but there was no answer. She knocked on the door leading into Walden's small office with the same result. Both doors were locked. It was five in the morning—where could he be?

She did a circuit of the house: front, sides, back, looking for an open door. There were none. Then she tried the windows. The window at the back of the storage building was unlocked. The windowpanes were frosted so she couldn't see inside. If Walden's car was parked there, then she'd know he was hiding in his house. Walden would have more than Mornay's bad temper to worry about if she found out he was cowering inside.

The window was old; it had two sections that swung out, like shutters. The center bits had been painted over for so many years, they'd become fused together. Claire used a small pocketknife to scrape away the paint and, using the point of the knife, slowly pried the windows apart far enough to give her fingers a grip. The hinges groaned, the wood creaked, and her fingers were numb with cold, but she managed to pull the window open wide enough to see inside.

A glint of silver caught her attention immediately. All she could see was the outline of a car, which was enough. Walden was home.

Claire went back to the car to get her torch.

She returned to the window to have another look, and make sure Walden wasn't ducking inside his car.

Instead of the familiar lines of the Grampian Police car she'd been expected to see, she was looking at a leaping Jaguar fixture. Lord Murdo Gordon's silver Jaguar was parked in the shed.

"You silly, silly man," she said aloud.

There was a noise behind her, and she turned around.

Neal Walden was watching her from the corner of the building. He wore a white Tyvek jumper, the sort worn at crime scenes. He had booties on his feet and green latex gloves on his hands. He'd wrapped wide adhesive tape around the trouser legs, sealing them over the tops of the booties. He'd done the same at his wrists. He'd pulled the suit's hood over his head, leaving only his face exposed. He was carrying a rubbish bag. He put the bag down and walked toward her.

"You're here alone, and you're calling me silly?" His voice was low, devoid of the high-pitched whine she'd grown accustomed to hearing. "You stupid cow."

His arm came up in such a blur, she didn't have time to avoid his fist as it hit the right side of her face. He hit her again as she was falling. The blow was so powerful that she was unconscious before she hit the ground.


More searchers had assembled by the time Mornay returned to Finovar. He asked after Claire and was told she hadn't returned. Before he could find out where Byrne or McNab was, his mobile rang.

It was Sergeant Rory Williams.

"I've been trying to reach you since Thursday morning. Where are you?" Rory asked.

"I'm at Finovar. David Lockwood's missing. I've been working all night."

"I've been working on your project these past two nights."

"What did you find?"

There was a note of caution in Rory's voice when he answered. "It's best that I don't say right now. Have you told anyone what you asked me to look for?"

If Mornay hadn't known Rory so well, he might've dismissed the caution. "What did you find, Rory?"

"Better to see it in person. I can be at Finovar by seven. I need to go home and apologize to my wife first, and change. I'll be there as soon as I can manage."

Troubling over Rory's cryptic phone call, Mornay went searching for Inspector Byrne. He found him in the library, talking to a tall Australian with a military bearing. Behind the Australian were Deborah and Eilish Lockwood.

Byrne's face was glowing with triumph. He passed Mornay a packet of photographs. After Mornay looked through them, he understood the reason for Deborah Lockwood's traumatized appearance.

"Who else knows about this?" Mornay asked Byrne.

"Just us, and that's the way it's going to be for the time being. Mrs. Lockwood has asked his lordship to come by for moral support. He'll be here within the hour."

"When will you tell the chief inspector?" Mornay asked.

Byrne grinned. "You just let me worry about him."


David Lockwood's body ached from shivering. He couldn't remember what it felt like to be warm. He was so cold that the pain from his various cuts and gashes was muted. Perhaps that was a blessing, not knowing the full extent of his injuries, but he knew now how easily he could give up and simply let the exhaustion and the cold work their way to the inevitable conclusion.

But he wasn't ready to give up.

He pushed again, the effort taking every bit of willpower he had remaining in his body.

The ground beneath David's head suddenly disappeared. His head dropped back, jerking painfully on his neck, giving him an instant panic sensation as he thought his entire body was falling through the hole.

But he remained pinned beneath the floor, his chest and neck muscles aching from the effort of holding up his head. He took several deep breaths of musty air to calm the panic and assessed his situation. He could feel the edge of the opening beneath his shoulder.

Cool air blew against his neck.

David pushed again, moving far enough over the opening to free his arm. He reached back, searching. There was only open space; even the wood floor had disappeared. Whatever building he was beneath appeared to have been built against a rock ledge or cliff, and within the cliff was a cavern. David craned his neck to the left to see if he could determine how far the cavern floor was below him, but he saw only darkness. His choices were to remain trapped between the timber and the rock wall—possibly dying from hypothermia—or to continue pushing until he fell into the chasm, perhaps breaking his neck in the fall.

David chose the chasm.

# Chapter Twenty-three

There was no sign of Walden or Claire when Mornay reached Walden's house. He tried the doors and windows on the first floor, shouting for Claire since her Peugeot was parked out front.

He heard a muffled sound coming from the small garage next to the house.

"Claire?" he shouted again.

The odd thumping grew more frenzied. All the doors were locked, but the side door was old, the wooden casing weathered, so Mornay took a running start and threw his weight against the door. The casing splintered from the stone frame and Mornay went crashing to the ground.

Cursing from pain, he stood, kicking shards of wood away from his feet. Then he saw the silver Jaguar.

The thumping was coming from the back of the

car. He found the release lever and popped open the boot. Claire sat up immediately, trying to pull herself out of the trunk, though her hands and feet were bound with tape. Her mouth was also covered in tape. He pulled it off and tried to calm her struggling.

"Claire, it's all right. Did Walden do this?"

"Yes, get me out!"

There wasn't much room to maneuver since his back was against the wall. He managed to get his hands under her arms and tug her out of the constricting space. He propped her on the floor and ripped through the binding on her feet and hands, then helped her to stand.

Claire was gagging uncontrollably. He walked her to the door and bent her body down over a patch of grass, propping her with one hand while he used the other to keep her hair out of her face as she retched.

"Claire, it's all right," he said over and over, until the retching had slowed to dry heaves. She was less wobbly when she tried to stand upright. He didn't have a handkerchief, so he tugged off his tie to let her use to wipe her face.

She stood without help. Her lips were still quivering, and her skin was as white as cotton balls. "Did you smell the car?"

"What?"

"The blood, can't you smell the blood? It's absolutely reeking."

"Where?"

She pointed to the Jaguar.

He found the light switch and walked back inside. "Why would Walden steal a Jaguar?"

"He was carrying that bag when he startled me."

Claire pointed to a black plastic bag next to the car.

"Did he do that?" Mornay pointed to her eye.

She touched the swollen lump under her left eye. "He surprised me."

"Find out what's in the bag; I'll have a look at the car."

The inside of the boot was clean, to Mornay's eye. The carpeting was dark gray. He leaned down and sniffed. There was a vague unpleasant scent, but it was too faint for him to make out.

He pulled at the carpeting to have a look at the spare tire. The tire was missing. Inside the wheel well was a pair of trainers. Children's trainers.

"Claire," he said.

She joined him. "Matthew's?" she asked. "Why are they here?"

"Gordon stashed them after Matthew died. Is there an odd tire?"

"Murdo Gordon?"

"David Lockwood had a security consultant following Lord Gordon these past six months. He's got over a dozen photographs of Gordon picking up male prostitutes in France. Very young male prostitutes. Most don't look over fifteen."

"Are you sure it's not a hoax?"

"I saw the photographs. He travels to Holland or France to find the boys. He makes the trips about twice a month. David might have confronted him, which is why he's disappeared."

"But why Matthew? He's known the Adairs for years."

Mornay slowly walked around the Jaguar. "I don't know. Maybe he's getting bolder, more arrogant. Thought he was untouchable." Mornay was at the front of the car. He knelt. "Claire," he said quietly.

She walked around the other side. "What?"

Mornay pointed to the Jaguar statuette. "Look at its shape." He leaned closer to study the leaping figure. The Jaguar's nose was quite sharply defined and narrow. Below the head were the figure's two front paws, one slightly forward of the other. "Hall wanted us to look for an irregular-shaped hammer. But those curled front legs could've made the pair of odd bruises below Matthew's wound. Look, there's a scratch just below there." He pointed to a spot below the figure. "Maybe a tooth mark." He straightened. "Matthew loved these cars; we know that from the photographs he kept in his lockbox. How difficult would it have been for an old family friend to lure Matthew for a ride and give him a drink laced with a sedative?"

"But Matthew's *dead*. Why would Gordon kill him?"

"Matthew must have realized something was off, because of the self-defense course. He must have tried to escape, and Gordon panicked. They struggled, Matthew put up a fight and was flung against the car and killed."

Claire was shaking her head. "I can't believe a man like Murdo Gordon would do such a thing. He's the one that formed the Pedophile Task Force."

"We'll know soon enough if he's our man. Remember what Mick Trenton said? He might have DNA evidence on our side. Let's get you cleaned up."

Mornay used his shoulder again to break into Walden's house. Claire went to look for the toilet while Mornay went upstairs, searching.

From the state of Walden's bedroom—doors

open, clothes strewn around—Mornay deduced that Walden had packed in a blind panic. He was on the run. Searching for clues, it took less than ten minutes to discover why: Walden had run up massive amounts of debt on his charge cards.

Mornay collected all the paperwork he could find and went downstairs to make his calls.

Rory Williams was waiting for Mornay when he and Claire returned to Finovar. Rory fell into step with Mornay.

"Does what you have to tell me have anything to do with Lord Gordon?" Mornay asked.

Rory's face went blank. "You knew?"

"A guess. Take everything you've got back to Aberdeen. I want you to camp outside Roger Donaldson's office until you get an appointment to see him."

"Seth, its not just what I found on Gordon." Rory passed Mornay a form. "Look at the names."

Mornay read them. Now he understood why Rory wanted him to see the paperwork in person.

"What do I do?" Rory asked.

"Are these the only copies?"

"I made them from old microfiche records."

"Could those be destroyed?"

"Easily, if they were properly filed. But the eyesight isn't what it once was. I can find them, but no one else will."

"Good man."

In the Finovar kitchen Mornay cradled his first coffee of the day, wishing he had a cigarette to go with it. He walked across to where Claire stood off in a quiet corner, eating an iced roll. He leaned against the wall beside her.

"How are the Lockwood women holding up?"

"Eilish is coping; her mother isn't. She's taken Alec Thompson to search the chapel. Apparently there's a secret chamber in the castle after all, below the chapel."

"How are you holding up?" Mornay asked quietly.

Claire turned and faced the window, pretending to be deeply interested in the stubbly remains of the kitchen garden.

"You don't have to be a stoic, Claire."

There was a funny catch in her voice when she said, "I've never been so humiliated in my life."

Mornay took another step closer, almost touching her. He could see the curve of her left cheek, the long line of her neck, and the swell of her breast. Some men would've given their eyeteeth for a view of Claire's breasts from this angle. He was more worried about getting a jab in his solar plexus from one of her sharp elbows, or his toes crushed beneath her heel.

"For what? Having a natural reaction to a traumatic situation?"

"I panicked. It was dark. And the smell of the blood."

"Anyone would've panicked. You've seen what I do at the sight of a needle and my own blood. It'll be our secret, right?"

They heard Eilish's voice. David Lockwood came into the kitchen supported by Alec Thompson and Eilish. His clothes were filthy, and he was limping.

"He was under the chapel," Eilish told them.

The pair of them got Lockwood seated, then

Lockwood pulled Eilish into a bone-crushing hug. Then he kissed her.

"There's nothing brotherly about that kiss," Mornay whispered to Claire.

"She doesn't seem to mind, does she? Let's give them some privacy."


Mornay was the first to greet DCI McNab when he arrived. "Sir, a word."

"Lockwood's well?" McNab asked, as they walked toward the front hall.

Mornay led him into the small lounge. "Well enough. Sprained his ankle. A few cuts and bruises. I need to ask you about something."

"Go ahead," McNab said.

"Where is your son?"

"That's none of your concern." McNab made a move to leave, but Mornay blocked him.

"Your son was in a terrible accident eleven years ago," Mornay said. "Now he's in a permanent coma. You were working on a case when that happened. Do you remember which one?"

"Aye," McNab said slowly. "A councilman's son claimed to have been abused. But he didn't know by who."

"Then your son has a hit-and-run accident, and you take a leave of absence. You're gone for nearly three months. Sir, has it ever occurred to you that someone didn't want you working on the councilman's son's inquiry?"

"You think someone ran my boy down on purpose?"

"You were close to realizing a terrible truth. Do you remember what else you were working on then?"

"I'd researched and found reports filed by five other boys who didn't know who their attacker was. They were all under the age of thirteen."

"The attacks that fit that particular profile stopped after your son was nearly killed. Geography wasn't the only similarity among those boys, sir. One or both of their parents knew Murdo Gordon."

McNab could have simply dismissed Mornay's theory, but the fact that he sat quietly, working it out in his mind, told Mornay that McNab had suspected something was off with those cases, and it'd stayed with him all these years.

"Murdo Gordon ran down my boy so I wouldn't continue with my inquiry?"

"No, sir. Roger Donaldson saw to that detail. I've proof that Roger Donaldson has been systematically covering up for his cousin, Murdo Gordon, for twenty years."

"What proof?"

"The original hard copies of those reports you were researching disappeared. There's no reference to them in the computer, either. The only record we've been able to find are on microfiche."

"I didn't realize we still had microfiche."

"Most people don't."

"Roger Donaldson," McNab said softly. "That's simply unimaginable. He's been a friend to my family for years."

"He's a man with a secret, and a cousin whose deviant behavior was growing out of control."

McNab was shaking his head, still not wanting to believe. "How did you even know to look for these reports?"

"Byrne has a map in his office with dates written

on it. They're all dates that correspond with reports
detailing a sexual assault. I've no idea how Byrne
came up with the list, or why he knew to concentrate
on the ones with the boys. I assume it's something he
learned while working on the Scottish Crime Squad.
I thought he might have used the information to
blackmail Roger Donaldson to be put back on duty
in Macduff, but he didn't have enough information.
Roger Donaldson probably brought him back to
keep a closer eye on him."

McNab raised his head, so emotionally wrung
out, his face was slack. "I told Byrne about those
boys, years ago. I'd always thought I'd missed something, and its been with me ever since. And when
Matthew was found, it brought it all back."

McNab sighed and rubbed his face, staring out
the window for a beat. "Donaldson didn't bring
Byrne back," he said at last. "I did."

"Why?"

"Byrne was diagnosed with prostate cancer just
after the Glen Ross inquiry. He went through surgery
three months ago and is going through treatments
now."

"Why would you let him return?"

"He was my friend once. And he was a good cop.
Being a cop is all he ever wanted to do. I couldn't tell
him no when he asked." McNab pushed himself out
of the chair. "Byrne hinted he was working on something; I didn't know what." He pinned Mornay with a
hard gaze, shades of his former self coming back. "If
you're right, then Donaldson will make sure there's no
evidence that links them directly to the attack on any
of the boys. Including Matthew Adair. We'll need that
evidence if we're to hope for any kind of prosecution."

"The information is safe. And we've got the Jaguar, sir. It's being moved to Aberdeen as we speak. It's our smoking gun."

"Let's hope you're right. Where's Lockwood now?"

"In the kitchen, waiting for you."


"Can you remember what happened yesterday morning?" McNab asked Lockwood.

They were seated at the table, Lockwood across from McNab. Eilish was to Lockwood's left. Deborah Lockwood and Alec Thompson to Lockwood's right. Mornay stood across the kitchen, watching. Claire was behind McNab, taking notes.

"Yesterday morning, Lord Gordon was in the kitchen when I came down," Lockwood said.

"Did you speak?"

"No. Which wasn't unusual; we rarely spoke."

"Odd behavior, considering he was going to be part of the family."

David Lockwood looked away.

"Tell him, David," Eilish quietly urged him.

Lockwood took a deep breath, then reached under the table for Eilish's hand.

"When I was eight," he began, "I was sexually assaulted. I never knew who did it. I went to bed, and sometime while I slept, it happened."

Deborah Lockwood's body went rigid. "David, why didn't you tell someone?"

"I didn't think anyone would believe me."

McNab intervened before Deborah spoke again. "Was that the only instance?"

"No," David said, forcing the word out. "It went on for nearly two years. The same, every time."

"You were ten when it stopped?"

"Yes, on my tenth birthday, to be exact. That's the day I broke my favorite mug. It was the mug I always filled with milk or juice and carried upstairs to bed. That night I broke it. I didn't tell anyone; I cleaned up the mess and went to bed. Later that night, the sound of my door opening woke me."

"There was someone in your room?"

"There were two people in my room. I recognized Lord Gordon, because he was a friend of my father and visited quite often. The other man I didn't recognize."

"Gerald would've believed you," Deborah said.

"I know that now. When you started dating Gordon, I didn't know what to do. I finally told Alec. We worked out that Gordon must have put something in my mug on the nights he intended to come to my room. We didn't know who the second man was. We'd hoped to discover the man's identity during Alec's surveillance."

"When were you going to tell me?"

"I'd planned to this weekend."

"Why would he attack you now? It doesn't make sense."

"I think he was afraid I'd finally remembered."

Outside, McNab lit a cigarette. "The hell those poor people have been through," he said quietly.

The sun had risen during their interview, but it was well hidden behind the clouds that stretched from horizon to horizon. Snowflakes were drifting lazily to the ground.

"Where's Byrne?" McNab asked Mornay.

"Haven't seen him for hours."

"Did you hear about Ian Harris?"

"No, sir."

"The dried blood in his workshop and on the hammer wasn't human. We found an old well filled with dozens of animal skeletons: dogs, cats, sheep. He seems to have only tortured animals."

"Sir," Constable Dunnholland shouted across the courtyard. The pudgy constable jogged to meet them. "Inspector Byrne's just rung. He's at Lord Gordon's house in Aberdeen." Dunnholland gulped in a great breath. "Says Lord Gordon shot himself. The lads from Aberdeen Division are there. And he wanted me to tell you Donaldson is gone."

Pamela's condition was worsening as Elrod's was improving. Elrod was awake and eating solid food. He would soon begin physical therapy to start walking again. Mornay spent an hour with him each day, then went upstairs to critical care and sat with Victoria. They'd made the funeral arrangements days ago. All that was left was the wait. And the regret.

Mornay was on the last day of his mandatory week's holiday. He was enjoying a leisurely breakfast at Nan's, reading through the property listings. He'd circled two, with the vague intention of calling the land agent later that day. If he was going to unpack, he wanted it to be somewhere he'd enjoy living.

The door to Nan's tinkled and Kathy Berra walked inside. Mornay's surprise at seeing her was eclipsed by his surprise at her appearance. She'd styled her hair differently and ditched the polyester outfit for jeans that hugged her curves, heeled boots, and a blouse with a plunging neckline.

"Look who I've found, at last." She joined him at the small table. "I've got good news and bad news," she said. "Which do you want first?"

"Bad," he said.

She reached for her purse and pulled out a slender wallet, which she passed to him. Mornay opened the wallet. It was identification for the National Criminal Intelligence Service. Kathy Berra's rank was listed as chief inspector. "I was brought in to work undercover to keep an eye on Maggie Cray's investigation."

"I didn't think NCIS types were allowed to leave their desks in Glasgow."

"Good thing for you that we are. We were getting too many reports about Maggie's unorthodox investigative techniques."

"The good news?"

Kathy smiled. "The good news is that your father was released from custody yesterday afternoon. Maggie Cray was inventive with her evidence against him."

"Where is he?"

"There." She nodded toward the boatyard through the window. "As far as I know, he's back at work."

"You've let him go, just like that?"

"Not precisely. Your father wasn't smuggling drugs or petrol. He was smuggling whiskey and selling it to buyers in Japan. Low risk; through-the-roof profits. Cobaj was his middleman. Unfortunately, with the *Sunward*'s destruction and Cobaj's disappearance, your father knows we've got no inquiry."

"Let me guess: He's hired a solicitor and claims to be a simple boatbuilder, and you're daft for thinking otherwise?"

"That's half a year, wasted. We're certain it was

Cobaj behind the attack on your friend Elrod Carlisle. He met your father several times at Elrod's."

"The security tapes," Mornay said.

"Right. Cobaj wouldn't want them in the wrong hands. We're assuming Cobaj wanted all the profits for himself. The attack on Elrod was meant to kill him and send a message to your father. Lucky for you, Carlisle is tougher than he looks."

"Cobaj killed the *Sunward*'s crew?"

"Most likely, but we'll never know for certain." Kathy nodded at his paper. "Thinking of moving?"

"Maybe. Does the NCIS hire former police officers?"

She grinned. "We could do; are you giving up the quiet life in Macduff?"

"I'm staying on for a bit, but I've a mate, Rory Williams, who's being invalided off the force. He's brilliant, Kathy; he's got an intuitive knack for finding information. He's the one that found the link on Roger Donaldson."

"Pity Donaldson's disappeared; that would've made an interesting trial. But that doesn't seem to be stopping your old pal, Teddy Whyte, from trying and convicting him. He's writing a book about the crimes, did you know?"

Mornay nodded.

"When it comes out, he'll have to explain why Gordon and Donaldson put Matthew's body inside the trailer. It was an incredible risk," she said.

"We think they planned to implicate David Lockwood in Matthew Adair's death. So that if David ever came forward with his sexual assault claim, no one would believe him. Murdo would be free to marry Deborah and hide his dark side forever.

"Donaldson used a pair of thugs he knew from his days as an inspector. They hid Matthew's body and drove the trailer. He arranged for their criminal records to be expunged from the database here, but he didn't count on them being in FSS's database. We've positively placed them in the Nissan and at Cosgrove's property in England."

"They get the land agent's cooperation?"

"Yes."

"How did they manage that?"

"The old-fashioned way: Donaldson threatened to expose Linley's past. He worked the streets as a prostitute when he was in his teens," Mornay said.

"Ah," Kathy said. "Well, I'll probably buy the book anyway. Teddy's revelations have been nothing less than startling. He must have quite a well-connected source on the force." She smiled, inviting him to share the secret. "Is it Byrne, the man of the hour? Or someone else?"

Mornay returned the smile. "Can I give Rory your card?"

She pulled out two business cards, writing her number on the back of one. "I'll see what I can do about your mate." Then she gave him another slow-burn smile. "Give me a call sometime."

Mornay watched Kathy walk to her car, a smile slowly spreading across his face. Behind Kathy, a blue-paneled van pulled up in front of his father's boatyard.

Mornay's gaze narrowed. The van matched the description of the one that was seen speeding away from the harbor the night Elrod was attacked.

He stood.

A man got out of the van and started sprinting away. Farther along the road, a black Mercedes stopped. The man jumped into the backseat and the car sped down High Shore.

Mornay bolted for the door.

The explosion ripped through the quiet morning, filling the sky with a flash of bright yellow. The blast's concussion shattered windows all along the street, including Nan's. Mornay was tossed to the floor like a rag doll.

He staggered to his feet and stumbled to the door, its glass only splinters in the frame. He could feel the heat from the fire.

The front half of Clyde's boatyard was a mass of twisted metal beams and crumpled metal siding, all of it charred. Walls and roof and doors were indistinguishable. The building across the road was just as damaged, flames were roaring from both sides of the road.

Sirens sounded in the distance. Mornay pushed through the wreckage of Nan's door and sprinted toward the ruins.

# The mystery never ends.

## The biggest names in crime fiction from Pocket Books.

**DENISE HAMILTON**
**Sugar Skull**
With murders marked by intricate
Sugar Skulls, the Mexican Day of the Dead celebration
takes on a horrifying new significance.

**MICHAEL MCCLELLAND**
**Oyster Blues**
Shell' em. Shuck' em. Shoot' em.

**S.W. HUBBARD**
**Swallow the Hook**
In a small Adirondacks town, a big-time scam can be lethal.

**ETHAN BLACK**
**Dead for Life**
A tragic mistake from the past holds the key
to stopping a killer bent on revenge.

**ERIN HART**
**Haunted Ground**
The truth never rests in peace…

**M.G. KINCAID**
**Last Seen in Aberdeen**
In a Scottish village, murder is just the beginning.

Wherever books are sold.

**POCKET BOOKS**
A Division of Simon & Schuster
A VIACOM COMPANY

**POCKET STAR BOOKS**
A Division of Simon & Schuster
A VIACOM COMPANY